Never Let Go

Gina Hejtmanek

First paperback edition September 2023

Book design by Gina Hejtmanek

ISBN 979-8-9882563-1-1 (paperback)
ISBN 979-8-9882563-0-4 (ebook)

This is for all the girlies who have a not-so-great relationship with your mom, or parents.
I see you.

Some content in this book could be sensitive for some readers.
Read at your own risk!

Triggers:

Domestic violence, abuse, abduction, drug use, alcoholism, light BDSM, pregnancy loss.

Chapter One

James

As I round the last corner to get home, the autumn leaves blow across the cobblestone road, the overcast sky low and threatening. The news is calling for an early October snowstorm, perfect timing to spend the weekend at home with my beautiful fiancée, Hazel.

I had stopped at the store on my way home to pick up some Bailey's, hot chocolate, and our favorite snacks. I have plans to binge *Harry Potter* with her all weekend– snuggled up and warm while the storm rages on.

As I pull up to our two-story brick house, I admire the beauty of it. Hazel and I have put a lot of money, blood, sweat, and tears into this place to make it exactly how we want it.

We started with the outside, getting rid of the putrid yellow siding, and laying the brickwork to have our dream Cape Cod home. It wasn't cheap, but this is our forever home, and we want it to look nice for a long time.

Although we had planned to have it all done by now, we're still working on the upstairs renovations two years later. I have to remind Hazel constantly that with three rooms on the main floor there's not a big need for us to hurry up and get it done.

Hazel's red Buick Regal is already parked in her stall of the garage. It's not often she beats me home, but I had to stop by the store to grab some snacks and Bailey's. I took a different route than normal just in case she saw me and sent her a text saying I was in a meeting with my boss, Jack, that was running longer than expected. Thankfully, staying late at work for a meeting is a regular occurrence, so she didn't suspect anything. She texted me back saying she loved me and she'd see me when I got home.

I park my black Honda Civic Type R in my stall and get out to grab the bags from the backseat, one of which had spilled its contents onto the floor. I pick the items up and put them back into the magenta-colored reusable bag that Hazel insists on using. I admire her for her concern about the environment, but why did she have to get such girly colors when I am the one who usually runs to the store?

That sounds very 'toxically masculine' of me, but black or blue are perfectly good colors for any gender.

Hazel sneaks up behind me and wraps her arms around me as soon I stand up from grabbing the bags from the car floor, causing me to jump 10 feet in the air.

"Jesus, Haz, warn a guy next time!"

"Sorry, Babe. I heard you pull up and couldn't wait for you to come inside." I turn as she's speaking, wrapping her in my bag free arm. She runs her fingers through my hair, pulling me closer with her other arm wrapped around my waist. Her perky breasts press against my chest as I deepen the kiss. She knows how to set the mood for our weekend.

As we start to get lost in our closeness—hands roaming and winding in each other's hair, the wind blows into the still-open garage door, making Hazel shiver from the cold and break our embrace.

"I should have thrown my coat on. I'll meet you inside." She winks at me before jogging away. I hate it when she leaves but watching her walk away is one of my favorite sights. Although, watching the way her ass bounces up and down as she jogs doesn't help my growing hard-on. I close the car door and follow her through the back door, closing the garage door with a click of the mounted remote inside the door.

"So, what did you get me?" She inquires as I set the bags on the island counter she's leaning against, one hip jutted out and her arms crossed over her chest. She hates surprises, whether it be birthday or Christmas presents, or in this instance, snacks. She constantly pesters me until I eventually cave.

"Oh, y'know, sardines, diet coke, and peanut clusters." All things she despises.

Our back-and-forth bantering is one of the things I love most about our relationship. Don't get me wrong, we take it too far sometimes and hurt each other's feelings, but we're always quick to make up. And the sex afterwards is always mind-blowing. I hand her the magenta bag of her goodies as she scoffs at my joke.

"Ooh, Reese's!" She shines a megawatt smile my way before digging deeper into the bag. "You know the way to a girl's heart. If I didn't snag you when I did some other hussy would have, then what would I be left with?" I roll my eyes at her ridiculous question.

I'm lucky she's my fiancée; she's so far out of my league it isn't even funny. She's 5'4" with long, dark brown hair, olive-toned skin, and the most gorgeous green eyes I've ever seen in my life. Meanwhile, I stand at 6'1", not buff but not a twig, and sandy blonde hair with shit-brown eyes. My skin is so pale I swear I glow in the dark sometimes. In comparison, I'm just average and she's model-level beautiful.

"I'm sure someone else would buy you the candies you love, but I'm glad it's me." I caress her cheek as I say this, looking into her green eyes with adoration. If only she could feel how much I love her, she would never second-guess anything about us ever again.

"They might. But will they not judge me as I devour an entire bag in one sitting and still call me the most beautiful woman in the world?" Her nose scrunches as she contemplates her own question.

"Probably not." She decides with a shrug. She kisses my cheek and brushes past me towards the other bags. As she starts putting the groceries away, I take off my coat and shoes, stretching after a long day in the office. I can smell the pork she has in the oven starting to cook. Usually I do the cooking, but occasionally, she surprises me and takes charge.

"I have the pork in, but you'll need to do the potatoes." She informs me as she's bent over putting groceries away. "In the meantime, how about you make us some of that Bailey's and hot chocolate? I could use a nice warm up." I slide behind her as she stands up, cupping her ass with one hand, grabbing her waist with my other.

"I know something else that could warm you up." I whisper in her ear, kissing just behind her ear. I smile at her devilishly as she looks back at me with her mouth slightly parted. She slaps my arm before moving away from me to finish putting things away. I chuckle and get to work making our hot chocolate, putting water in her nana Rose's blue tea kettle. As that warms up, I grab our favorite mugs and set them on the counter.

Hazel lets our Shiba inu, Kiba, outside before filling his food dish. We adopted him from a rescue about a year and a half ago. He fit right in, his antics always making us laugh.

As I watch Hazel do this everyday task, it hits me that this is what I've always wanted in life. The only thing missing is a couple of kids running around causing a ruckus, but that will come in time.

For now, I enjoy my time with just Hazel and me. We have the freedom to do what we want whether that be lying in bed all day and ordering take out or going on a spontaneous trip out of town. The dog complicates that enough, children would make it even harder. But if she were to get pregnant now it wouldn't be a bad thing. Hazel would make a great mother, thanks to her Nana.

Hazel's father was never around when she was growing up and her mother, Lynn, was a prostitute with a raging alcohol and substance abuse problem.

I'm not one to give Lynn many props for how she raised Hazel, but I do acknowledge the effort she put in to make sure it didn't affect Hazel too much. She was always making sure Hazel had some sort of activity to go to while she worked or sent her to Rose's when she was getting too carried away with her addiction.

Rose got custody of Hazel when she was 12 after her mother ended up in jail for the sixth time due to drunk driving—this time killing a pregnant woman. She went to prison for 20 years and got out a couple years ago.

She comes by once in a while, but Hazel tries to keep her distance.

Rose was 62 when she took on Hazel—who had a plethora of trauma and issues, but she did so gracefully, and Hazel turned out great. Hazel's father tried contacting her when she was 19, but she cut that off quickly when she realized he wasn't the father she'd always dreamt of. Not that she expected him to be perfect, but a drug-addled pain in the ass wasn't something she was looking to add to her life while trying to juggle college and work.

Hazel got her bachelor's degree in communications and now runs a public relations firm with her business partner Jefferson. It's small, but they've made quite a name for themselves. She's close with the mayor and other big-wig politicians of the state, always running coverage for their fuck ups. Some of them should be in prison for the shit they've done. But thanks to the lawyers and Hazel, they're still out there making laws and fucking their mistresses while their wives happily spend their money and ignore their marital and family problems.

As her fiancé, I'm privy to all the ins and outs of their lives. She needs someone to vent to, after all. She also has her therapist, but she tries to focus more on her trauma than work related issues when she meets with her.

These guys are real pieces of work and it takes a huge toll on Hazel's mental health. I've held her as she's cried multiple times because she's so full of guilt at helping get these guys off the hook. She's a genius for some of the ways she gets them out of hairy situations with the press. She has a know-how for this stuff thanks to all the excuses her mother always gave for her addictions and prostitution.

That's probably why she still does it, even though she's thought about quitting multiple times. She feels like she's obligated to use her skills to help shitty people do shitty things because that's all she knows.

She's incredibly intelligent and could do anything she wanted, but she's decided to stick with it for now and I support whatever decision she chooses.

The tea kettle starts screaming as Hazel lets Kiba inside; I grab it from the stove and pour the boiling water over the hot cocoa mix, leaving enough room at the top to add in some Bailey's.

"Mm, better hurry with that or I'll freeze up and die." Hazel says, making me chuckle at her overdramatic demands.

"You're not going to freeze and die. It's 72 degrees in this house, ya damn reptile." She scoffs at my jab.

"It feels like it's the arctic! If I could be on a sandy beach with a margarita for the rest of my life I'd be set!"

"See! Exactly like a reptile! You need warmth and humidity to make you happy!"

"I am not a damn reptile! I just prefer not to freeze my ass off. You should be thankful. I know how much you love my ass." She takes her mug from me and lets the steam frame her face as she breathes in the sweet aromas.

"You're damn right I do. It's perfect." I give her ass an appreciative slap that makes her jump and spill some of her cocoa out of the mug.

"JAMES!" She moves to get a towel to clean up the spill, but I beat her to it.

"Sorry, babe. I got a little carried away." I bend as I apologize, wiping up the spilled cocoa. I look up at her from my place on my knees, our eyes locking. The atmosphere is thick with the sexual tension that started in the garage.

I want to rip her clothes off and worship her body right here in the kitchen, but she clears her throat, moving on from the moment.

"So, you got treats, and deliciousness…what are your plans for this weekend? The weather is calling for a ridiculous snowstorm."

Tampering down my disappointment, I stand and throw the towel in the washer to be washed later. "Well, to be honest, Haz, I have a really important meeting on Monday, and I need to work on my presentation." I hope my lie sticks even though I hate lying to her, but I can't ruin all the surprises in one go.

I don't think she'll fall for my lie about having to work this weekend because this isn't like me. I never work on weekends. I have worked very hard to have a good work- life balance and the weekends are my time to unwind and relax. Work stays at work, home stays at home. Hazel seems dismayed at this confession of mine, though.

"Well, I'll be around here when you're done. I'm not going out in this shit." She gestures towards the window where the first snowflakes have started to fall. She takes her mug into the living room and curls up with her Sherpa blanket in her chair, grabbing her latest read, *The Confidence of Wildflowers* by Micalea Smeltzer, from her side table.

While Hazel dives into her fictional world I start on the potatoes: washing, cutting, seasoning. 15 minutes later they're ready to join the pork in the oven.

According to Hazel I'm a thriving producer, but I'm just an ad-maker. My job is grueling sometimes, but I love making people believe in a product and I take pride in my commercials…when they make the cut. It's a highly competitive company. I love the work I do, I just wish I worked somewhere else.

Hazel's ex-boyfriend, Ryan, is my coworker and he's always trying to outdo me in everything. I know he wants Hazel back and to show her how much he's changed, but she despises him. Unfortunately for me, Jack is his uncle and gave him a job when he got fired from his last three places for sexually harassing the receptionists and other female staff.

We were both going for the production manager position a few months ago. I thought for sure Jack would give it to Ryan, but I got the position. The look on his face was worth it. Now he is essentially my bitch and I get to make the calls on how production goes for our commercials.

I'd be lying if I said I didn't turn his ideas down sometimes just out of pettiness.

After putting the potatoes in the oven, I look up through the kitchen doorway to admire Hazel in her natural element. But as soon as my eyes reach her, I see her staring at her phone with her brow furrowed, worrying her lip. *Uh oh, this can't be good.*

I make my way into the living room, taking a seat on the arm of her chair, smoothing her hair. "What's up, Haz?"

"It's my mother. Apparently, Paul is off the wagon and is being an abusive ass to her again. When will she learn?" Her voice breaks with emotion. She takes a deep breath to regain her composure before continuing. "She wants to come spend the weekend with us to let him cool off. What should I tell her?" She looks at me and the torn look on her face guts me. She worries her lip while her brow furrows. I can tell she's struggling with this decision, but I don't know what to say.

Paul is Lynn's on and off again boyfriend of five years. They met as pen pals while Lynn was in prison. They fell madly in love through letters and Lynn was dead set on moving in with him when she was released on parole. She wouldn't be relying on her daughter; her pride was too great for that. But she expected Hazel to bail her out whenever things got dicey between her and Paul...which seemed to be at least twice a month, sometimes less, sometimes more. I really don't want Lynn coming over, but I understand it's Hazel's mom, so I'll deal with it if Hazel agrees.

"That's up to you, babe. But you know how it always goes. If your mental state is up for it then that's what we'll do, but if not, tell her we're out of town and won't be back until Sunday evening." Lynn drains Hazel's mental battery more than anything. She is full of complaints and demands and never considers how her actions affect her daughter.

I know that if Lynn comes, my weekend plans are kaput, but I know that Hazel would feel responsible for her mother being out in the cold during a snowstorm. She has nowhere to go but here. Since Nana lives in Ridgewood, the assisted living facility over on Burr, Lynn isn't allowed to spend the nights there.

She tried it once and we got a call at 2 A.M. to come get her. She had hidden in the closet anytime a staff member came in to check on Nana. After the midnight check, Lynn had fallen deeply asleep on the couch and didn't wake up to the footsteps. The nurses were not pleased and almost kicked Rose out over the situation. Only Hazel's compromising skills had gotten them to agree to let Rose stay.

Those skills consisted of Hazel doing some digging into Russ Waymire, the owner of the facility, and discovering him living a second life.

Russ has a beautiful wife who is two years younger than him. They have two sons, 16 and 14, both in multiple sports and top of the class academically.

But Russ also had a pregnant girlfriend 20 years younger than him. They'd been together for two years when Hazel discovered the scandal.

She threatened to tell his wife if he didn't let Rose stay. Not ideal, and he wasn't happy at first. But since then he's sought out Hazel's skills to help him.

"Well, if you're going to be working on your presentation it wouldn't hurt, I suppose. The company could be nice." *Well, I can't tell her now, can I?* I'd seem like an asshole and like I'm coming up with an excuse to not let her mother come over. While that is enticing, I know Hazel couldn't enjoy herself while her mother was out in the freezing temperatures. "I hope there's enough food for her as well. She probably hasn't eaten in days." If there isn't, I'll find something else to eat. I won't make Lynn eat frozen pizzas; last time I did that it was almost World War III.

"Okay, Babe. But if you need me to be the bad guy, just say the word. She doesn't bother me the way she bothers you. I'll kick her ass out if need be. I don't care about the weather. She needs to respect you and our house, or she can leave and figure it out on her own." Hazel smiles at me, but it's unconvincing; she knows what's about to happen, she's already tensed up, waiting for the inevitable.

I'm not sure why Hazel doesn't just get her mom a motel room, but I don't suggest it. I'll probably regret not doing so, but only time will tell how Lynn is going to be this weekend. Sometimes she's not so bad, I've only had to kick her out three times in the last two years. But we constantly have to ask her to calm down or not be so rude. It's draining on both of us, but I don't let it show, nor do I talk about it with Hazel.

Hazel dives back into her book after sending off a text and I move over to my spot on the couch, opening up Reddit on my phone. I go to my favorite subreddit, r/twosentencehorror.. They freak Hazel out, but I find most of them fascinating. When I'm on my fifth story, Hazel drags her blanket to the couch to cuddle with me. I love it when she does this. I don't mind if she prefers to sit in her chair, but when she sits next to me, I feel at peace.

And given that our weekend is about to be ruined by her mother, I'll take every shred of peace I can get. I put my arm around her, and we both go back to our own worlds until the oven timer goes off, causing both of us to jump.

We reluctantly leave the comfort of the couch and head to the kitchen. I get the pork and potatoes out of the oven while Hazel gets our plates out.

As we're sitting down to eat, a knock sounds at the door. Kiba starts barking as Hazel and I glance at each other, I smile gently at Hazel and squeeze her hand, trying to send calming energy through her body. She takes a deep breath and goes to let her mother in.

Chapter Two

Lynn

"Are you fuckin' kiddin' me right now, Paul? You're gonna kick me out in the middle of a fuckin' snowstorm?!"

"Well, if you weren't such a bitch I wouldn't have to, now would I, Lynn?" Spit flies from his dry, cracked lips as he screams at me. He turns into such an asshole when he's not drinking or using.

Shit, who are you kiddin'? He's always an asshole. Just when the withdrawals kick in, you're his punchin' bag. I rub my ribs where Paul had punched me the week before.

The same ole shit as usual. Arguing over alcohol versus bills. All of our utilities are either shut off or about to be. I'm trying to explain to him we're gonna have to pay to have the gas turned back on, so we have heat come winter. He says he don't give a fuck about the gas bill, that's what space heaters and the fire pit are for. "You do realize the fire pit is outside, right? You can't bring it in the house, you'll burn the trailer down if you do that."

"No shit, Sherlock. I'm so glad I have you here to tell me how fuckin' dumb I am. What would I ever do without you hounding me about my bad ideas? We ain't got the fuckin' money for the gas bill. Those cocksuckers want 500 fuckin' dollars from last year. I ain't got it. And you sure as hell don't got it so why are we even talkin' about this?" He marches past me, shoulder-checkin' me so hard I hit the paneled wall to my right; picture frames fall down around me, my breath knocks out of me. As I struggle to breathe, he slams the bedroom door, shaking the trailer from the force. Maybe he'll just go take a nap and wake up in a better mood. "GOD FUCKING DAMN IT, LYNN. WHAT THE HELL IS THIS!?"
What is he on about now?

"What are you talkin' about, Paul?"

"There is piss all over our bed. You pissed in the fuckin' bed, you bitch." He comes marching down the hall, grabs me by the back of my neck and drags me into the bedroom. I know what he's about to do, and try as I may, I'm powerless to stop it.

He rubs my face in my urine like I'm a dog. When I don't give him the reaction he wants, he throws me to the crusty floor, my face pressing into the food flaked floor, the smell of ashes, dirt, and rot invading my nose. He strides over to me and starts kicking my abdomen, belittling me the whole time.

"You fuckin' sick cunt." Kick. *"I can't believe you fuckin' did this."* Kick. *"You make me fuckin' sick."* Kick.

I thought I had just sweated through my pajamas. I didn't know that I had pissed myself. I haven't been feelin' the best, but I knew Paul won't let me go to the doctor, so I hadn't said anything. He would just go on and on about how it cost money we don't have, and that he doesn't trust those rich fucks, anyway. All they want to do is dope everyone up and then condemn them for their addictions. As if he's one to talk.

A week later and I still don't know how long it had gone on for. I just kept hoping he would let up; the pain was more than I could bear. I protected my abdomen as best I could with my arms, but his aim was impeccable, or maybe just lucky. How I didn't end up with broken ribs, I will never know.

I still hadn't made it to the doctor about my pissin' the bed, but now I was being forced into the freezing cold because of this jackass. *I have to ask Hazel if I can stay at her place. I have nowhere else to go…please, God, don't let me piss myself at her house.*

I walk out the door and head across the dry yellow yard to my neighbor Sandy's house to use her phone. I can't afford the bills here— let alone a phone, so if I ever need to make a call, I have to use her phone.

I don't even knock when I come over anymore as I'm here almost every day having coffee with her. She's the only solace I have in this fuckin' trailer park. And I'm beyond grateful to her. She knows it without me saying anything to her about it, too. We have a bond, me, and Sandy. We've seen some shit and we're living with it.

I walk into her house and find her sitting on her sofa watching *Oprah*. She looks up as I step inside, "Hey, girl. You see this crazy weather we're gonna be having this weekend? Gonna be a doozy."

"Yea, I heard. I'm not lookin' forward to it." She gives me a knowing look and hands me her phone. While Sandy is my best friend, I would never impose on her to stay at her house. I'm sure she'd let me, but that feels like it's crossing some line that has never been drawn. Paul already hates her; I don't need him hating her more for letting me sleep on her couch.

I sit down next to her and take the Motorola from her hand, "Thanks, girl. I appreciate it." She nods and goes back to her talk show. I reluctantly send Hazel a text—

"I need to come stay at your place for the weekend. Paul is on one again.

Please."

Why did you put please? Now she's going to know something is up. You just sold yourself out, dumbass. I'm desperate to be able to have a warm place to sleep for the weekend. Come Monday I'll figure something out, but I need the help and if I come off as nice and respectful in text, she'll be more likely to allow me into their home one more time. God knows I need all the help in that area given that my behavior there hasn't been the best.

When I finish sending my text to Hazel, Sandy turns off her program and turns to look at me. She has this sad, resigned look in her eyes.

She won't speak on it, though. She never does.

Instead of lecturing me about my life choices, she tells me she's got a new boyfriend and she really thinks he's the one this time. It's the same song and dance as the last 50 she's had, but she doesn't pass judgment on me, so I'm not about to do it to her.

Even though it takes everything in me to not do so. She's definitely a better friend than I am in that regard. Although I try not to pass judgment on her, I can't help but tell her to be wary of his intentions.

If there's one thing my life has taught me, it's that everyone has ulterior motives.

"I hope he's better than Charlie was, Sandy. He may have been worse than Paul and that's really sayin' somethin'." Sandy laughs and rolls her eyes at the memory of her former boyfriend. He was a retired marine with a mean streak like I've never seen. Where Paul won't hit me when there's people around, Charlie had no issue doing so.

"He really was something, wasn't he? But let me tell you, Lynn. Those toxic ones really know how to use what the good Lord gave them. And we're gettin' up there in age now, so really, how picky can we be?"

God, is she right. The toxic ones are the best in the sack. I know from all my years prostituting to provide for my daughter. The ones who beat the hell outta ya were God's gift to earth in the bedroom. Too bad they couldn't have some manners to go along with it. I hate that she brings up our age, like we're already too tired and used up to love and be treated decently. I s'pose she ain't too wrong in that, though. If she was, I don't think I'd allow myself to stay with Paul, but men hear about my past and they get scared and run or they judge me for the decisions I had to make to provide for my daughter.

I wasn't perfect and I never claimed to be, but no one has ever given me credit for what I did for her and how I protected her the best I could, given the circumstances.

Sandy's phone chimes, pullin' me from my thoughts. It's a response from Hazel:

"Of course, Ma. Come on over."

"Hey, Sandy, could you take me over to Hazel's? I'm gonna go spend some time with her this weekend." It's too cold to walk across town with no coat, so I hope she's willing to take me over there. If not, I'll have to ask Hazel for more favors and I need to avoid that at all costs.

"Of course, Lynn. I think it'll do you good to get some quality time with her." I know Sandy knows what happens to me, she can hear it through the thin walls of the trailers. I know because of the looks she gives me sometimes, just like the one she's been giving me since I walked in. Not judging, but a knowing pity is in the depth of her eyes.

Thankfully she never speaks on it. If she did, I'd probably lose her as a friend, too. She also knows how bad Paul can be. But she doesn't hold it against me.

It had started snowing while we were waiting for Hazel to text back, the roads already covered in white. We get in Sandy's car and head across the tracks to Chaplain, a fancy neighborhood that I never thought my daughter would live in.

I'm proud of her for not following in my footsteps even though they say it's more likely to happen when you grow up in that environment. But she kept a good head on her shoulders and worked hard to be nothing like me. I have my mom to thank for that, too I s'pose.

I'll never tell her that, though. She'd hold it over my head until her dying day. I told her thank you for helping me with Hazel once and she gloated for years, always rubbing it in my face that I couldn't take care of my own child. *Not all of us can be mother of the fuckin' year.*

The drive seems to take less time than I thought it would– or maybe I'm just not ready for this. My stomach does somersaults as we pull up to Hazel's house, a two-story brick mansion and I hop out of the Challenger. "Thanks a lot, Sandy."

"Any time, Lynn. If you need a ride home, let me know and I'll come get ya."

"Nah, I'll be just fine. See ya 'round." I close the door and head up the walk, taking a deep breath to get my mind in check.

Coming here always gives me anxiety. I'm not used to living with no worries of where my next meal would come from, let alone the cleanliness of the place. I felt if I got a speck of dirt on anything it would be permanently ruined. I feel out of place and like I have to pretend to be someone I'm not.

There's also the matter of James and how I know he don't like me. Whenever I fuck up over here he's always kicking me out. He's so damn quiet around me. I know no daughter of mine would be with someone so quiet. I know it's because he's holding his tongue around me.

I just don't know why. I'm not gonna judge him for anything he has to say. I may get pissed about it and voice my opinion on the matter, but that's what mothers do, right?

I walk up their shrubbery-lined sidewalk despite the freezing temperatures, hating that I even have to be here. I go up to the door and take one last breath before I rap my knuckles against the dark, smooth oak door.

I immediately hear Kiba on the other side. I hate that dog with a passion, and he seems to feel the same about me. For some reason he sees me as a threat even though I've never done any harm to him, or anyone in this house for that matter.

Chapter Three

Hazel

I really didn't want to let my mother come over this weekend. I was hoping James would tell me he had some secret plan to cuddle all weekend and relax.

Maybe I could have convinced him to have yet another *Harry Potter* marathon.

But since he has to work on his presentation I couldn't justify saying no to her when I'd be spending most of the weekend on my own. Not to mention, if I refused her, she'd be sleeping in an alley somewhere.

I know what this weekend is going to consist of– my mother and I arguing, her pushing boundaries, James stepping in and her following those boundaries for a short time before having to be reminded endlessly that she is in our house. *A house she has no right to control with her negativity.*

I'll have to call the cleaning company on Monday and have them come do a thorough cleaning; God knows what my mother is going to bring in with her.

One time she gave us bed bugs and denied that she had. Not that she had the money to treat it, but she could have at least apologized. Kind of impossible for us to get bed bugs when we hadn't gotten any new furniture and everywhere we go is clean and well-kept, unlike her and Paul's mobile home which is one of the nastiest places I've ever stepped foot in.

I shudder whenever I think about the place my mother lays her head at night. Especially considering whenever I get home from there, I strip in the garage and throw my clothes away; the smell alone is enough to make me never want to wear those clothes again.

It's probably more wasteful than I need to be, but I don't want to bring that filth into our house when we've worked so hard to make it so nice.

Thankfully James and I earn a good living and we were able to get the bed bug issue taken care of. She wasn't allowed over until their house was treated as well—which we had to pay for. Paul certainly doesn't have enough money for that kind of thing and wouldn't go without his addictions so that he and mom wouldn't get eaten alive by the parasites. Although, getting him to agree to let us treat his house was a whole ordeal and he only agreed to it when we bought him booze.

I was at their trailer when I had the conversation with him, given neither of them have a phone. He originally denied any likelihood that they had any bugs at all. I pointed out the roaches crawling across the walls, the moldy food laying on all available surfaces, and the trash scattered across the floors. I told him just based on that there was a huge possibility that they had creatures other than roaches and flies living with them.

The unmistakable smell of piss burned my nose and I wasn't sure what to attribute the smell to– rats or humans.

He was worse about accepting help than Lynn was. He tried blaming her for it, saying she was the worst at keeping the house clean. I didn't disagree, but I'd rather die than agree with him on anything.

I chose to be the bigger person and ignore him. My therapist was impressed with my growth, and I can't say I wasn't impressed with myself, too.

My mother has a lot of faults, but I'm not about to team up on her and make her feel worse than I'm sure she was feeling at the time.

My mom didn't speak to me for two months after that. She's a very prideful woman and anything that threatens that pride is immediately removed from her life. Her pride is all she has left in life, so I don't blame her for being the way she is.

I just wish she knew she didn't deserve the life she was living. She may have been a terrible mother to me, but I know she was doing the best she could with the hand life had dealt her. James told me I was being too understanding to a person who wasn't the least bit thankful for the amount of money we shelled out to treat both houses.

But that's just the way my mom is, and I'm used to it. While that may be sad, it's the truth of the situation. I've come to terms with it as best I can with the help of Miranda, my therapist.

I walk down the hall to the front hall to let my mom inside. Kiba is at my heels, ready to protect me if need be. We never trained him to be a guard dog, but he's very protective of me. The smallest sound and he's at my heels, ready to pounce on anything that moves. He's the best dog I've ever had.

That's not saying much, I've only ever had Kiba. My mom never wanted the responsibility of animals around, and Nana was too old to care for anything other than me.

She did a great job raising me, despite me bugging her endlessly about at least having a fish or gerbil. But she was dead set on no animals in the house. In case my mom got out of prison early and got me back she didn't want to be responsible for said animal.

I don't blame her, but the probability of my mother getting out early was slim; she kept getting into fights in the pen. She spent most of her time in solitary because she was so hostile towards anyone who looked at her the wrong way. We were all surprised she didn't get time added for the fighting. One woman had ended up in the hospital, needing serious surgical operations after my mom shanked her for trying to steal her lunch. Our best guess is the guards were tired of dealing with her and wanted her gone. I'll give it to Mom, she's a tough old lady, I just wish she had a soft side too.

I would do anything for a hug and an "I love you" from my mom, but that's not who she is; she's never been that way. Every once in a while, she tries to be motherly, but it always falls short of everything I need from her.

Bang, bang, bang. "Come on, Hazel. Let me in! It's freezin' tits out here!" She calls out as I reach for the deadbolt to let her in. My hand hesitates on the lock, I rest my head against the door and steady myself for the force that is my mother.

I'm so not ready for this. I take a deep breath and open the door to let in my mother—who has no coat on.

Kiba growls deep in his throat, but when he realizes it's my mom, he runs back to his bed, away from the cold that is flowing into the house.

"It's about damn time, Hazel. I about froze to death out there!" This is where I got my overdramatic nature from. While it was freezing outside, she surely wouldn't die from it. She's too vile to go that easily. She stomps her snow-covered boots on our rug, shrugging out of her light jacket as she does so.

I will my nose to not scrunch at the smell radiating off of her, stale cigarettes, piss, and musk. I've seen her bad, but this is something worse.

Her gray-blonde hair is plastered to her head, her eyes have smeared mascara around them. Her lips are dry and cracked, sores sit in both sides of her mouth. My heart squeezes at the sight of her standing in my home, so obviously broken.

"Mom, where is your coat?" I know I shouldn't ask, but I can't help it, the temperature has dropped drastically since James got home and I met him by the car.

"That jackass burned it in the fire pit last week. Said I was being ungrateful and that I didn't need to go anywhere so why would I need one anyway? As if I'm not the one who goes to buy the groceries and his liquor." Her voice is deep from years of chain smoking and drinking. Her skin hangs off her body as if it's melting away from her corrupt soul.

"I think I have a spare one in the closet. I was going to go through my old stuff here soon and donate it, but I'm glad I haven't yet." I go to hug her, but she stiffens when I lift my arms, so I drop them back to my sides and let out a breath.

"You don't have to do that. Don't take pity on me. I'll just go get one from the thrift store when Paul's disability comes in."

"Didn't he just get that, Ma?"

"Yes, last Thursday, but he spent it all on booze. We didn't even get to pay the electric bill so I'm sure that'll be cut off soon. That stupid asshole doesn't know how to budget his money and is more concerned with partyin' by himself than havin' a suitable place to live. At least my bills were always paid."

As if my mom has any room to be talking about Paul paying his bills on time, or at all, with his meager disability check, let alone to judge him for his drinking considering she drank just as much as he did. Granted, her bills were paid, but it was by her working as a prostitute, but no one wants an old haggardly woman when there are pretty 20-somethings to use instead.

I look back at James, and I can see my feelings are reciprocated. His brown eyes are concerned but reserved.

We know there's not much we can do for her if she doesn't want it.

"Well, how about you just borrow it and then when you go buy one you can just donate this one for me?" We both know if she takes the coat it has to be on a loan, but it'll never get donated or returned, not that we would want it back from that pig stye anyways, but we've learned that the hard way when letting my mom borrow things.

We once lent her one of our cars and it got "stolen by some hoodlums." It was actually sold to some sketchy guys on Randolph for meth. Thankfully it was already paid off, so when we got the call that the car had been found in a river, there wasn't much sweat off our backs. The people who stole it survived, at least we're assuming they did because no bodies were found, just some needles and empty beer cans.

We didn't press charges against my mom because she wasn't the one who wrecked it, at least we didn't have proof of that. And the only thing that would come from that is her going back to jail. I was adamant that my mom had been through enough in life and didn't need us to add to the list, but James fought tooth and nail to have some sort of repercussion from the events. We almost ended our engagement over that fight. But we love each other too much to let my mother tear us apart. If we can survive my mother, we can survive anything.

We came to a compromise; my mom wasn't allowed to borrow anything of value from us again and she had to do community service for three months. She refused at first, insistent that she wasn't the one who wrecked the car. She finally agreed when I told her if she didn't follow through with it, she was no longer welcome to be part of my life. I didn't think it would make that much of a difference to her, but it got her to agree.

"Yea, all right. With this weather I'll catch pneumonia and die if I don't have a proper coat. That mother fucker, kickin' me out in this shit."

"Ma, calm down, please." The cussing doesn't bother me, but the tone of her voice caused my heart rate to spike and I could feel sweat building in my hairline. I was going to have a panic attack if I didn't get her to calm down.

"Ah, that's right. You're too prim and proper now to have someone express themselves honestly. Fuckin' sissy." I feel my face drain of color. *This is going to be a long weekend.*

James takes this time to step in and set some boundaries. He knows I have a weak spot for my mom and while I *can* set boundaries with her, it takes a lot for me to do so. Something I'm trying to work through in therapy.

"Lynn, please. It's not that we don't believe in expressing ourselves, it's that there are better ways to do so. If you're going to be a guest in our house, we only ask you to follow a few boundaries. If that is too much for you, you are welcome to leave." He doesn't like being an asshole to guests, but you have to be firm with my mom, or she'll take everything from you, beginning with your sanity. And even though I know this on a cellular level, I still can't do it until it's too late.

She rolls her eyes at me as she pushes past me and makes her way to the kitchen. She's never had a problem making herself right at home.

It wasn't until she was already helping herself to the Bailey's that I realized I'd forgotten to put it in our room; our mugs will be the only helping that we get all weekend. She will have it gone by 9.

"You made a decent meal for once, James. I'm shocked you're not having frozen pizzas or a fend for yourself night." You'd think for someone who's used to eating cold ravioli out of a can she'd be thankful for any warm food she was given, but she expects to be treated like a queen when she comes here. It's one of the many things about her that drive James mad.

"He cooks quite regularly, Ma. It was one time we had frozen pizzas and you decided to drop by unannounced. That's not our fault. Whenever you let us know you're coming, we always make a nice meal for you. So please stop making jabs at James. He hasn't done anything to you. In fact, he's welcomed you into our home, the same as me. Please be respectful." I don't bother to mention that I'm the one that cooked the pork; it'll only make her poke at James more.

My watch buzzes, letting me know I received a text,

"Just say the word and she's gone, Haz.

She's already starting and it's only going to get worse."

I look at James, my inner turmoil written on my face and shake my head. I'm not going to say the word, I see the bad state my mother is in, and we can smell that she hasn't showered in weeks. Her hair is matted to her head with grease, the stench of cigarettes permeates the air around her, and there's a visible layer of grime covering her scabbed skin.

"Yea, yea, yea. You don't have to keep remindin' me. Can't you two take a joke?" It wasn't a joke, James and I know this, but don't comment on it because we don't want to start off with a fight. We let it go and my mother picks up my mug of hot chocolate that's half empty and sits at the breakfast bar to drink it. As she does, James' phone starts ringing.

Chapter Four

James

Ring, ring. I check my phone to see my boss calling, he never calls me on the weekends. He knows my schedule and how serious I take my time off, but if he's calling it has to be an emergency. "Excuse me, ladies.

"Yea, Jack. What can I do for ya?"

"Your wife has a PR firm, right?"

"Yes, why? What's going on?" My defenses immediately raise; Jack may be my boss, but I'm not dumb. He's a piece of shit and the sooner I can get out of his company the better. I may have just accepted a promotion from him, but it was good money and I couldn't turn it down.

"I'm being slandered, that's what's going on! These bloodsuckers want all my money, and I don't want to give it to 'em so they're spreading rumors and it's leaking to the media! Have you seriously not read the news today?" He's yelling and while that's normal for Jack, his tone is frantic, manic. The bloodsuckers he's referring to are his ex-wife and her lawyers.

This explains why he wasn't in the office today.

It was a nasty divorce, and she took him for everything he had. She almost got the business, too. Thankfully, the judge felt sorry for the schmuck. The rumors she's leaking to the media are true, of course. Mistresses who may or may not be of age, a gambling addiction, drugs, you name it, and Jack has his hand in it. But he's an understanding guy and gave me a chance when no one else would. As long as he keeps me out of his personal business and signs my checks, I begrudgingly turn a blind eye to the truth of who he is as a person. Work is work, after all.

"Can't say I have, Jack. I've been quite busy with work and then Lynn showed up this evening as we were sitting down to eat."

"Fuck. I really need to talk to Hazel, James. It's serious business. If my reputation gets trashed, so does yours. You don't want that for your future in the biz." I pull the phone away from my head to exhale a breath. *I don't need this shit right now.*

"No, I certainly do not. Let me get Lynn settled and I'll talk to Hazel for you and have her give you a call. But let's not make this a regular occurrence, yea? Our weekends are not for business."

"I'm sorry, pal. If it wasn't important, I wouldn't have called, you know this." Him calling me pal always puts me in a sour mood. He's like that creepy uncle at Thanksgiving that drinks too much and either makes sexual jokes to the underage kids or says the most racist things he can think of. It seriously grosses me out.

"Yea, I do. I'll talk to her, and we'll get back to you." I hang up, running my hand through my hair. *Just what Hazel needs, more stress. But maybe this will help her keep calm while her mother's here.*

I go back out to the dining room. Lynn is ravenously devouring her pork and potatoes as if she's never tasted something as heavenly as baked meat. Lynn isn't even using her utensils and is instead shoveling the food into her mouth with her hands, resulting in food all over her face and clothes. *Good thing we have clothes here for her.*

Hazel is taking her time, eating delicately as if her mother's mannerisms sicken her to the point of not being able to consume the food in front of her. I don't blame her; I take my place at the table and meet Hazel's inquisitive eyes. I wink at her and start eating myself.

I'll fill her in when we're done eating. It's none of Lynn's business and if I tell Hazel right now she'll go eat in her office. Which probably wouldn't be a bad thing, but she has a tendency to get lost in her work and let her food go cold.

Mealtime was uneventful, if you consider a nice romantic meal ruined by the sounds of a cow chewing cud as such. It's 7 o'clock and Lynn is three-quarters through the bottle of Bailey's. This is impressive considering she's been here an hour and hasn't mixed it with a single thing.

When I'm finished I take my plate to the kitchen. On my way back I hear Hazel carefully suggesting her mother go shower.

"How about a nice warm shower and some new clothes, Ma?" Hazel's voice is quiet and calm. One misspoken word and Lynn will flip shit on her.

"That would be great." I walk into the dining room just as Hazel's eyes widen at her mother's easy acceptance of a shower and change of clothes. "That ole bast—" She stops herself, taking a deep breath. "Paul wasn't letting me shower, saying I take too long and…" she stops herself before she says anything incriminating. But we know how he is even if she doesn't say what she's thinking. "You know how he gets sometimes. I'll be out in a jiffy." She goes to take a shower, head held high, pride unshakable. It's moments like these that make it hard to hate her for everything she does. She's a woman who has been beaten down by society and forced to make her way somehow. But there were other options for her, using drugs, drinking incessantly, and prostitution was not the way she should have handled it.

But who am I to judge?

"I'm surprised she stopped herself, honestly." I say as I sit at the table next to Hazel, trying to lighten her darkening mood. "Usually, she just blathers on without considering what we think or how we feel."

"Yea, but that just shows how bad it is there. I just wish we could help her more." Her eyebrows scrunch together as I take her hand, both of us thinking of a scenario in which we can help Lynn and not screw ourselves over in the process.

There's not a single thing we've done that has helped so far. Unless she's willing to let Lynn go to rock bottom and sit there for a while, her efforts will be wasted. I can't tell her that, though. It'll just result in us arguing about her mother *again.*

"Haz, you know that doesn't go over well. Remember last time it got this bad and we tried to help her? She stole all of Nana's jewelry and pawned it off because we wouldn't buy her booze." We'd had Nana's valuables in a lockbox in our closet, she had pried it open with a butter knife and took it all. The only thing Hazel had left was a diamond band she wore on her index finger.

"I just keep hoping one day she'll wake up and realize we could help her and give her a better life than what she has. It doesn't have to be like this. We could put her in rehab and get her a job down at the gas station. She doesn't need to depend on him to make it by, which she's barely doing by the looks and sounds of it. I think she's lost 30 pounds since I saw her last. She looks sunken and it breaks my heart." Tears form in her eyes, threatening to spill over. She blinks them back, knowing if she lets them fall they won't stop. Then her mom will be wondering why she's crying; that's a whole bag of worms neither of us want on the first night of Lynn being here. *I should have suggested that motel room…maybe it's not too late.*

"I know you want to help her, babe. But you have to remember that you can't help those who don't want help. She's fine with her life the way it is. Regardless of her bitching about it all the time, she doesn't want to change. If she did, she would accept our offers."

"You're right, per usual." She smiles sadly at me, getting up from her spot at the table. She comes over to me, standing next to my chair. I look up at her and can see her want in her eyes. I stand up and wrap her in my arms. The embrace is not the sensual one we shared earlier, it's just love and support, strength in this trying time. She wouldn't be able to handle her mother if it weren't for me and we both know that. I am her rock. I'm about to bring up the idea of a motel room, but she starts talking as I open my mouth. "Who was that on the phone?"

Loosing a frustrated sigh that I missed another opportunity to get my fiancée alone this weekend, I kiss her head and fill her in on all things Jack.

"It was Jack. He needs your help with a PR thing."

"Jesus, what did he do now?" She releases me from the hug, stepping back to lean against the table.

"To be honest, I'm not sure. He kept rambling on about the bloodsuckers who want his money and how they want to ruin him and his business. Which tells me it's about his ex-wife. But as for what he did? No idea. I told him I'd talk to you about it and if you decided to help him, you'd give him a call. But if it's too much with your mom here, you don't have to. I'll tell him an emergency came up and we were busy." I should have told him that to begin with. The idea of Hazel helping him just sets me on edge.

"No, it's okay. This might give my brain the break it needs from my mom's incessant tirades and allow me to think of anything else besides her woes. Give me his number and I'll give him a ring." I do so and she enters her office to start running Jack's cover story.

She's a fantastic story weaver. Someone was caught with a 15-year-old prostitute? That was their niece, and they were giving her a ride home and some cash for a birthday they missed. Someone was caught with large quantities of drugs? They found it on the street and were taking it right to the police station to turn it in; test their pee, it'll be clean. And sure enough, every test, every story adds up. She's wicked good at what she does. Not that I condone what she does, it's disgusting that these people are still out on the streets thanks to my fiancée, but I give credit where credit is due. And Hazel is the best in the business.

"Where'd Hazel run off to?" Lynn looks a million times better now that the grime has been scrubbed off her skin and her hair has been washed. Not to mention her clothes aren't stained with God knows what and stinking like last year's trash.

"Working away, as usual." I'm in the process of picking up the plates from supper; Lynn doesn't offer to help or step in. It doesn't surprise me, but it does irritate me beyond belief. I set my stack of dishes down as Lynn starts in on her bickering about my personal life. I know I shouldn't entertain her words, but sometimes I just can't let it go.

"You should take a page from her book. It would do you good to hustle the way that girl does." She walks into the living room, sitting down in my spot on the couch.

"I know, Lynn. I'm not nearly as dedicated as her. But I'm also not in charge of keeping people's lives intact like she is. I make commercials, she runs damage control." She rolls her eyes at me.

"You could be doing something else productive with your life, ya know. Like a second job or a hobby." This was a conversation we had had many times and Lynn never got tired of berating me for not being good enough for her daughter. I tend to tune her out when she gets on her tirades or, like tonight, try to change the subject.

"Have you been to see Rose lately? She got a new neighbor that drives her crazy." I don't miss the way she tenses up at the mention of her mom.

"No, I've been too busy with Paul and his ridiculous ideals on what a clean house should be to do anything but be at his beck and call. I'll have to go see her one of these weekends." I knew the real reason why she hadn't gone. Last time she was there she smelled so badly of urine and feces that she had been asked to leave. Paul didn't believe in a clean house, he didn't care what his house looked like, as long as he had his drink and smokes. And Lynn certainly didn't keep a clean house, or she wouldn't show up here looking so dirty and smelling the way she did. But Lynn did everything in her power to make people believe her life wasn't as bad as it was.

We'd have to be incredibly dense to believe a word of it, though.

Lynn gets up off the couch, she heads to the front hall where her purse is. "I'm goin' out to smoke." I just nod at her, going back to cleaning up our supper mess.

As I'm wiping off the table, Lynn comes back in, sitting in the same spot on the couch. She looks at me, "You gonna watch anything on the ole boob-tube?" Nothing about our TV says boob-tube, it's a 75" Samsung. I'm not about to get into her with it over that, though. I know how to pick my battles and this one is so miniscule I just bite my tongue.

"No, Lynn. Knock yourself out." I finish what I'm doing and retreat to Hazel and I's bedroom. I'll do my jog on the treadmill while Hazel is on the phone and hopefully when she's done Lynn will be sleeping peacefully on the couch.

I change out of my gray slacks and baby blue button-up and throw on some black gym shorts. I don't bother with a shirt because Lynn won't come in here. Even if she did, she's seen enough male chests in her lifetime I don't think it would phase her.

But I don't want her ogling me, and that thought has me rethinking my decision and throwing on a *Bueller's Mowing* cut off and throwing on my Nike running shoes. I turn on the TV and find the weather channel. I know we're getting a snowstorm and it's going to be bad out, but I want to know just what we're in for and if we'll be stuck with Lynn for more than a couple days.

"10 inches of snow is expected tonight alone, folks. I hope you all got your last-minute supplies. After this commercial break we'll tell you the things you need to do to be prepared if you lose electricity. This is Patrick Melbourne. K19 news."

Great. I start my jog at a slow pace to warm up my body. I don't want to overdo it, but I don't want to underdo it either. I should have stretched beforehand, but I was too eager to get lost in my running. I'm stuck in a house with my future mother-in-law who I cannot stand, and I may end up losing my job if Hazel can't figure out a way to help Jack.

I don't doubt her abilities, but Jack has a lot of demons, and I don't know if her abilities can get him out of it this time. I should probably start looking for another job, but I have to hold out faith for my fiancée. If I don't, she'll feel like I don't believe in her and that's the last thing she needs right now. The only thing I have going for me right now is this treadmill

50

and sleeping with my fiancée tonight. *This weekend is turning up daisies.*

I can't focus on the weather, so I put my earbuds in and crank up *Misery* by Stephen King, it's a classic. I increase the speed on the treadmill to start my bursts and get lost in the thumping of my feet, the whirring of the treadmill, and my audiobook.

Chapter Five

Hazel

I close the door to my office and give Jack a call.

"Hello?" His voice is gravelly and has a tremor in it. The sound grates on my eardrums.

"Hey, Jack. It's Hazel. James said you needed my assistance?" I'm kind of hoping he will tell me never mind and that it all blew over in the hour between his call to James and me calling him.

But life doesn't work that way for me.

"Yes, thank you, Hazel. My ex-wife, Lauren, is trying to ruin my fucking life. I had this beautiful girl over to my house the other day and apparently Lauren had access to my cameras in my living room…I–I don't know. What I do know is she has this video and is sending it everywhere."

"Okay? Well, before we get started, Jack, we need to talk about rates. I like to think I'm worth what I charge, but some people think otherwise, and I don't work for free."

"Of course not. I wouldn't ask you to. I'm offended you would think so." He scoffs.

"I never said that, Jack. I'm just being upfront with you."

It takes a half hour before we come to an agreement.

"Going back to your wife having a video of you having intercourse with someone else; I don't see why that's such an issue. You guys aren't married anymore. Tell me what's really going on, Jack. I can't help you out if you're not honest with me." I sit in my chair and grab a notepad and pen to take some notes.

He sighs into the phone, the sound loud in my ear causing me to flinch. "I was hoping you'd have picked up on it from what I already said, so I didn't have to admit this more than once."

I hold my breath, waiting for him to drop this bomb on me.

"She was 16." I can't help the gasp that escapes my mouth. "Now, look. I don't need your judgment. So if that's what you're gonna do then forget about it."

"No, Jack. It's fine." It wasn't. "I just wasn't expecting that."

His grunt is the only response.

"Okay, so the good news is the age of consent is 16. The bad news is, she's still a minor and a lot younger than you."

"Yea. Listen, that's not all of it." *Oh God.* "I paid her. She was standing outside of that convenience store on South street. She asked me to buy her some booze. I couldn't help myself.

"She was wearing this short dress and her tits were about to pop out the top. Her hair was a mess and her mascara was running down her face. I know it's fucked up. But I took a look at her and knew she needed money. Whatever had happened, she needed an out of it."

My stomach rolls over, and I have to force myself to swallow the bile creeping up my throat. He reminds me so much of Ryan it's absolutely appalling and I don't want to take this case. But if I don't, James might lose his job.

He's quiet on the end of the line for a minute and I hope that's the end of his admittance. Just as I'm getting ready to ask if there's anything else, he starts talking again.

If I wasn't as well-versed in these situations as I am, I'd think he was ashamed at what he was saying, but I know better.

"I bought her the booze and asked if she needed a ride somewhere. She looked around and I could tell she didn't really want to get in my car. That's when I offered her the money." He didn't sound sickened by his actions, just mad that he got caught.

"How much did you offer her?" I don't know how my voice sounds so strong, but I send a thank you to the universe for the strength I do not feel.

"A thousand all together." I release a breath. I have my work cut out for me.

"Is there anything else you need to tell me, Jack?" I hope to God he's done. I don't know how much more I can stomach.

"No, that's it. Listen, Hazel. I need this taken care of fast. We all know what happens if I get caught up in this. It won't be pretty for anyone." His threat hits home, my pulse picks up as I think of what would happen if I don't get this cleaned up.

"Okay, Jack. I'll keep you updated. This is probably going to take a day or so. Sit tight." I hang up before he can respond. That probably pissed him off, but if I had to hear one more word out of his mouth, I was going to lose it.

I need a vacation.

I turn on some music to help me calm down from that disgusting phone call. Dandelions by Ruth B. starts playing and improves my mood a little. This song always makes me think of James. I start thinking about how we first met: bumping into each other at a 24 hour diner after a wild night out with Jayden. I wasn't paying attention, his head had been turned to his friends—we ran right into each other, his soda exploded all over the place, soaking our clothes. Instead of yelling about him ruining my white dress, I busted out laughing.

He hadn't asked for my number then, but weeks later I received a text from an unknown number asking if I'd like to go to the local book store and have coffee; the rest is history.

I still don't know how he got my number, or how he knew about my love of books and coffee, but I have a feeling Jayden had something to do with it.

I relish thinking about our relationship, but then my thoughts remember the secrets I kept from him for so long about my mom. I still feel incredibly guilty over it.

The guilt causes me to think about the guilt I feel with my mom and how I know there's something I can do to help her. But then I remember how she dismissed my hug when she arrived. I don't know what I was expecting, but it wasn't that. My mom may not be the most affectionate of people, but she's never not hugged me before.

I keep fooling myself into thinking one of these days she'll change, she'll ask for help out of her situations, but she doesn't. It isn't good for my mental health to continuously worry about her; it's not fair to me having to constantly worry about her, and it's not fair for James to have to pull me out of my rut whenever she leaves.

I just keep holding onto hope, but I know in my soul that she doesn't want help. So why do I keep extending the olive branch? Why do I keep offering?

I should have told her she couldn't come this weekend. I could have used a break from reality and spent some much-needed one-on-one time with James, but there's just something about her pathetic situation that I feel bad for. I mean, she is my mother, but she wasn't there for anything in my life because she was in prison; Nana was there.

Speaking of Nana, I really need to go see her soon, it's been a week and I can tell by our phone conversations that she's starting to go stir crazy. I'll have to take her to get a pedicure or something.

I feel like I'm going insane, my mind is jumping all over the place, and I can't get it to slow down. All this pressure to be perfect and have the best life imaginable. The thought of kids, marriage, all of it. It's almost too much at times. But I'm lucky I have James. He's my rock and so patient and kind to me. Him and Nana are the only people in my life that I can truly rely on.

This is quite the pity party. And that thought has me scrambling back from my thoughts of defeat and woe and to something I *know* I can fix: Jack and his fucked-up life.

This one is going to be a little harder than my other ones, for the simple fact that Jack is related to Ryan, I'll have to focus harder on keeping my emotions out of it.

I sit at my desk, pull my hair back into a ponytail, open my MacBook and get to work. I'm going to start by digging into all the news outlets and reading the articles written about him. That way I can know firsthand what we're dealing with on that front, then I can start my story on how his ex-wife is just a wicked old witch.

Focusing proves to be impossible with my racing thoughts and ill-feelings in regards to who Jack is. I know I need to get this done so our lives can go back to normal, but I don't want to. I have so much on my plate right now that I just want people to stop relying on me for two seconds.

My mother is stressing me out more than I thought she would.

I decide to call it a night, I know when my brain has had enough and no matter how hard I push, it won't go anywhere helpful if I keep going. I close my laptop and shoot Jack a text that I'll have some solutions for him by tomorrow evening. If I don't keep him updated on where I'm at he'll keep blowing up my phone for updates. For a man in the production company, he's one of the most impatient people I know. But he's also not willing to shell out any more money than he is to make sure this gets done overnight.

I walk into the living room to see what James and Ma are up to, hopefully James hasn't kicked her to the curb yet. I haven't heard any yelling, so I take that as a good sign.

I want to try to talk to her and learn more about what happened when I was a kid and why I wasn't ever enough for her to change. I know this conversation won't go anywhere; I've tried before. All I ever get from her is excuses and her telling me she tried her best to provide for me any way she could. But what was it about alcohol, drugs, and men's bodies that was so appealing that it caused her to give up responsibility for me? I enjoy a drink as much as the next person, but I could never put it before my child.

Not that you would know how you would handle having a child. I shake my head and my hair falls out of my loose ponytail. I don't know why my thoughts are being so awful today, but it's not helping the mood for the weekend. I need to do something that makes me happy, maybe a nice hot bubble bath.

I find Mom stretched out on the sofa, sleeping peacefully, James is nowhere to be found. *I wonder how long it's been since she's gotten a good night's sleep...* I go grab her a blanket from the hall closet and hear the treadmill going. I take the blanket to my mom and tuck her in. I'm not sure if she'll stay here all night, but if she does, she'll want a blanket because we keep our heat low at night.

Seeing her looking so peaceful in her sleep loosens some of my resentment. I kiss her forehead; even if she wasn't there for most of my life and still doesn't like to be a part of my life very much, she's still my mom and I still love her. Life has treated her badly, that's not her fault. My interrogation can wait, because that's exactly what it is and it's not going to be pretty when it happens. I want answers and I've waited long enough to get them.

I go to the bedroom and sit on the bed to watch James while he runs, he should be done soon. His muscular legs are pumping, his breathing heavy, but even. He's wrapped up in his audiobook and hasn't noticed me come in. I lay on the bed, watching him and admiring his sweaty body, I let my thoughts wander.

What are we going to do about Jack? He's in some deep shit and we need to come up with a good story. The girl's legs over his shoulders, and his fat, blubbery body pumping in and out of her like there was no tomorrow. His breathing sounded as if he was dying.

He rasped out, "You like that, you whore? Who's daddy's little whore?" I was surprised he could speak due to how out of breath he seemed to be. She laid there, pretending she was enjoying it, but you could tell from her open, blank eyes that she was contemplating her very existence. *I wonder if this is how my mom felt when she was a prostitute? Why is this girl doing this? I should help her…somehow.*

I'm jolted from my thoughts by James caressing my cheek. I jump and grab his wrist in a self-defense move I learned when I was 10. My mom used to send me to self-defense and dance classes, so I'd be out of the house while she worked. For the longest time I had no idea how she afforded it, but one day school had got out early, I walked home, and found Mr. Walowitz, my dance teacher, leaving my house. It all made sense then. She slept with my teachers to pay for my lessons.

"Woah, Haz, it's just me. What is going on, Haz? What were you thinking about?" I immediately let go of his wrist, yanking my arm back to my body like I'd been burned.

"Are you okay? I'm so sorry, I was just thinking of how to help Jack. Nothing out of the ordinary. I don't know why I did that. I'm so so so sorry." Panic rises in my chest, my breathing is rushing in and out, my mind reeling at what I just did. James holds his wrist in his other hand, rubbing the sore spot where I had grabbed him.

"It's okay, Babe, I'm fine. You sure you're okay?" He brings his good hand to my face, slowly caressing my cheek this time, as if he's scared I'll hurt him again. Concern takes over his face, his brow furrows.

"Yea, I'm fine. I was just spacing out and my instincts kicked in, I guess. It must be all the stress of my mom being here. I've been worried about her for a while and now it's just bubbling to the surface when it hits me in the face with how bad it is." My words rush out of me, trying to explain to myself and James why I did what I did, even if it makes no sense. I'm not a violent person.

"I know you have, babe. Just know I'm always here for you if you need to talk about it, okay?" He kisses the top of my head in his delicate way. "I'm going to go jump through the shower then we can watch a movie or something, okay?"

"Don't you need to work on your presentation?" He bites his lip and looks away; it's his guilty tic and the realization he lied to me about working this weekend slaps me in the face. I feel stupid for falling for it.

"Actually, that was a lie." When I go to respond, he rushes on with his explanation, "I know we don't lie to each other in this relationship, but I really wanted to surprise you this weekend with us just laying around watching movies and eating junk food. Then your mom texted you and I couldn't come clean about it then or it would have seemed like I was lying about *that* to keep Lynn from coming over." He blows out a breath, running his hands through his hair, relieved he finally told me. I'm a little taken aback because he doesn't ever do anything like this, but at the same time I understand his desire to spend quality time together.

"It's okay, Babe. I'm not mad at you. I just ask that next time you tell me your plans and not lie about them in the first place. I would have figured out something else for my mom, like a motel room or something so we could have had time together. The only reason I agreed to her coming here is because I thought you would be busy." I grab his arm lightly and kiss his wrist, letting him know I forgive him and I'm very sorry for hurting him.

"I guess the only good thing is that now you have something to do so you don't have to be stuck with your mom all weekend arguing?" I laugh at that; he always finds the silver linings. Even though I do want to spend time with my mom to figure out things from my childhood, it's a good thing I have Jack's problems to worry about. If I questioned my mom, it would turn into an all-out war and if we're stuck together all weekend who knows how it would turn out. "I love you, Hazel Jane." He kisses the top of my head.

"I love you too." He smiles down at me before heading to the bathroom.

As soon as he's gone, I start berating myself for hurting him. *What the hell was that?* In the seven years James and I have been together I have never been physically harmful to him. *Maybe make an overdue appointment with Miranda.* I've worked through a lot of heavy shit with her, and I know she'll have some sort of insight as to why this happened. I haven't met with her in a month because things were going pretty well, and I didn't want to take time away from people who needed her more than I did. I mentally make a to-do list for tomorrow, on the top is texting Miranda.

Chapter Six

James

I kiss Hazel on the top of her head, grab my clothes and head to our bathroom. *What the hell was that all about?* When I'm out of her line of sight I stretch out my wrist. She's much stronger than I give her credit for.

Turning on the water, I run through what could have caused Hazel to act like that. I know she's stressed with this whole Jack thing and her mom being here, but we've been through bigger stressors and nothing like this has ever happened.

I step into the shower without checking the water and burn my back in the scalding hot water. "Ow!" I turn the cold water up and the heat down; perfect.

"Are you okay, Babe?" Hazel calls through the door. I must have yelled louder than I thought.

"Yea just turned the water too hot. I'm fine." As I wash up, I start to feel better about the situation. My wrist still hurts a bit, but nothing major. The last thing I need is for her to feel bad about hurting me on top of everything else she has to worry about.

I get out and get dressed, looking forward to cuddling with Hazel and watching some stupid movie we find. I hear her talking in the other room, assuming it's her mother who has awoken and come to chit chat with her. But it sounds like a one-sided conversation, and I don't hear Lynn. *She must be on the phone with Jack again. Sheesh, he's needy today.*

I go out to our bedroom, where Hazel is sitting on her side of the bed, her back to me. Her hair covers her face. She's still talking, but it's too quiet for me to understand. I go to nuzzle her neck to let her know I'm done and realize she's not on the phone, but instead talking to herself.

"Haz, you okay?" I get off the bed and kneel in front of her, it's clear she's been crying.

"I didn't mean to hurt you. I swear I'm not a violent person. I was so wrapped up in my thoughts that you startled me. I am so sorry, James." She starts sobbing and I wrap her in my arms, offering her solace in her world of despair.

"It's okay, Babe. I'm perfectly fine. I'll just have to keep your awesome kung-fu moves in mind next time I try to scare you while we're watching a scary movie." I chuckle as I pull back to stare into her emerald eyes. She's really beating herself up over all of this, but it really isn't a big deal. My wrist hurts, but it'll be fine by morning.

Hazel rolls her eyes at my bad joke, but she stops crying and gives me a little grin. Before she can carry on our conversation, her mother knocks on our door.

"Come in." Hazel's voice comes out nasally due to her crying.

"I'm gonna head onto bed." Lynn looks at Hazel's face and sees she's been crying. "You all right, Hazel? Why you cryin'?" It's almost comical to me to see Lynn being motherly, but the amusement dies down as I see her dart her eyes to my face full of accusation. I ignore it because if I say anything the entire situation will explode in my face.

"Yea, I'm okay, Ma. Just a little stressed. I was thinking of making some chamomile tea to soothe my nerves, would you like some before you go lay down?"

"I don't know 'bout all that fancy tea." Lynn's face contorts with discomfort. She's never been one to try new things and this evening is beginning to be full of them, from being concerned about Hazel's wellbeing to trying a new tea. Lynn is out of her depth.

"I promise it's delicious." Hazel goes to her mom and puts her arm through Lynn's, and they leave the bedroom. *I adore that woman.*

I stretch across the bed and remember our kiss from earlier. I really hope she's in a better frame of mind when she comes back because I'd love to continue where that was going. I think she could use the distraction as well.

I browse news articles while I wait for Hazel, same shit different day. There's a lot going wrong in this world and sometimes it makes me not want to have any kids. What kind of world would it be when they get to be my age? I don't want them to have to suffer because of *my* want.

As I'm reading a depressing article on the war raging in Africa, Hazel comes back in with her big white mug. She isn't looking at me and I know she's still feeling guilty. When she gets like this it is so hard for me to get through to her. But I still try because she deserves every effort I have to give.

She rounds the bed and sits on the edge, placing her mug on her coaster that lays next to her book on the bedside table. She made us custom coasters when she was in her resin pouring phase last year. I can't say I've used them much, but she uses them every chance she gets. It's one of the projects she was happiest with.

They're beautiful and I think that's why I don't use them—I don't want to ruin them. They're a dark purple with golden swirls going through. They remind me of an amethyst, if it had been interrupted in its growing process by gold ore.

I roll over and rub her back as she stares at the floor. Her back heaves with her deep breathing. I hope she's calmed down enough to at least let me hold her while she sleeps, if not let me fuck her senseless.

She turns around and looks deeply into my eyes. "Make me forget for a while, James. Please." My heartbeat spikes, and I know that's my cue. Not hesitating I wrap my hand around the back of her neck, pulling her into me. Our tongues tangling around each other, hands exploring and removing each other's clothes. We act as if we'd die without the feeling of the other's skin on our own. I know we both need this time together and I'm so desperate to bury myself inside her, I don't give a damn if her mother is in the house.

As she leans back into her sea of pillows, I follow her, unwilling to break our connection for one singular second. My hands roam over the curves of her body, skimming her sides until I reach her round breasts. I kiss the corner of her mouth, making my way to her neck where I nibble and bite at her, one of her hands is buried in my hair while the other squeezes the arm I'm using to hold myself above her.

She tastes so sweet.

Licking down her abdomen, I put my weight on my knees so I can get her leggings off. Her clean-shaved pussy is so wet and suddenly I'm parched and only her sweet juices will quench my thirst. I devour her, my tongue making slow circles on her clit, my left hand traces up her leg as she writhes beneath me with both hands in my hair. Her breathing grows more frantic with every rotation of my tongue. My left hand finds her center and I slide one finger in, she's soaked for me already and she hasn't even cum yet.

I sink another finger into her wet pussy and massage her g-spot while I increase the speed and pressure of my tongue. She moans my name and it takes all my willpower not to stop eating her pussy and sinking my cock into her wet heat.

With another flick of my tongue, I have her coming undone for me, her body spasming around me, her thighs squeezing my head.

I remove my fingers and get off the bed so I can remove my sweatpants, my dick bouncing up and down as I pull them down. Hazel watches me with hooded eyes, mewling.

I keep eye contact with her as I crawl back up her body, taking my time even though I'm itching to be inside of her already.

Dipping my head, I kiss her stomach and make my way up her body with my lips and my tongue, her hands wandering my body. When I'm parallel to her, I look deep in her eyes, "I love you, Baby." She returns the sentiment by simultaneously grabbing my neck and pulling my face to hers and grabbing my cock and lining it up to her entrance.

I don't need any more prompting, my dick hurts from how hard it is for her. She's so ready for me it takes no effort to enter her. I have to bite back my growl. That's one of the many downsides of Lynn being here. I can't have my fiancée the way I want her, discretion is needed. I bury myself inside of her, her pussy clenching around me. I pull out until only my head is inside of her and then I slam back in.

Discretion may be needed, but as my cock moves in and out of her soaked pussy, I lose all inhibitions. I no longer care if Lynn hears us, this is our house and I'll do as I please. Even with that mindset, as Hazel moans her pleasure, I still put my hand over her mouth to soften the sound.

"Your pussy feels so good wrapped around my cock, Baby." I growl in her ear as I start to fuck her, she tries to wrap her legs around me, but I stop her. I need to be deeper inside of her. I grab her legs and put them on my shoulders. Her hand is skating down her body towards her clit. I grab both of her hands and pin them by her head in one free hand as I lay over her, contorting her body in what must be an uncomfortable angle, but I don't give a fuck. "Only I get to make you cum tonight."

I pick up speed, pumping into her. The sound of our skin slapping together is loud in the quiet room. I growl in her ear,

"God, you're so wet for me." Her face is divine, sweat shining on her hairline, mascara smudging under her eyes.

Normally she would respond, but my hand refuses to let her move her lips. She closes her eyes as the sensations get to be too much for her. I remove my hand from her mouth, trusting her to be quiet. As soon as my hand is gone, she opens her mouth to moan. I spit in her mouth and cover it again. She looks at me, shocked, but her pussy clenches around my dick as she cums. It's something we've only done one other time when we were drunk. But God damn, we both have things to forget tonight, and I'll make damn sure that happens. I thrust hard three more times and she bites down on my hand while she cums all over me.

I move back and flip her over, "Ass up, baby." I grab the lube and her wand from the bedside table and squirt some lube on my hand, rubbing it onto my cock and her puckered hole. She lifts her head and looks at me, unsure.

"I don't know about this, James." Her voice quivers with concern. She never knows if she wants anal, but I know she loves it. She cums harder when I fuck her ass.

"You wanted to forget, let me do my job." I slap her ass and she takes a deep breath, lowering her head back down to the mattress, accepting that I'm going to do it and her denial has no place here.

Lining myself up to her ass, I turn on the wand and put it against her clit, her hips start rotating as it vibrates against her bundle of nerves. When she starts moving faster, I slowly push into her ass, making sure it doesn't hurt her and giving her time to tell me to stop if she really doesn't want to do this.

Instead of telling me no, she pushes her ass into me, giving me the green light. I slide into the hilt, pausing to give her body time to adjust, she moans into the comforter. When she starts squirming against me from the wand and my cock in her ass, I start to fuck her. I don't go as hard as I did in her pussy, I don't want to hurt her, but hard enough she'll be really sore tomorrow. I slap her ass and push the wand harder onto her clit. She buries her face into the comforter to try to muffle her moans.

"That's it, Haz. You're such a good girl." I growl to her, increasing my speed, I can feel my balls start to tighten. I'm on the brink, but she needs to cum first. "Take the wand." Releasing my other hand, I reach up to pinch her nipple between my fingers and tug. With another thrust, she's coming so hard, she squirts all over me. And that's all it takes for me to empty myself inside of her. "Fuuuck."

I pull out of her and pat her ass, "I'll go get a towel." My head reels from my orgasm as I go to the bathroom for a towel. When I get back to the bedroom, she's still in the same position, eyes closed. I clean her up and push her onto her side. She opens her eyes, smiling at me. "We need to get a different blanket." She laughs at me and gets up to go to the bathroom to finish cleaning herself up.

"It's your fault, so you go get it." She says over her shoulder as she saunters away and starts a shower.

I laugh and go to the hall and get a new blanket. *God, she's so perfect.*

She comes back to bed twenty minutes later smelling like peaches, hair wrapped up, skin shining. All she has on is a robe and she takes it off before climbing into bed and snuggling into me. "I love you."

"I love you, too." She barely gets the words out before she starts softly snoring. She sleeps peacefully for about an hour before she starts tossing and turning, nightmares plaguing her.

Chapter Seven

Lynn

I follow Hazel to the kitchen, my eyes taking in how nice their house is. I am always surprised when I come here, she did not get her decorating skills from me. Her big kitchen has dark gray cabinets with black trim and stainless-steel appliances. The kitchen we had was absolute shit compared to this.

The peeling wallpaper was from the fifties and stained yellow from decades of smoking and cooking grease. I probably coulda got em clean, but who the hell cared anyway? The kitchen did what it was intended to do and kept our food cold in the fridge and cooked our food on the gas stove. Ain't no need for it to be magazine perfect. I wasn't running for no mother of the year award. She was fed, educated, and bathed. That's the best I could give her. None of my clients cared what state my home was in anyway, and most times we'd go to a motel or just fuck in the backseats of their cars.

She's filling up Rose's tea kettle. My mother was obsessed with that fuckin' thing. Always making some nasty smelling drinks in it. I don't know what the big deal is about these fuckin' teas. It tastes like absolute shit.

She's quiet and I can tell there's something botherin' her, but I don't know how to bring it up. I'm not the communicating type. I say what needs to be said and leave the emotional shit to settle itself. I have too many secrets to go blathering my mouth around like some ninny from church.

"If you wanna talk, you can. I'll listen. Can't promise I'll have anything helpful to say, but—" Hazel looks at me as if a snake just snuck up and bit her ankle.

"I'm okay, Ma. Just stressed. I'll be fine tomorrow." She goes back to focusing on the tea and it drives me mad that she won't talk to me. I can't say I blame her, but I'm her fuckin' mother. I deserve some level of communication from her, especially when I ask.

I stew in my anger while Hazel makes our tea. I'm startled back to reality when Hazel puts a mug down in front of me. I almost knock the mug over as she sets it down, only stopping myself at the last second. The steam rises up to cup my face and the smell is quite pleasant. *Maybe this won't be so bad.*

Hazel raises an eyebrow at me that I choose to ignore. If she won't speak to me, I certainly won't open up to her.

Hazel watches me like she's waiting for me to say some foul thing about her attempt to bond. "It smells good." I manage to get out despite being angry at the way our relationship is and hiding that she startled me.

"Try it, it tastes even better. And it'll help you get a good night's rest." Her eyes close as she takes a sip. She visibly relaxes after one sip. *Fuck it. Worst case, I pour it down the drain.* I take a small sip and the flavors explode on my tongue.

"I don't usually like all these fancy teas, but this ain't half bad, I s'pose." She aims a smile at me; the first I've seen for *me* in years. I look away because I'm not good with all these emotions I'm feelin'. I love my daughter, as any mother does. But I'm just not motherly, that's not who I've ever been.

"I'm glad you like it. I'm going to take this to my room and read a book. You're welcome to sit in the living room and watch TV or go to the guest room. Night." I wave her off and am left to wander my thoughts alone.

After 20 minutes of runnin' my mind through the ringer of my situation, I decide to go lay down. My bones are tired. I haven't slept well in months and this tea is making me sleepy.

I'm laying there tryin' to get some sleep and I can hear them in the other room. I'm happy they have a good relationship, but one thing a mother never wants to hear is her daughter havin' sex. Guess I'm up for a while despite the tea's effects on me.

My grogginess makes my mind think of real weird shit. Like Hazel's father, someone I try my hardest not to think about, but the thought of him always weasels its way in when I'm around Hazel. She's the female version of him.

My mind also likes to think of him when it's late and I can't sleep.

I was in love with that man and would have changed everything about myself had he wanted me to. He was tall and muscular, and his shoulder length brown hair was the most gorgeous hair I'd ever seen. He was a bad boy, the best kind. He treated people like shit if he didn't want somethin' from 'em or didn't care about 'em. And at first, he treated me like a queen.

On our first date he picked me up on his Harley, my mom didn't approve of his mode of transportation, but I didn't give a damn. It was freeing being on the back of that bike. When we pulled up to the lake, I saw a red and white checkered blanket sittin' there with a bottle of Jack and some sandwiches waiting for us. I didn't know why he left it here, anyone could have stolen it, but I was swooning for this man, so I shook that thought away and we enjoyed each other's company. He seemed genuinely interested in getting to know me and I opened up like a book for him, mind, body, and soul.

That fantasy lasted about two months before I walked into his house one night while he was havin' a party and found some brunette bimbo blowing him in the middle of the living room. I ran out of the house so fast, bawling my eyes out.

I found out two weeks later I was pregnant, and I had gonorrhea and chlamydia, which could have come from any of the five guys I had slept with since. I was trying to erase the thought of him, but nothing worked.

I saw him around town, but I never spoke to him again. I was crushed, I had seen forever with him, but I was just a quick little fling to him and when he got bored, he found someone better. Last I heard he was in trouble with the police for sellin' dope down by the liquor store. Funny where life takes people.

Hazel and James finally finish up with their fuckin'; I can hear the shower runnin' and the hall closet open and close. I can finally get some sleep. I hope my dreams are good and wholesome like Hazel and James' relationship. Lord knows I need a break from reality for a while.

But my thoughts followed me in to sleep. I can't even get a break from them there. They ranged from fighting with Paul and him punching me in the face to back when I was with Hazel's dad, Steven, and he was overdosing on coke on the bathroom floor.

Not all of the dreams were about struggles. There was one where I was in a stream with beautiful rays of sunshine coming through the trees. There were birds chirpin', squirrels runnin', and bugs galore. I dipped my toes into the warm water of the stream, relaxin' more and more as I spent time in this paradise. It reminded me of the camping spot my mom and dad used to take us to when I was a little girl. As I was just starting to fully relax a loud annoying sound started interrupting my peace. It sounded like someone talking.

I jerk awake to the sound of Hazel's voice telling me that there's coffee and muffins in the kitchen. I can't tell if I'm still dreamin' or not because my clothes feel soaked, like I fell in the stream, but I don't recall doin' that. I jolt all the way awake and realize it wasn't water from the stream soaking my clothes, but piss. I'd done it again, only this time in my nosey daughter's house. She's gonna kick me out and I'm not gonna know where to go. *Shit.*

I start pulling the bedding off the bed and notice there's a liner on the mattress. I must have been so tired last night I didn't even realize it. I'm thankful it's there, though, otherwise they'd have to get a new mattress altogether instead of just washing this mess.

I start cursing myself out as Hazel opens the bedroom door to see what the commotion is. If I was faster, I'd have blocked the door, but as she comes in, I drop the bedding to the floor, mortified to have her catch me.

Chapter Eight

Hazel

I really thought I had forgotten all my problems after James and I had sex last night, but my dreams determined otherwise.

I yawn into my hand as I knock on the guest bedroom door.

"Hey, Ma, coffee is ready and there are muffins on the counter for you! I'm going to go take a shower and then work on Jack's stuff." I usually let her sleep until she wakes, but I'm slightly worried because it's 10 A.M. and she is usually awake for a while by now. As I turn to walk away, I hear her talking to herself.

"Fuck, fuck, fuck. You stupid bitch. How could you do this?!"

"Ma? You okay?" I open the door to the guest room and am hit with a smell I hadn't smelled in a long time but knew instantly what it was. "Ma? What happened?"

"Hazel don't—shit, I—I'm so sorry. I don't know what happened. I had a cup of tea and passed out. I was so tired I must not have woken up to pee. I am so sorry, Hazel." She's crying and obviously mortified.

I'm slightly taken aback at seeing the tears, she usually doesn't let those show.

"Ma, it's okay, these things happen. We can clean it up, no worries." I walk further into the room to help her with the bedding. She's frozen to the spot, eyes wide open. When I'm three steps into the room she snaps out of her frozen state, waving her arm like a game show host towards the bed.

"I know that; I see there's a mattress cover on here." She looks at me accusingly as if we put it there for her. Which is true, but I won't ever tell her that. We got it after I took her to a doctor's appointment a year ago. I had walked into her house and was hit with the smell of urine so strongly that I had to wait for her in the car, so I didn't vomit on her floor.

"We wanted the mattress to stay nice and decided this was the best idea for having guests over. Good thing, too, because when Jayden and Isaac were here one night, they spilled some wine on the bed. Mattress was perfectly fine, so it'll be fine now."

The story about Jayden and Isaac is true, unfortunately.

Jayden was my college roommate, and we became best friends, Isaac is her husband. We had had a game night, and all got a little too drunk, Jayden took her glass of wine to bed with them and Isaac wasn't paying attention. He was tickling her, and she accidentally spilled. I had to throw out that bedding set because the stain wouldn't come out no matter what I did. Jayden replaced it despite my telling her she didn't need to.

"So, what's going on, Ma? I know this isn't the first time and has been happening for a while. Are you on drugs? Are you sick What's going on?"

"What the hell are you talkin' about? I'm not on drugs. How they hell would I know if I'm sick? Paul doesn't like those rich fucks and won't let me go."

I want to punch him in his throat. I have my issues with my mom, but she deserves better than that; anyone deserves better than that.

"I just...I have accidents sometimes. It's embarrassing but nothin' wrong with me than an old, used up bladder."

"Sometimes? Mama...I don't want to be insensitive or make you embarrassed, but I know this isn't just a sometimes thing. When I took you to the doctor when you had pneumonia I couldn't even stay in your house because of the smell. So, I mean, unless Paul is pissing himself when he's drunk, I know this isn't just an every once in a while thing."

"It's too early in the Goddamn mornin' for this shit, Hazel. Can we please talk about it later? At least let me have a cup of coffee first. And maybe a shower."

"Definitely a shower, Ma. There are clothes that should fit you in the closet."

"Now Haz—"

"Ma, I got them at Goodwill, just in case we ever came across this current situation of you staying here with no clothes. It's fine. I spent like 50 bucks. It's okay."

"Okay, fine. But I will pay you back some day. You know I don't take no charity."

"I know, Ma. You can pay me back in full." I knew she wouldn't. She was getting too old to work and if this bedwetting was something serious, she wouldn't be working ever again. But if it made her feel better about taking the clothes by believing her own lie, then I'd let her say it. I leave the room so she can get her clothes in peace. She follows me with the bedding.

"I'm not gonna let my daughter wash my pissy sheets. I'll at least get them in the washer. I washed your piss-soaked sheets, I'll be damned if you do it for me."

"Okay, Ma. Thank you. The detergent is in the cupboard above the washer." I leave her to her shower and coffee and go into my home office to start on Jack's case. I have to start doing damage control or he's going to be blowing up my phone and then refuse to pay me.

I have a hard time focusing when I start. I've never had this problem before. After last night I worry about it happening again, any time I get lost in my thoughts I worry I'm having another episode and I'll hurt James again.

I cannot believe I did that.

But James is jogging on the treadmill, so it's okay. He'll be busy for at least 30 more minutes, if not longer. It's his time to think about things. He prefers to jog outside, but since the weather is so bad, he's stuck watching the weather channel and staring at our walls instead of the elm trees and squirrels. He says it doesn't bother him, but I know being cooped up inside gets to him sometimes.

I turn on *Spotify* and start looking over my notes and plan what to do with the information Jack gave me on the phone. The drugs were his son's, and he didn't want him to get into trouble with the law. We can get my partner, Alex, to pee for him. Hair follicle test? We have plenty of wigs in storage for just this type of thing…*But isn't Jack bald?* Fuck. Okay, a blood test…how are we going to get around that one? Fake veins don't work because they take it from different places now. Last month they took it from Greg Fincelli's leg. Granted, it was the only vein that wasn't blown out, but they can get creative. But if Jack doesn't use for a while, he'll be okay...or should be.

As if he could stop using. That jackass has been using for decades. Yes, but if we could convince him... *Convince him to jump off a cliff maybe.*

Jesus, we can't do that, this is my livelihood; how I make my living. Without people like this, we would have nothing.

Helping pieces of shit is what you want to do with your life? Have at it, darling. But they'd be better off dead.

That may be, but he isn't, and we have bills to pay.

The voice in my head is relentless and reminds me so much of my mom that it truly bothers me sometimes.

The only part of this problem I'm having a really hard time with is the video of him fucking the 17-year-old girl. There's no way I can come up with a cover for that. I need to bring in reinforcements.

I email Alex to have him help me brainstorm some ideas and notice how quiet the house is. I don't hear the treadmill running or the TV. Has it already been 30 minutes? I've barely got anything done. If time goes by this quickly, maybe I can get through this weekend in one piece.

My mom cracks open the door and I mute my music. "How's it goin'?" I'm surprised she seems concerned about my work. She's never been interested in it before.

"I can't seem to concentrate and I'm not sure why." That's a lie, I know why I can't concentrate. Her voice keeps circling my mind with terrible ways of how to help Jack and everyone else I help with my talent. On top of that, my dreams were incredibly fucked up last night. While the chamomile tea usually helps me sleep, I tossed and turned all night and was plagued by a continuous nightmare of hurting James. Every time I woke up, I fell asleep to continue where I had left off.

Only this time when I hurt James, it wasn't just a simple wrist control technique.

We were in a grimy shack in the middle of nowhere. I tried to see if there were any houses nearby, but from where I looked out the small, dirty window, I couldn't see any. All I could see were birch and cottonwood trees and a narrow gravel path that could barely fit a car. The shack was surrounded by the same gray gravel, giving this place a grim feeling. There was a sliver of pond or lake visible from the window as well.

"Where the hell are we, Hazel? Why are we here?" James is standing behind me. We had tried the door but found it locked when the padlock knocked against the boards and the chain clinked against the doors handles when we tried to open it.

"I don't know, James. I've never seen this place before." Even as the words left my mouth, I knew that I had, but the memory eluded me. James starts pacing, he doesn't like confined spaces. That's why he prefers to run outside. If he could walk everywhere, he would.

As I stared out the window trying to recall the memory of this place, we heard a car approaching. The motor was quiet, but the tires driving over gravel were almost deafening in the silence. James came to stand next to me as the sound of car doors reached us.

"There's at least two of them." He whispered as if we were hiding. But if we're locked in here then we needed to bang on the walls and door to get the people's attention. Unless these were the people who put us here. My breathing accelerated as I heard the sound of them unlocking the door. "If we both rush them then maybe we can escape."

We both looked around the barren shack trying to find quick, useful weapons, but there was nothing. He grabbed my hand and looked at me. Despite feeling absolutely useless, the determination in James' eyes is what kept me grounded. I nodded to him and took a deep breath.

When the door opened, we were blinded by the light that came in. All I knew from their shadowy outlines is that there were three of them, and at least two of them were massive. Their silhouettes reminded me of body builders—pure muscle. I could only see the head of the one in the back, he was taller than the other two by at least four inches. My heart fell to my feet. We couldn't rush them. We couldn't escape.

The two big men parted to make room so the man in the back could enter the shack. He sauntered in, taking his time. His confidence was envy-inducing; he knew as well as I did, we were not leaving here alive. This knowledge was confirmed when I saw the cruel, twisted smile on his otherwise unrecognizable face as he entered the tiny shack. "Hazel, it's been a while."

The man had forced me to stab James five times. And then he left, one of his cronies locking the door behind them as they left. I was left in that terrible shack with James bleeding out. I had a concussion and kept falling in and out of consciousness.

After having a dream like that, I'd love to see someone be able to focus on someone else's life and make it better so they can succeed.

If I lost James, I would have nothing. He was my everything. I had just wanted one night of peace; *No such luck for me, I guess.*

"I know you'll figure somethin' out for him. I'm gonna go watch some TV. I switched over the laundry, so don't worry about doin' that." I don't know what's gotten into her today, but her being supportive is out of character. I know she feels bad about her accident, but this is completely unlike her.

"Thanks, Ma." Before she can leave, James walks through the door.

"What's up ladies?" He smiles that beautiful smile of his. I couldn't stop myself from smiling even if I wanted to.

But my mom rolls her eyes and leaves the room without saying anything.

Chapter Nine

James

I can't focus on my run. I know Hazel is still feeling guilty about last night. She kept me up all night with her constant moving and sighing. But I knew if I had woken her up and said anything last night it would have made the situation even worse than it was. So, I suffered in silence and pretended to be sleeping.

It killed me; I thought I had done my job in helping her forget her troubles, but I was wrong. I would do anything to make sure she was okay. But I can't help her with this if she doesn't forgive herself. It's not like she broke my wrist, just hurt it. It's not even sore today, so no big deal. I've been through worse.

I go check on her in her office. I know she wants to get ahead of this problem with Jack. He's not one to sit back for a weekend and worry about it on Monday. When you're a famous person it's easy to ride out the controversy, but Jack barely had a name for himself with *Windsor Advertising*. I understood that he couldn't ride this out. I just wish he hadn't used Hazel to get him out of his own fuck ups.

I walk into the office, and Lynn is there freshly showered, talking to Hazel. *Damn, she must really be enjoying our hot water. Good for her.* I've never seen her shower that often, no matter how many times she stayed with us. It was usually days between her showers. I've obviously missed some of the conversation because as I enter Lynn stops talking and looks at me like I caught her stealing cookies from the cookie jar.

"What's up, ladies?" I smile to try to lighten the mood. Hazel blesses me with her gorgeous smile, but Lynn rolls her eyes and walks out of the room, bumping her shoulder into mine. "Is everything okay with you two?"

"Yea, Ma was just checking on me." So we're not going to acknowledge Lynn's disrespectful behavior. Noted.

"I haven't got much done this morning and I can't get my mind to focus, but I'm going to give it one more hour and then call it quits for a bit." If I hadn't spent a night next to her troubled sleeping, the bags under her eyes would have given it away, she looks exhausted. *We need a vacation.*

"Sounds good, Babe. Do you need anything? Water? Granola bar? Reese's?" She smiles at me as the stress starts to recede from her body.

"No, thank you. I love you and I'll come and join you in the living room soon. Please shut the door on your way out."

"I love you, too." I wink at her before closing the door and heading to the living room.

As I enter, Lynn is headed to the front hall to go out for a smoke. I'm surprised to see her grabbing Kiba's leash and taking him outside. She hates that dog with a burning passion, but Kiba is very persuasive when he wants to go out.

I take a seat on the couch and turn on the TV. I won't get much time out here watching what I want, Lynn doesn't like the shows I watch. Even though I don't like her, I try to give her a reprieve of the shitstorm that her life is when she's here. I take what I can get and try not to let it bother me too much. Luckily, there's nothing that exciting on anyway.

She comes back inside, taking off Kiba's leash and shucking off her coat and boots. She comes in and sits on the other end of the couch; snowflakes melt in her hair, her nose is red from the cold, and the smell of cigarette smoke wafts around her. I hate it, but she won't quit so there's nothing I can do about it.

"You gonna watch anything?" Her eyes flit around the room, avoiding eye contact with me.

"Nah. Nothing is really catching my eye." I pass her the remote and she starts flicking through the channels, not speaking to me. But I catch her throwing glances my way every once in a while. She has something to say, but I'm not going to pry. If she wants to talk, I'm all ears, but I'm not going to bring it up. She's an adult and it's time she learns how to communicate when she has an issue with something.

She tosses the remote on the coffee table and looks at me. For once, she doesn't look like she hates me. I see concern in her eyes, and I know what she's about to say has something to do with Hazel.

"What's goin' on with my daughter, James? I know I haven't been a good mother to her, but I know when there's somethin' goin' on with her, it's instinctual. So, you better start tellin' me what it is right now." She glares at me when she's finished.

So much for her not looking like she hates my guts. I knew she couldn't stay civil with me even if it was a matter of life or death. This woman despises me and how I make her follow our boundaries when she's here. I'm the villain in her story, and that's fine with me, as long as I'm the hero in Hazel's.

I'm shocked that she was so straightforward with me, though. She either beats around the bush with these types of conversations or avoids them all together and we have to pry it out of her, which usually ends in her screaming at us.

I wasn't going to push her, but if she wants to know, I won't lie to her. There's no point anyway because I'm honestly not sure what's going on with Hazel other than stress from her mother and work.

"I really don't know, Lynn. She's stressed out between you being here and now doing this job for Jack. That's all I've got." I shrug my shoulders. Her eyes get wide and then darken with anger. *Fuck.*

"*MY* bein' here?" Her voice raises with each word she speaks; *I've really screwed the pooch now.* "What the fuck do you mean by that, James? My daughter said I could come stay with y'all this weekend. It's not as if I just showed up and demanded y'all take me in!" *Shit.* I rub my hand down my face, I need to run damage control before this escalates any further, but I'm so tired of Lynn coming here and causing chaos in our lives. It's time she found out exactly what she does to her daughter; she's been living in denial for years now. I sit forward on the couch, turning slightly towards her, my arms resting on my knees.

"Well, Lynn, I'm not going to sugarcoat it for you. Your presence in this house really wears on Hazel's mental health. She loves you and would never let you be outside in this cold, but that doesn't mean you don't affect her in a negative way by being here."

"Had I known my bein' here with my daughter was such an inconvenience I would have never asked. And you can bet your ass that after this visit you'll never see my sorry ass *ever* again."

"Lynn—" She's already storming out of the living room towards the guest room. Before I can get off the couch, she's slamming the bedroom door.

Thankfully I saw Hazel put in her soundproof headphones, so she won't be bothered by her mother's tantrum. But if she doesn't calm down before Hazel is done working, I'm going to have some explaining to do.

I find it hard to believe Lynn didn't know how badly she affected Hazel. If she could sense something was wrong with her with her "intuition" then she should have been able to tell how Hazel acted when she was around. Then again, maybe not because she doesn't know a different side to Hazel. But I do and I see the difference every time Lynn is here and it kills me inside. If I was an asshole at all, I'd never let Lynn over, but I know it means a lot to Haz to be able to spend this time with her, no matter how painful it is. So, I let it happen time and again. I'm getting tired of it, but if this is what Haz wants, then I'll support her. I bite my bottom lip,

97

trying to come up with ways to fix this before it blows up in my face.

I turn the TV to Comedy Central to try to lighten my dark mood and give me some background noise while I consider my options.

There's a Dave Chappelle special on. I've seen it a million times already, but it is funny. I go grab a bottle of water and settle onto the couch. Kiba comes over and looks at me as if he knows the shitshow I just made for myself.

"I know, Kiba. I don't need your judgment. I'll deal with it." He whines at me and then lays on the ground, huffing in annoyance.

His annoyance isn't only with my predicament, but also the fact we haven't gone on a walk today. The temperature had dropped to -12 degrees Fahrenheit, completely unheard of in October. The snow has picked up tremendously and I don't want to take him out in it and both of us get frostbite. He'll get over his irritation later. In the meantime, I'll just ignore his relentless huffing and whining.

I should go apologize to Lynn, but I'm still too mad at her lack of empathy to look at her. I'll finish watching Dave Chappelle and then go talk to her. That should, hopefully, be adequate enough time for us to both have clear heads.

Chapter Ten

Lynn

That cocksucker. Telling me my own daughter doesn't want me here. She would have told me she didn't want me here if it bothered her that much.

You sure about that, Lynn? I don't know what to think anymore.

My life is in shambles, and I just want a way out. I can't keep dealin' with this shit. I sit on the edge of the bed, contemplating my whole sorry existence. Ain't nothin' been easy for me and I'm tryin' to fix it. I'm tryin' to do better, but I keep finding myself in this same fuckin' cycle and I don't know how to break it. If I was alone, I'd scream at the top of my lungs. That's always worked in the past.

But I'm not alone and if I start screamin', they'll come running and that's the last fuckin' thing I need.

I gotta get out of here. Kinda fuckin' ironic that the one place I thought I'd always be welcome is the one place I'm not wanted. Why wouldn't she tell me? She knows damn well that I wouldn't come here if she wasn't okay with it. Sure, I've shown up uninvited and without permission before, but God damn it, what else was I supposed to do?

I need somethin' to help me forget this whole shitty situation. My own fuckin' daughter hates me and there ain't shit I can do about it. What a sorry excuse for a fuckin' mother I am.

The worst part is I don't blame her.

I pace the guest room thinking over my options. There's not many. If I ask one of them to borrow a phone, they'll know I'm trying to leave, and I don't want to ask them for anything else. I don't want to be more of a burden than I already am.

James is in the living room, so he'll see me if I go out either door. I walk over to the window to see if it's got nails holdin' it shut or if they painted the seams, but my luck has held out there and it looks clear. I grip the smooth ledge and lift up, it glides right along, lettin' in the cold air, I hurry and close it before it lets in too much cold air. *I'm gonna need to layer up if I'm really goin' out there.*

We could probably talk this through, but that's never been me and it never will be. No matter how much Hazel needs me to be. If she had such a problem with my bein' here, she shouldn't have agreed to me coming. But since she didn't and her fiancé did, I'll just remove myself from her life so she can keep on bein' happy and not worrying about my well-being.

I never wanted kids, especially after Steven left me high and dry for that bimbo. I tried to abort her, I tried drinkin' and doing every drug I could get my hands on, thinkin' that would get me clear of this huge responsibility I wasn't ready for. It didn't work. My belly kept growing, I kept getting sick, and eventually here she came. Shockingly she was perfectly healthy, if only a little underweight. My mother wasn't happy I was havin' a baby, but she wasn't surprised either. I remember I told her the day I found out because I didn't know what to do.

I walk into the living room where my mom sits in her plastic-covered chair, sewing up some socks that have holes in the toes. We aren't poor, but she is determined she can fix our clothes if they get holes.

"Mom." My voice shakes, givin' me away the moment words leave my mouth.

"What did you do, Lynn? What kind of trouble are you in?" She sets down her sewing, staring at me standing in the doorway. "I swear to God, child, if you got caught by the cops doing God knows what with that boy, I'll hang you both from your toes in the tree out back!"

I take a deep breath, hoping it calms me down, but my stomach is queasy, and I can feel myself fighting back tears. "It's not that, Mom. I'm—I'm pregnant, Mom."

"LYNN JEAN BROKER!" I jump out of my skin at her raised voice. If she's yelling, I know I fucked up. I knew she'd be mad, but I was hoping it wouldn't be this bad. She's so understanding most of the time. But I'm clearly a fool in more ways than one. "Do you know how expensive babies are? Do you know the first thing about babies? No, you don't. Yet you go around spreading your legs for any boy that shows you attention. I can't believe this." She shakes her head at me. "Go to your room, I can't look at you right now. We'll discuss this later."

I turn around and burst into tears as I run down the hall to my bedroom. I hate her assuming I've been sleepin' around town. I may have recently had a promiscuous streak, but I just wanna get over Steven the way he's getting over me. Before Steven I had only ever been with one guy, Tony.

Tony was my best friend growing up. Our moms worked together, and we would have dinners together every Saturday until they moved away two years ago. Tony and I were curious about the opposite sex and who better to find out the ins and outs than your best friend? Our moms were at the grocery store and would be gone for a while, as they always were, so we thought it was the perfect time. We were *nervous and both shaking, but we managed. And we kept doing it until he moved away. We had a mutual understanding that this wasn't a serious thing, just two kids havin' some fun.*

I fall onto my stomach as soon as I reach my bed, not carin' if it hurts my baby or not. This is the worst thing that could have ever happened to me. What the fuck am I gonna do?

My mom eventually came around to me being pregnant, but the first few months was like walking on eggshells and any little thing set her off as if she was the one carrying the baby and having her hormones all over the damn place.

After that, I tried not to trust her with anything again. I didn't have a choice in Hazel moving in with her when I went to prison. If I did, she wouldn't have got my daughter. I didn't know where Steven was, and all my friends were drugged up or drunk. My mom was the best place for her, and it still irritates me to this day to admit that.

I haven't thought about doing drugs in years despite Paul going on benders, but right now I want to be as numb to the world as I can. How I'm gonna manage it is beyond me, but I'll figure it out. I have to, but first I need to figure out what to wear so I don't freeze to death out there. There's not a coat in here because that's in the front hall closet. So, I'll have to make do, ain't nothin' I'm not used to. I've been figurin' my way around for decades now and I haven't lost that talent.

I go over to the closet and open the door, lookin' over my options. There are a few sweaters, but they don't look very warm. If I layer them up, they should work though and that's all I need. I throw 'em on the bed and keep looking to see what else I can find. I throw a few pairs of pants on the bed with the sweaters along with a few socks.

Then I realize my shoes are in the front hall. *FUCK*. Well, at least I'll be able to grab a coat and maybe find some gloves. I'll just have to wait until they go to bed tonight. I lock the bedroom door so they can't come in and bother me. I can't face either of them right now. I just need to get the fuck outta here and never come back.

I move the clothes onto the dresser by the door and go back to the bed, the bedding is still in the dryer, but I don't wanna go out there, so I lay on the bare mattress and close my eyes, hoping sleep takes me for a while so I don't have to keep running my head in circles on all my fuck ups in life.

What feels like a few hours goes by and there's a knock on my door.

"Lynn, can we talk?" His voice is muffled through the door, but I can hear the sincerity in his voice and it pisses me off.

"Leave me alone, ya prick. I don't wanna talk to Hazel and I *definitely* don't wanna talk to you." I roll over and put the pillow over my head to drown out his voice. If he thinks he can come in here and apologize to me and make everything better, he must have lost his damn mind. I'm done with them just as they want me to be. I will never rely on them for help ever again. I'm not just hurt that Hazel couldn't tell me how me being here was affecting her, but also that I didn't see that I'm not actually welcome here. I've been too inside my own problems to look outside myself. That's just who I am, I guess. Because even though I see it now, I can't pull myself out of it. I know that if I just change my ways and apologize for the way I've been acting everything would be fine.

But I can't. All I can think about is gettin' the hell out of here.

The sound of James' feet walking back to the living room loosens the bunched up muscles in my shoulders. I don't want to fight with him right now. I would have if he would have kept pushing, but I really don't have it in me.

I must have fallen asleep at some point because I get scared awake at the sound of a knock on the door,

"Ma, it's me. I know you're not speaking to us right now, but I really wish you would. We'll be up for a while longer if you want to come talk to me." I don't bother with a response. It's not worth it to her to hear the pain in my voice and I don't have the energy to speak. What would I say to her, anyway? Anything said after learning about how she feels would just seem weak and stupid.

I don't know how long I wait, but as soon as all is quiet in the house, I make my way out of the room. I use the time to layer on the clothes I had laid out earlier. When I'm sure they're both sleeping, I make my way to the front hall where my shoes and the coat Hazel told me I could have are.

I'm gettin' the hell out of here. I tiptoe to make sure I don't wake them. I reach the front door and pull on my shoes and coat. I find some gloves on the closet shelf and a fuzzy hat. *It's almost as if this was all meant to happen this way.* What a depressing thought.

They had locked their door and that will have to be the only sign that I left because I don't have a way to relock the deadbolt. Nothing I can do about it, so I just head out into the freezing cold.

A part of me wishes I could have just apologized for my shitty behavior and stayed because this weather sucks. But it's the principle of the matter. My pride wouldn't let me. So here I am, on my way to the alley on Elm. It holds the answer to all my problems.

I haven't been here since I got out of prison. I was trying to make better decisions, but clearly, I've been doin' it wrong this whole time. I walk down the alley to one of the burning trash cans. Three men stand around the fire, warming their hands. I don't recognize them in the dark, the firelight is playing tricks on my eyes.

"Lynn, it's been a while." I stop in my tracks as that voice sends my life into a further tailspin. I haven't seen him in decades, and here he is, like no time has passed at all. My heart falls to my stomach and I start questioning the decisions I made to get here.

"Steven—"

Chapter Eleven

Hazel

I finally manage to make some headway with Jack's case after a phone call with Alex. I'm glad I hired him despite Jefferson's reservations. He thought Alex was too young and didn't have enough experience to be of any real use. Alex has proven him wrong time and again, he's given us insight onto new methods of drug testing, comes up with brilliant cover stories, and is just an all-around good guy.

Pulling up Jack's number, I lean back in my chair. He's going to be ecstatic to finally hear from me. He picks up on the third ring.

"Please tell me you have something, Hazel. I'm losing my fucking mind."

"We've got it handled, Jack. I can't promise you'll get out of everything, but most of it is covered. I'll send you the details, what's your email? Give me a call back when you've read it over and we can fine-tune it as best we can."

"Thank you, Hazel. You're a Godsend. I could kiss you right now." I shudder at that thought but laugh at him so he doesn't know how much he repulses me.

"Don't get too ahead of yourself, read it over and then decide how much of a Godsend I am. Talk later, Jack." I hang up with him and run my hands through my hair, letting out a breath. I really hope this works for him. If not, I'm not sure what else we can do for him. Given the type of person Jack is, it's probably not enough, but he royally fucked up and he needs to be held somewhat accountable.

I turn off my computer and go out to the kitchen where James is cooking chicken stir fry. He's facing away from me, so he doesn't notice me coming in. Kiba is sleeping in the living room or else he'd give me away. I sneak up on James and wrap my arms around his waist, making him jump and yelp.

"Damn it, Hazel. You could have hurt yourself with the oil!" He's laughing so I know he's not mad at me.

"Wouldn't be the first time and it won't be the last, Mr. Bacon-Is-Life." I give him a tight squeeze before letting him go and sitting on the barstool at the island. "Where's Mom at?" He stiffens when I ask that, and I have a sinking feeling in my stomach. *What now?*

"Uh, well—fuck. I'm sorry, Haz. I really am, but I was so tired of how she was treating you and how she doesn't give a damn how her being here affects you. She asked me what was bothering you and I told her what I knew."

"And what was that, James?" My words come out harsher than I intended, but I would be lying if I said I wasn't mad that he said anything at all. I was going to handle it, I just needed time; time that I was spending on his boss.

"That her being here and Jack's case had you stressed. That's all I know that's bothering you because that's all you've given me. If it's anything else, I'd like to know, but I'm also not going to push you to talk to me. I'm not your therapist and I understand there are some things you reserve for her. I respect that, but when she comes at me in an accusatory way, I get pissed." He looks genuinely upset about the fact he said anything to her. I can only imagine how that conversation went.

"Why didn't you come tell me?"

"You were working, Babe." He turns back to finish up the stir fry. "And given how long you were in there, I figured you were making good progress."

"Ugh. This weekend has been absolute shit." My head drops to my arms resting on the island. I practice my breathing exercises Miranda gave to me to help calm down my anxiety. When I get to the count of fifteen, I feel James' hand running up and down my back.

"I'm so sorry, Haz. I really didn't want to add to your stress. I thought maybe she'd be receptive. She hasn't seemed to be in such a bad mood this weekend. I was wrong." He sits on the stool next to me and brushes my hair from my face and I turn to look at him. I give him a small smile to let him know I'm not upset with him. I mean, I am upset, but I know his heart was in a good place.

"Is she in her room?" I stand up to go check on her and he grabs my arm. I look back at him and from the look on his face it isn't good. "What?"

"I tried talking to her afterwards. She doesn't want to talk to either of us, she locked the door. You can try, but I'm just giving you a heads up." My head drops back on my shoulders in defeat, *I can't believe this.*

"I'm at least going to tell her supper is ready. She can come if she wants, and if not, we'll make her a plate and put it in the fridge. She should be better in the morning." Her mercurial moods don't typically last long with me, but James isn't me so I have no idea what to expect. If it's like any other time he's kicked her out, she won't come back out until she leaves. I shake that line of thought out of my head, hoping I'm wrong.

Knock, knock, knock. "Mom, supper is ready. We're having stir fry." She doesn't respond and it's quiet behind the closed door. She's either choosing to ignore me or she fell asleep. Sighing, I go back to the kitchen. "She's not coming to supper."

"I didn't think she would." James gives me a sad smile and wraps me in his arms. We stand like that for what seems like forever and a millisecond at the same time. He calms my storms and I'm so thankful for him.

He didn't know about the shitshow that is my mom until we were well into dating and had already told each other we loved each other. He'd met Nana, of course, and he asked about my parents, but I always gave him some lame excuse and hurriedly changed the subject. Then one night I got drunk and emotional and bawled while I told him all about it. James never changed how he felt about me, even knowing what my mom did as a profession while I grew up. Most people find out and shun me as though I was the one selling myself to pay bills.

There wasn't much to complain about with my mom, she provided for me monetarily. I had everything I needed, and I was thankful for that, but the reason I cried whenever I talked about it is because she lacked an emotional connection to me. I didn't know if it was just that she wasn't a maternal person or if I was conceived in a horrible way. When I was 16, I asked Nana about it, and she told me that was "just the way Lynn was." She never really went into details about my mom with me, so I stopped asking.

To this day my mom is still an enigma to me, and I feel like I'll go crazy trying to figure her out. I try not to think too hard about her, but when she's here I can't ignore the gnawing thoughts and questions in my head. I was fully prepared to ask her all types of questions this weekend, but then Jack called and here we are.

I'm pulled from my thoughts when James places my plate of food on the counter in front of me, the sweet and spicy aromas making my stomach growl loudly.

"Did you eat anything today?" He raises an eyebrow at me, and I know he's about to lecture me because I hadn't. I'd gotten wrapped up in my work and didn't even have one of my granola bars I have hidden in my desk.

"Yea, totally." The sarcasm is thick in my voice, and he shakes his head at me before grabbing my plate and heaping more food on it.

"You know better than to do that, Hazel. Eat all of this and then we'll break out the Oreos and chocolate ice cream while we watch a movie." The smile I give him is the first genuine one I've given him all weekend.

"That sounds amazing, Babe." I kiss him before digging into my food. I don't know how big he thinks my stomach is, but this is entirely too much food. There's no way I'm going to finish all of this despite not eating all day, but I'm going to do my best.

We talk about Jack's case while we eat and he's, yet again, impressed at how we spin the whole thing. The only thing Jack is currently facing trouble for is the drugs. Alex had been thinking the same thing I was about the underage girl and had been working on that for the last 24 hours. He bought her silence, found someone who could pass for her and paid her a lot of fucking money to give a statement that it was her in that video. How he pulled that off, I will never know. I don't ask questions; I just ask for results, and he provides. He's probably still going to face jail time for the drugs, but it's better than prison for fucking an underaged girl.

He's telling me about his book when I look down at my plate and realize I only have three bites left. I turn to look at him with eyes as big as my dinner plate and he chuckles, pleased with the progress I've made.

"Good girl, Haz." Despite the shitty weekend, my thighs clench at those words, and he smirks like he knows exactly what he just did.

We don't hold our sexual desires, likes, dislikes, or fantasies from each other. I've never been as sexually liberated as I am with James. Not that I slept around a lot before him, but I had my fair share of lovers, especially in high school.

I bite my lip, thinking about last night and what I want him to do to me later. It's been a while since we used the bed straps and given my celebratory mood over Jack's case and my frustration over my mom, tonight seems like the best night to do it. *Maybe I'll even let him gag me.* I silence a moan with my last bite of food, so he doesn't know just how turned on I am.

I pick up our plates without looking at him and take them to the sink to rinse them off before putting them in the dishwasher. It's like he has a sixth sense or something, because he comes up behind me and hooks one arm around my neck, his free hand landing on the inside of my thigh slowly making its way up, teasing me. He breathes heavily in my ear, making goosebumps raise on my arms. I try to turn around so I can kiss him, but his grip around my neck tightens. His upper body pushes against mine, making me bend over the sink, my hands going out to brace myself on the back of it. He grinds his dick against my ass. He's already as hard as a rock.

I was already wet from my thoughts, but now I'm soaked.

As much as I would love to let him fuck me in our kitchen, I can't consciously let him knowing my mom might come in here at any moment.

"James, we can't. At least not right here." He growls in frustration but moves away from me. "Finish up the dishes and come to the bedroom when you're done." I wink at him and saunter away, feeling his eyes devouring me.

I go into the bedroom and get out the ball gag, red velvet sleep mask, and get the bed straps out from underneath the mattress, leaving the drawer open: invitation for him to use whatever else he deems fit. I set my items on the comforter then go to my closet to choose which lingerie I want to wear for him. Given his mood it can't be something I like, or it'll get ruined. He'd prefer me naked, but I like to challenge him; it adds to the fun.

My first pick is a light blue lace top with matching thong and garter, but the way it compliments my skin makes it one of my favorites. Instead, I go with an all-black silk set that I've had for a while. It's still in excellent condition, but I could live without it. I hurry to put it on, knowing he's rushing the dishes to get in here. I lay on the bed and put the sleep mask on, I don't want to know what he's going to do or when. I consider putting on my noise canceling headphones, but I love it when he talks to me, and I don't want to miss a word he utters or a sound he makes.

I lay there for what feels like forever. *What is taking him so long?* I go to take the sleep mask off, but he stops me with a sharp *tsk*. My heart hammers in my chest. *How long has he been here?* I don't care, it turns me on more knowing he was standing there enjoying the view.

"Looks like my girl wants to play." I whimper at the huskiness in his voice, knowing he's just as turned on as I am. I nod my head, not trusting myself to speak. "Then play we shall. Though, it would be a lot easier if you were naked."

"What's the fun in that?" My voice shakes with unbridled lust. He growls at my response, placing his hand on my thigh, causing my breathing to hitch in my chest. He moves both of his hands to my leg, taking his time going down to my ankle. When he gets there, he grabs it and yanks it to the side of the bed where a strap lies in wait. When that leg is secure, he does the same with my other leg.

This was a good idea when I had it, but now I'm impatient and just want him inside of me or touching me or something.

"You forgot something, baby." He's securing my left ankle in the cuff when he speaks, tightening one notch too tight, just the way I like it.

"What's that?" He slaps my inner thigh, making me cry out from the shock that rings through my body.

"The handcuffs." My body shivers at the promise in his voice. His hand leaves my thigh as he turns to grab the handcuffs from the drawer, and I already miss his touch on my feverish skin.

I jump when he returns just as quickly as he left and grabs my hands in one of his, locking my wrists in the metal cuffs. We could have opted for those sex shop fuzzy cuffs, but this feels more risqué. He tightens them tight enough I can't get out, but not tight enough that they hurt me. Perfection as always. He bends down to kiss me as he raises my arms above my head to put them over the spindle in the middle of the headboard. I'm his to do with as he pleases; no escape, and once the gag is in place, no way to say stop. *This is exactly what I need.*

I hear the click of his pocketknife opening and then he's running it over my skin, caressing me with the blade. Goosebumps dance along my body and my breathing is accelerating with each pass of the knife on my skin. He traces the blade up my arm and cuts one strap of my negligee, dragging the knife across my chest to the other one to repeat the process. I try to stay as still as possible, so he doesn't accidentally cut me. Knives make me nervous, but I trust James with my life and know he won't hurt me, but if I move just right it won't be him hurting me, but myself.

He cuts a small slit in the top of my negligee and then rips the rest of it off me. This is why I chose something I didn't love. I knew this would happen, well, not the knife bit. I'm not complaining, though.

I feel his lips on my skin, kissing me where he had dragged the knife across my chest; showing me he loves me after showing such an act of aggression. He moves his mouth down and onto my left breast, taking my nipple into his mouth, teasing it with his tongue and then biting down with the right amount of pressure to get me to arch my back, pushing me further into his mouth. His hand grabs my other breast and pinches the nipple, I try my hardest not to squeal, but then he pinches harder, and it leaves my lips.

He releases me from his mouth.

"That was a test. You failed." I can hear the devilish grin in his words. I don't know what my punishment will be, but I am more than willing to find out. I feel him get off the bed and I wish I didn't have this mask over my eyes so I could see what he's doing; the anticipation is killing me. I can still feel him in the room, or at least I think I can. And then the bed is dipping beneath his weight again. My body is shaking from the adrenaline of giving him this power over me. "Move your head forward." I do as he says, I'm his to control. I'd do anything he told me to at this point. "Open your mouth." He inserts the gag into my mouth, running the straps behind my head and securing them. He grabs my hair and yanks my head back to where it was. Then he runs his tongue up the side of my face. I try to move away from him, but his grip in my hair holds me in place. He slaps me where he just licked, the saliva making the slap burn more than it normally would. I breathe deeply through my nose. I can feel drool already dribbling down my chin.

He caresses the side of my face, then grabs my cheeks in his hand, "You're mine, Hazel. No one else's, ever again. You belong to me." Then he kisses my forehead. I'm melting in a puddle of love and lust and anticipation. I don't just want him inside of me, I *need* him. He runs his hand down my face, to my neck, and keeps going, furthering his descent. I'm not sure where his destination is, but I know where I want him to be.

I hear a bottle pop open, and I know what my punishment is. *He's going to fuck my ass.* As soon as I have the thought, I feel him putting the lube on my hole and I instinctively clench.

"Relax, Haz. We both know you love this. Take a deep breath and let all your reservations go." I do as he says, and then he's putting a finger inside of me, testing the tightness. I'm sore from last night, but I'm too turned on to care.

He follows his first finger with another, stretching me open with his fingers. His other hand has found the Holy Land and is rubbing my clit to help me relax more. I buck my hips off the bed, and he slaps my pussy.

"Be still, Haz. Unless you want to be punished more." His voice is husky with lust; I know he wants to punish me, but that would mean I have to wait for him to fuck me senseless.

He removes his fingers from my ass, and I feel his head at the entrance. I suck in a breath through my nose, trying my best to relax. He goes back to massaging my clit while keeping his head at my ass, not thrusting, not moving, just massaging me and getting me comfortable. My whole body tenses as I cum for him, my moan muffled by the gag in my mouth. He keeps massaging as I ride the wave, body tense, breathing huffing in and out of my nose.

As soon as my body relaxes, he thrusts his dick into my ass. It takes everything in me not to tense at the intrusion. He did the work right, so it doesn't hurt that much, but it's a wild sensation, nonetheless. He growls in the back of his throat, his fingers still massaging my sensitive clit, his other hand gripping my thigh. He stills when he gets all the way in, giving me a chance to get used to the fullness.

He must be watching me closely for any signs of discomfort because when I give a small nod to let him know I'm ready, he pulls out almost all the way and goes back in slowly a few times. I'm whimpering behind the gag. I can't help it; his dick feels magnificent. He slams into my ass, and I yell out behind the gag. He removes his fingers from my clit and shoves them into my soaked pussy and I buck my hips again. It's involuntary and I wonder if he noticed.

He's either too focused to do anything about it or doesn't care because he doesn't stop his assault on my body. He slams in and out two more times, his fingers matching the strides of his cock and I tense around him, squirting all over. I feel the waterfall leave me and his answering moan almost pushes me over the edge again. He keeps slamming in and out of me and I think I may die from how many orgasms I have. They're back-to-back and I can't catch my breath. When I think I may pass out from the blood rushing to my head, he growls out my name and empties himself inside of me.

He slowly pulls out of me and crawls over me to take the gag out and the mask off. I blink in the bright light. He smiles down at me and kisses me deeply. "I love you, Hazel. From now until the end of time."

"I love you too, James." We just lay there for a moment, basking in the aftermath of everything.

"I'm going to go run a bath for us. I'll be right back. Don't go anywhere." He chuckles as he gets up to go to the bathroom. I'm still handcuffed to the headboard and my legs are still spread wide in the bed straps; escape isn't an option.

"Jackass." I giggle, too, because while it was a ridiculous joke, it *is* kind of funny. *I absolutely love that man.*

Chapter Twelve

James

"Jackass." She's giggling, letting me know she doesn't actually mean it. I'd love to let her go so she can move her arms into a more comfortable position, but I want to be there when she does to make sure she's okay. I need to rub the feeling back into her arms and shoulders. If I let her go, she'll do it herself and tonight is about me taking care of her.

I go into our bathroom and start the water, letting it warm up enough to relax her tense muscles. As soon as the water is at the right temperature, I put the plug in the drain and add in some of her favorite essential oils: ylang ylang, lavender, jasmine, and tangerine. We're going to smell like a damn flower shop after this bath, but it'll be worth it to make her happy. The lavender will help her sleep better tonight, too, which she is in desperate need of. I put the oils back on the counter and go get my fiancée.

I can't wait to call her my wife and spend the rest of our lives together. One more year and she'll be mine completely. We'd do it sooner, but she wants a big fancy wedding and the venue we want is booked out. We got the soonest available date—June 15th, 2024. I was shocked at first, but then Hazel took me on a tour of the place, and it made sense.

The venue had an entire wall of windows that face the west and will make a perfect backdrop for our evening wedding. The woodwork is a dark-stained oak, the pews are made of matching wood. Our wedding colors of black, maroon, and silver will complement it well. The price for the place wasn't bad either, we paid a little extra for their cleaning services as well. We just have to make sure to get our decorations down. We didn't want to have to postpone the reception, so we hired people to take them down for us. I don't mind, though. As long as it makes Hazel happy, I'd spend every last penny on this wedding.

I go back into the bedroom to get Hazel; her beautiful green eyes meet mine and she smiles at me like I'm the sun to her universe when I walk through the door. "You better hurry, I think my arms are going to fall off." I roll my eyes at her. She's barely been tied up for an hour, they're not going to fall off, but I go over and undo her legs from the bed straps, making my way up, my hands exploring her body until I get to her neck. I reach over and grab the key to unlock her cuffs and let her go. Her arms fall to her sides as she winces. "I'm getting too old to be doing all that kinky shit with you."

Laughing at her, I rub her shoulders, "You're only 35. You're far from old; it was just a weird position to be in." She relaxes against the bed as my fingers dig into her muscles. I slide one of my arms under her neck and the other behind her knees and lift her from our bed. "I'll finish massaging your arms and shoulders in the tub. The hot water will help a lot more than just my hands." She nuzzles her face into my neck as I carry her to the bathroom.

"Going back to the topic of my age, in the olden days I'd be considered an old maid. Not married, barren, worthless in the eyes of society. A total sham."

"Well, it's a good thing we're not living back then, huh? You know I'd have already married you if you weren't so in love with Peak's Hall." I set her down in the tub of hot water, reaching over to turn off the water.

"I know, I'm just teasing you. I am getting close to 40, though. So as soon as we're married, we're going to have to pump those three babies out really quick." I'm almost certain my eyes are going to pop out of my head when I look at her. "What? You know I want three kids; this isn't a surprise to you. And biologically my clock is ticking down. It'll be hard, but we'll make it work."

I know we've agreed to have three kids, but my brain hasn't really processed the fact that in a year, if things go as planned, we'll be expecting our first child. Everything changes after that. No more just Haz and me. I've gotten so used to it just being us, I'm going to mourn the loss of that time. I know we'll still have time together, but it won't be the same. Then adding more children just complicates it more and more. I would be lying if I said it didn't give me anxiety.

As if she can read my thoughts, Hazel reaches for my hand and drags me into the tub with her. "We have months to discuss it more and work out the details. For now, focus on the here and now. Plus, you still owe me that massage after ravaging my body." She smirks at me and places my hands on her shoulders.

"I can't give you a good massage like this. Turn around." She does as I ask, carefully, so she doesn't spill the water over the side of the tub. Once she's settled between my legs I get to work on the knots in her shoulders. Knots that aren't only from what we just did, but also the stress she's been under. "I know this is probably a bad time to talk about it, but I can't help it. You need to decide, Haz. Either stop letting her affect you so badly or stop letting her come here." She tenses under my fingers.

"Jam—"

"Before you say anything, listen to me. Please." I interrupted her and I know that's one of her biggest pet peeves, but if I don't, she'll just go on a tangent and that's not the goal here. "I know she's your mom and you're hoping you can mend the gap you two have. But you have to have realized by now that it's never going to happen. That's not who she is. She doesn't want anything other than a place to crash and to mooch off of us."

"I know, James. Trust me, I fucking know." She takes in a shuddering breath and hangs her head; her hair falling into her face. *She's going to shut down.* I grab her hair and tuck it behind her ear.

"Don't shut down on me, Haz. Talk to me, we can figure this out together—as a team." She lifts her head and stares at the wall. She's gotten a lot better at pulling herself out of her thoughts and talking to me. I'm incredibly proud of her and thankful to Miranda for getting her to this point.

"I just don't know how to build those walls around my heart when it comes to her. I feel so much empathy towards her because I know her life hasn't been easy, and she's been trying to fill a void. I know it's not my responsibility, but I still *feel* responsible for trying. I'm all she has left. If I give up on her like everyone else, she has no one." She's crying now, her sobs are wracking her body. I wrap my arms around her and lean back against the tub, bringing her with me. I kiss her head.

"I'm sorry, Haz. I really am, for all of it. I know you mean well, but it's my job to make sure you're okay too. She makes you not okay. I know that sucks, Baby. I get it. You should call Miranda in the morning. She won't mind that it's Sunday if you say it's about your mom. I'll keep Lynn occupied while you get advice from a non-biased person."

"Yea, that's a good idea." She's still crying, but she's not as tense. I squeeze her to me, offering her endless support in whatever she decides to do. My selfish hope is that she cuts Lynn off. I'm not that delusional, though. Lynn will be a part of our lives until the day she dies. I let go of Hazel and tap her shoulder. "Sit up, I'll wash you up and then we can go to bed." She nods as she leans forward.

I take my time washing her, showing her a soft side after what we just did in our room. When I'm done, I hand her a big fluffy towel and dry off quickly with my own. I need to get a new comforter for our bed before she goes to lay down. I kiss the top of her head and wrap my towel around my waist before leaving our room to go to the hall closet. I can see the guest room door is open from where I stand. Lynn is probably in the bathroom or the kitchen. I'll have Hazel go talk to her before she goes to sleep. I'm the last person Lynn wants to talk to right now. Hazel might be able to get through to her, but it's doubtful when Lynn gets into her moods. That's where Hazel learned the art of shutting down when her feelings get to be too much.

I go back to the bedroom and carefully remove the comforter from the bed. While her juices should be dry by now, you can never be too careful. When the comforter is off, I realize it soaked through to the sheet as well. I give myself a mental high five and a pat on the back and go back to the hall closet to get a new sheet as well. I'm not worried about the mattress because we have a cover on it just like the guest bed. I go back into the room and glance in the bathroom to see Hazel is still in the middle of her self-care routine. She's rubbing her lotion into her toned calves, and I know I only have a few minutes before she's done. I hurry to put the sheet and comforter on. I want her to be comfortable when she's done talking to Lynn if she decides to go talk to her.

As soon as the comforter settles on the bed, she walks out of the bathroom wearing nothing, I take a moment to appreciate the view before breaking the news to her. "Your mom left her room finally. I'm not sure where she's at because there weren't any lights on, but her door was open." She falters in her walk to bed. She's torn between going to sleep or going to talk to her mom. I have no idea which she'll choose, but I'm hoping it's bed.

"I should go see if she's okay." She heads to her closet to get a nightgown and I can see it's stressing her out after I just worked so hard to relax her. She was looking forward to a good night's sleep and she's going to be up for a while if she goes to talk to her mom. Her exhaustion is going to catch up to her sooner or later and it's not going to be good.

"She's probably fine, Haz. You can talk to her tomorrow. Just come to bed and get a good night's sleep before talking to her. It'll help you think more clearly with her and not be as emotional as you would be right now." I shouldn't have said that, but I can't in good conscience let her go talk to Lynn like this, neither of us will get sleep if she does.

She turns away from the closet to look at me, sadness heavy in her eyes. "You're right. I just hate that she's upset right now." The internal eye roll I give to that statement makes my eyes physically hurt. Lynn is the least deserving person for Hazel's empathy.

"She's always upset about something, Haz. One night isn't going to kill her—or you for that matter. Come to bed." I open up her side of the comforter. She hesitates for a few more seconds, glancing at the bedroom door, then nods to herself and joins me in bed. I pull her against me and tell Alexa to shut our light off.

"I'm sorry this is all so fucked up, James."

"You have nothing to be sorry for, Haz. You didn't ask to be born to her. You've survived so much and I'm glad you're here with me. I love you to the edge of the universe and back times infinity." I kiss the back of her head and squeeze her to my chest.

"I love you too, James." Her voice is already heavy with sleep, and I know she made the right choice in waiting for morning. I close my eyes and follow her into sleep.

Chapter Thirteen

Hazel

My brain wakes up before my body is ready to. It keeps telling me to get out of bed, there's something I need to do. I'm at a loss as to what that is in my sleepy state, but I have to pee anyway, so I sit up and look at my phone to see what time it is. 12 P.M. *Holy shit.* I must have been exhausted. I look over to James' side of the bed and find it empty. I get up to go to the bathroom and when I round the bed, I hear the shower running. My body is sore from last night, but I feel so rejuvenated after sleeping for so long.

"Good afternoon, Babe." I yell over the sound of the shower as I sit down to pee.

He pokes his head out, water dripping off his chin onto the floor. "Hey, Sunshine. How'd you sleep?"

"Great. If I dreamt, I don't remember it. I can't believe I slept so late. When did you get up?"

"About 10 minutes ago." He seems sheepish about this. I'm not sure why. Out of the two of us he's the one who prefers to sleep in on the weekends.

"Nice. I wasn't sure if you'd seen my mom yet this morning. But that answers that question. I'm going to go make some coffee. My brain may be awake, but my body is not having it and I'm praying to the gods that the caffeine will kick it into high gear." I give him a kiss and wipe the water off my face.

"Sounds good, I'll be out in a minute. Can you throw a bagel in the toaster for me? I'm starving."

"Sure thing." I grab a hair tie before leaving our bathroom and throw my hair into a messy bun. I don't have the energy for anything else right now. I go back to our bedroom and to my dresser to get some leggings and thick wool socks and then go to the closet to get a sweatshirt. Comfort is of the highest priority today. Once I'm dressed, I head down the hall and see my mom's door is still open. My stomach sinks at the sight of it and I'm not sure why. "Mom?" I call out to her and hear nothing.

Kiba comes over to me, nose to the ground and tail between his legs. I bend down to pet him. "What's wrong, Baby? Are you hungry? I'm sorry I missed breakfast." He perks up at the mention of breakfast and I kiss his head before standing up to go to the kitchen. He follows me with his tail wagging.

I go to the kitchen and freeze. There's no coffee and the bathroom door is open. My mom isn't here. As I start to panic, I try to rationalize with myself. She could have called Sandy to come get her. She could be in the living room, and I just overlooked her. Shit, maybe she's just outside having a cigarette. But as I check the living room and the windows, I realize she's not here. *What the fuck?*

My breathing hitches and gets lodged in my throat, my heart starts beating rapidly. I know something is wrong. Even though I told myself she could have called Sandy, I know there's no way she could have because our phones were in our room with us. *Maybe she snuck in while we were sleeping.* That's a good idea. I go back to our bedroom and grab James' phone off his nightstand. I go to his call log and there's just the call from Jack. I check his texts, nothing. I do the same to my phone and find the same.

James comes out of the bathroom as my legs give out. I fall hard to the floor, and he rushes over to me. "Haz, what's wrong? Are you okay? Are you faint? Do you need some food? Water? What is it?" Kiba comes into our room, whining. I promised him food and I didn't get it. But I can't focus on him right now, my brain is working overtime and I can't get a clear thought in my head. I don't know how I get the words out, but somehow, I manage to say, "She's gone." I can't breathe. I think I might pass out.

"What do you mean she's gone, Haz? Who? Your mom?" I know he means well, but his questioning isn't helping my meltdown. My heart is pounding and I'm gulping breaths.

"Who else would it be, James?" His utter cluelessness in some situations really pisses me off. He rubs my back, and while that would normally calm me down, it's doing the opposite right now. I need space. I need to think and breathe and find her. It's so cold outside and it's still snowing. I know she's a grown woman, but I can't help but worry about her.

"It'll be fine, Haz. Just breathe. We'll find her. I promise. She probably went back to Paul's."

"Please stop touching me. I can't deal with this right now." He immediately stops rubbing my back and sits on the edge of the bed. He's far enough away that I don't feel suffocated, but close enough that I know he's there if I need him. "Why would she go back there? He kicked her out. She'd have to walk and that's clear across town. This is all your fault, James. She wouldn't have left if you hadn't said anything yesterday. God, we were fucking, and she was leaving. I should have gone to check last night. I knew it. I felt it. I'm the worst fucking daughter ever." My words come out in a fast, jumbled mess. I'm taking my worries and anxiety out on James and I know I shouldn't, but I need an outlet and he's right here.

Kiba comes over to me, nuzzling into me, whining. I throw my arms around him and the floodgate that was holding my tears back breaks. My body shakes with my sobs. Kiba licks my arm in a comforting gesture. I hate it when he licks me, but I'm too far gone to tell him to stop. I need to pull myself out of this and figure out where she is. I have to know she's safe.

James hasn't said anything since I yelled at him. I know it wasn't fair, but I can't apologize, not yet. Not until I figure out what the hell is going on. Maybe not even then. I'm so damn mad at him and her and myself.

My crying slows to a point I can breathe normally, besides a couple of hiccupping breaths here and there. I get up off the floor and grab my phone. I leave the room without looking at James. I want to drive home the point that he needs to stay the hell out of my way right now. I call Sandy while I head to the kitchen to make some tea. I could use coffee, but my stomach can't handle the acidity right now.

"Hey, Lynn." My heart sinks at this greeting. She doesn't know my mom left, so she's not with Sandy. Not that Sandy's car could get here in this snow. "Do you need a ride? I don't think Paul has calmed down any. Between his yelling and blaring music all night there was no peace and quiet over here."

"This is Hazel, not Lynn." I try to sound strong and not like I'm on the precipice of losing my mind, but I can hear my voice shake.

"Did something happen to your mom? Why are you calling me?" She sounds offended and worried all at once. It does nothing to ease my worry.

"I don't know, Sandy. I wish I did. She left sometime last night and I don't know where she went. I was hoping you knew. Can you go to Paul's and see if she's there?"

"Shit. Yea, I'll get dressed and head over there. Give me 15 minutes. I'll call you back. She'll be fine, girl. Don't you worry; she's a strong woman."

"I know she is, but she wasn't in the best frame of mind last night. Her and James got into a fight, and she didn't talk to us all day, then this morning she's gone." The words are like vomit and I can't stop them. Somehow, I find myself slowing down, breathing. "Thank you, Sandy. Talk soon." I hang up and set my phone down on the counter before I chuck it across the room. My head falls to my chest, my hands reach up, grabbing fistfuls of my hair. I can feel James' eyes on me, but I don't acknowledge him.

"Haz, my love. I'm sorry about yesterday and I'm sorry your mom thought she had to leave. I just wanted her to know—" I spin to face him, rage clear on my face.

"I DON'T GIVE A FUCK, JAMES." My one string of sanity has snapped, and I can't do this anymore. "It wasn't your place to tell her anything. Yet you ran your mouth."

"Haz, I was just trying to help. I'm so sorry, Baby. I didn't mean to piss her off this bad. I just wanted her to get her shit together and be better for you." Logically I know he's right. The look on his face almost has my resolve crumbling, but my anger is running hot through my body, and I can't let it go yet...not until I know she's okay.

"How many times do I have to tell you to let me handle it? I know I need to, and I will. But you have to keep meddling in our business." He jerks back like I slapped him. "Just leave me alone for a while, James. Please. I just need some space." I turn away from him and put my head back in my hands. I want to hide from the world, but I have so much to do.

"Okay. I can do that. I love you endlessly." He backs away from me with his hands raised. I already hate myself for how I treated him, but his overbearing nature is the last thing I need right now. As he exits the kitchen my phone rings.

"Was she there?" *Please, please be there. I know it's a shitty place to be, but please be there, Mom.*

"No, he hasn't seen her since he kicked her out." My heart drops to my stomach and the tears start flowing again. "I'm sorry, Hazel." Something about her tone tells me she's not. She knows how tumultuous our relationship is and tends to blame me for the issues. I can tell by the way she looks at me whenever I see her. She thinks I should do more for my mom, but there's nothing more I can do that she'll accept.

"It's okay, Sandy. It's not your fault. I appreciate you going over there. I'll call you if I find anything out. Please, if she shows up, call me."

"Of course, hon. She's too headstrong sometimes. She probably managed to get a motel room and just needs to cool down." I bite back a bitter laugh; we both know my mom doesn't have the money for a room. Sandy is trying to help me and I'm not about to piss her off with my sardonic attitude.

"I doubt it. We both know she's broke. So, unless she managed to convince someone to get her one, that's not a possibility."

"You know your mom, though. She can be very persuasive when she wants to be. Could have been a lawyer if she'd had better support." She's giving my mom more credit than she deserves, but I don't say that.

"Okay, Sandy. I'll talk to you later. I'm going to make a few more phone calls and see if I can track her down."

"Sounds good, Hazel. I'll call you if I hear or see anything. Bye." She hangs up before I can say bye. She probably has some idea of where my mom could be but didn't want to tell me. Shit, for all I know my mom is camped out at her house and she's covering for her. I have no way of knowing unless I go over there. But that would show mistrust and I'm not that desperate yet. I'll call the motels around the area and Nana and see if she's at any of those places. Then I'll call the hospital and jail to see if she's there. If that's a dead end, then I'll go out and start looking for her. I just hope I'm not too late when I do find her.

Kiba whines at me from where he sits in front of his food bowl. "Fuck, I'm sorry Kiba." I get him some food and water before making more calls.

Chapter Fourteen

James

I really fucked up this time. I don't know if or when Hazel is going to forgive me. I didn't think Lynn would take off in this weather. I thought she'd sulk for the night and then come out with guns blazing as usual. I read the situation wrong and now there's nothing I can do. Hazel is trying to figure out where she is, and while I'd love to help her, she doesn't want me around. Not that I blame her, it's just how she is when she gets this worked up.

I throw on my winter gear and head outside. My breath comes out as a thick fog. *God, it's cold out here.* I need to clear my head, though, and my treadmill isn't going to cut it today and Hazel needs some space. So, I'll brave the cold and walk for a few blocks then come back. Hopefully that's enough time for Hazel because if not, I don't know what to do.

I turn left on the sidewalk, heading towards the business district. If the flower shop is open, I'll stop in and get Haz some flowers in an apology. She'll probably hate them, but it'll help me feel better. And I'm hoping the gesture shows her that I still love her and that I *am* sorry. I know I have a lot of making up to do, but I would do anything to make it right. Even scrubbing the floors with a toothbrush or cleaning the toilet for the rest of the year. I just want her to stop being mad at me. I *need* her to stop being mad at me. If we're not a team in this, we won't get very far. We work better together, and two heads are better than one, especially when the one is clouded with emotions.

Oleander's Flower Shop is open, so I go in and pick out a beautiful bouquet of lilies, marigolds, and some type of grassy filler. It's breathtaking. They put a plastic bag over it to help protect it from the cold, I pay and thank them then head back out. The inside of Oleander's was a great reprieve from the cold, but it made going back out in it that much worse.

It didn't take me as long to get here as I thought it would, so I go get a cup of coffee at Bucky's Coffee Shop across the street. I order a mocha espresso before finding a table to sit and sip at. I set the flowers down and shed my jacket, pulling out my phone hoping to see something from Hazel. There's not. I didn't expect there to be, but I had to be sure, just in case she needed me. Even though I'm not at the house to help, it doesn't mean I can't help from here. I'm about to start making calls to hospitals and the police station when Isaac walks through the door and sees me. He walks over and sits across from me. He points to the covered flowers, "Fucked up, huh?"

"How did you guess?" It doesn't surprise me that Hazel would call Jayden and tell her what's going on. What does surprise me is that Isaac knew where I was.

"Jayden told me that Hazel called her and all she said was that she needed Jay and that you weren't there. I dropped her off at your house to help Hazel figure out what to do. I knew I'd be in the way and a nuisance to Hazel. I figured I'd go for a drive since I didn't know where you were. Then I saw you crossing the street to come here and thought what a better way to strengthen our bond than over a cup of joe." He laughs, but I fail to see the humor in the situation.

"Thanks, man. I appreciate that." I do feel less alone with him sitting here. I feel like I can actually get through this and figure out a way to make it up to Hazel. We'll find Lynn and everything will work out just fine.

"No problem. I'm going to grab a coffee. I'll be right back." He gets up and goes up to the counter. I settle into my seat more comfortably and get ready to spend however long here. I take the bag off the flowers so they can breathe while we talk. He comes back a few minutes later with some caramel smelling something or other and takes his coat off, knowing we'll probably be here for a while too. It's just as bad, if not worse, than I thought it would be. "Those are really beautiful, she'll love them."

"I hope so." I find it hard to look at him right now, but I try to keep eye contact. My guilt is eating me alive.

"It's not entirely your fault, you know that, right?" I divert my eyes from his knowing gaze. *If only he knew.*

"I appreciate you trying to talk me down. But you don't know the story." I fill him in on everything that happened. He nods here and there, paying attention to every detail. "Now Lynn is missing, and Hazel is blaming me. Like I'm the one who took her somewhere and dropped her off." He raps his knuckles against the table, one of his weird tics he does when talking. It's not rude, but it certainly gets the attention of whoever he's talking to.

"Fuck that, man. Hazel is your girl. You were protecting her and trying to work through shit with her mom so you guys could be at peace. If Lynn doesn't face the harsh reality of her life, nothing will change. And, no offense, but Hazel is too chicken shit to face her mom like that. You know that as well as Jayden and I do. She feels protective and scared to bring up sensitive topics like that to Lynn." He's right, of course. He's known Hazel just a few months longer than I

145

have so we both know how she is. If anyone else talked about Hazel like this to me, I'd tell them to get fucked. But Isaac has this calm presence about him, and a no bullshit attitude and I don't feel defensive listening to him talk reason into me.

"So, what do I do, man? How do I fix this shit show?" I wrap my shaking hands around my coffee cup. I don't want him to see how emotionally fucked up I am even though I'm sure he knows. It just seems so non-macho; not that I need to be macho around Isaac, it's just the principle of the matter.

"Shit, I don't know. I think the flowers are a good start. Other than that, you know best, man. She loves you with her whole heart, she'll come around. But until Jayden texts me that it's clear to go back, we're stuck here. So, tell me what's been going on lately. Any new commercial pitches?" I chuckle and start to relax..

I start telling him all about this new commercial pitch I've been trying to work the details out on. It's for Dave's Automotive up on Wert Ave. The guy is a con-artist if I've ever seen one, but he's willing to pay our fees, so I'll make his commercial. The issue is, his lot is ridden with potholes, the cars have a thick layer of dust on them, and his small building looks as if it hasn't been repainted since the 80's, some of the wood panels are rotting away. We may make the commercial, but he's not going to get any business if his place continues to look like that. It's not my place to say anything to him, so I ran it by Jack and he's going to do some finagling with him. Hopefully by October we'll be able to shoot the commercial and get some business headed his way.

And even when I'm trying to relax and forget about Hazel for a while, she's there at the back of my mind, a nagging feeling that I need to go back home and make amends.

"What about you guys? What's new with you? It's been a while since we've seen you guys." We live in the same town, but we're all adults with lives and other friends of our own so we don't spend as much time together as we would like. We keep trying to remedy that, but life is hectic.

"We were actually going to invite you guys to dinner next weekend, but now all this shit with Lynn is going down. Fuck, this might not be the best time to tell you, but shit, man. I'm gonna tell you anyway. Jayden's pregnant. We're gonna be parents, dude." His smile could light a pitch-black town. His smile is so infectious, I feel myself smiling too. He's excited and I can't help but be excited for them. Jayden will be one of those Pinterest moms who always has those little goody bags for teachers and little snacks for parties. It goes hand in hand with her interior design gig. Isaac will be good if it's a boy, he was an All-American athlete in high school and can't wait to teach his son the ways of the field. If it's a girl, I'm not sure what he'll do. He doesn't seem the girl-dad type.

"Man, that's so awesome. Congratulations! How far along?" Hazel is going to freak out when she finds out. I know Jayden won't be able to keep it a secret until we get back and that thought dulls my good mood a bit. Her reaction would be amazing to see right now.

"12 weeks on Wednesday. We wanted to keep it a secret until she popped, but I couldn't keep it in any longer. I had to tell people. We compromised and decided to have dinner Friday with our families and tell them and then next weekend with our friends, but you're the first friend to know. I thought it would help lighten the heavy mood over you guys." He looks a little guilty over telling me about this now, but his excitement wins out.

"Thanks, man. That's really awesome. I'd say we'll still come to the dinner, but it depends on what's going on with Lynn at the time and how Hazel's mental health is holding up. You know how it is." I shrug my shoulders and he nods, having experienced many cancellations due to Hazel having a breakdown or over-planning her weekends.

"Yea, that's all right. If you guys are awesome, if not, no hard feelings. Especially now that you know. This shit with Lynn is way more important."

We both grab another coffee and chit chat about life for another hour and a half before his phone chimes with a text. "It's Jay. We're good to go back to the house now." I feel relieved and also scared. Jayden is a fierce woman and I know she's probably going to lay into me.

"How's Hazel?" The look he gives me makes me feel stupid I asked. It's full of sympathy and pity.

"I don't know, she didn't say." My heart sinks. She could still be mad, or she could just be withdrawn. I don't know what to expect when I walk into the house. As we get up from the table, my phone chimes. I check it and my heart skips a beat when I see Hazel's name. My heart soars as I read her text.

We throw some money down on the table, throw our coats on, and I put the plastic back over the flowers before I grab them, and we head out to his custom painted aquamarine Audi R8. This car has been a point of envy for me since he got it, it's so damn beautiful.

"You're gonna have to trade this beast in when the baby comes." His eyes bulge out his head as he whips his head toward me. I clearly struck a nerve.

"There is no way in hell I'm getting rid of Rachel. Don't put that bad juju on me, James. You'll hurt her feelings." His words would be funny enough, but the fact that he means it makes me bust up laughing. I've never been a huge car guy, but Isaac lives and breathes cars when he isn't working.

"All right, man. Sorry for saying it." I hold my hands in front of me, showing I mean no harm.

"Don't apologize to me, apologize to her." His words have a double meaning that he didn't realize, and I take the advice. I apologize to Rachel as I climb in and tell her how beautiful she is.

Isaac peels out of the parking lot, driving like a bat out of hell. It makes me a little nervous, given it's been snowing for the past 24 hours, but he handles it like a pro. Although I'm nervous of his crazy antics, I'm glad he's driving so fast because it means I'll get back to Hazel faster.

Chapter Fifteen

Hazel

As soon as I hear the front door close, I call Jayden. I can't be alone, but I also can't stand to be around James. I need space from him, but I still need support from someone. I feel guilty that I can't let James be the one to help, but he's just too much right now. Jayden will give it to me straight and not bullshit me.

While the phone rings, I let Kiba outside and plan out what I'll say to Jayden. But how do you explain to your best friend that your fiancé caused your disaster of a mom to leave in the middle of the night in freezing temperatures?

"Hey, girl! How are you?" She's met with silence. "Hazel, are you there?" I can see her, in my mind, pulling her phone away to make sure the call is connected. "Haz. What's going on, Hon?"

"I need you." I finally manage to whisper into the phone. All the words I had planned to say to her scattered the moment she picked up.

"Give me 20 minutes. I'll be right there, Babe. Hang on, okay?" There's a ruffling sound on the line as she pulls the phone away to hang up, but before she does, I hear her say, "Isaac, go get the car started, I need you to take me to Hazel's." She hung up without me confirming anything.

While I wait for her, I call the police department and hospitals, and Nana's nursing home to have them check her room without worrying Nana. Not surprising, she isn't at any of these places. I had to hope she was with Sandy or went back to Paul's place. But my mind keeps envisioning her laying frozen and dead on a park bench.

I let Kiba back inside, he shakes the snow from his fur. Some of it lands on me, but my mind is so far gone that I don't feel the cold. I go to the living room and curl up on the couch, sobbing my eyes out. I haven't felt this heartbroken and alone in a long time. The last time was my sophomore year at college…I don't let my mind go there, I can't. The guilt and trauma eat at me too much.

When Kiba starts barking 15 minutes later, my heart starts pounding in desperation. I *know* it's my mom, it has to be. I run to the door and throw it open and am met with a mixture of disappointment and joy when Jayden stands there instead, even though I knew she was coming, my face falls from its hopeful look and she doesn't miss it. "Damn, you said you needed me. I didn't expect you to be so upset seeing me here. Early, at that."

"Sorry Jay. I thought you were my mom." She perks up at that. She has always been one for gossip, especially when it comes to my mom. Her face is this mix of sadness and intrigue, causing her nose to scrunch and the left side of her mouth to lift in a snarl.

"Why the hell would I be your mom, Haz? What happened?" I sigh and step back from the open door, trying to keep Kiba from jumping all over the place in excitement.

"Come on in and get comfortable; it's a lot." She frowns, but steps in and takes off her boots and hangs her coat in the hall closet. "Do you want something to drink?"

"Yea, I'll just have some water." I look at her oddly, she always takes a soda when she comes over. I let it go, not having the energy or mental stamina to ask questions. I bring her water to the living room where she's curled up on the couch with a blanket draped over her. "Thanks."

"Of course." I sit on the edge of the couch and put my face in my hands, taking a deep breath to prepare myself for the words I'm about to speak.

"Where's James?" I dread this conversation with every ounce of my being. I know Jayden is one of my people and she'll support me in everything I say, but it's the fact that I even have to say it that's bothering me so damn bad.

"I don't know. He left right before I called you. We got into a fight." She sits up at this. It's not common for James and me to fight and even less common for him to leave while we are fighting.

"What is going on, Haz?" Concern is etched into her face.

I exhale a big breath and jump in to telling her how this weekend got so fucked up. From my mom crashing here, to working on Jack's case, to James saying something to my mom about how she bothers me so much, and now she's missing, and no one will tell me where she is and it's my fault as well as James'. Because if I had had more of a backbone, I could have told her no, gotten her a motel room, and enjoyed our weekend together.

But the soft spot I have for my mom won't let me do that.

Never has and never will, I will always be her crutch. And that sickens me beyond belief.

Jayden listens raptly, when I'm done, she whistles out a breath. "Damn, girl. That *is* a lot. I'm so sorry you're dealing with all of this. Have you called around?"

"Of course, I have. I did it while you were on your way here. She's nowhere. The only other thing I can think to do is walk around town trying to find her, but it's so cold outside. At this point I have to believe that she found someone to get her a room somewhere or is at Sandy or Paul's and just refusing to speak to me."

"Honestly, she could be. That sounds like some shit Lynn would do. She's an absolute nut job." She laughs when she says this which kind of pisses me off. How are these people taking this situation so lightly? This is my mom we're talking about, and yea, she's shitty, but she's still my mom.

I take a deep breath to calm myself down. I may be upset in general, but I know Jayden means well, so does James. While Jayden hates my mom, she also finds her somewhat iconic for all the shit she's been through. It's a bit of a sore spot in our friendship, but I get it in a sick, weird way.

"What are you going to do about James?" I shrug my shoulders and shake my head because I don't know.

"Forgive him, obviously. What else is there to do? He didn't expect her to leave like this. I know that. But I am so damn mad at him for speaking out of place on *my* feelings and *my* experience with her. He should have left it to me, no matter how long it took me to finally tell her." She's nodding her head in agreement, her messy blonde bun flopping on top of her head. "Even though I could have punched him earlier, I miss him now. I need him here now. I was such a bitch." I'm on the verge of crying again, but I take a deep, ragged breath to keep the tears at bay.

"He was just trying to help, and I know you know that. I'm just here to talk you through it all. James is a good guy, the best. Although quirky and strange and definitely not who I ever envisioned you with. But he's honestly perfect for you. His actions may have been wrong, but they weren't misguided nor were they meant to make Lynn leave. You know that, or else he would have told her to get the fuck out like he has before. He really just wanted her to understand what her being here does to you."

"You're right, per usual. I need a vacation, Jay. Away from my mom and work. I just need a break." I slouch back against the couch, defeated by the weekend's events.

"That sounds so great. I could definitely use a beach right about now. Sadly, it'll have to wait a bit, though." She smiles shyly at me. My eyebrow arches as I try to put it all together, but my brain isn't putting the pieces together.

"What? Why?" I sit up and tuck my leg underneath me.

"Well, this is probably a shitty time to tell you, but... I'm pregnant." I scream and Kiba starts barking and running around, trying to figure out what's going on.

"OH MY GOD, JAY!!! THAT'S SO EXCITING!" I jump up from the couch and go hug her. She's going to be the best mom there ever was or will ever be.

"Sorry for telling you about it right now. We were going to invite you to dinner next weekend with the rest of our friends to tell everyone together, but I thought you could use some happy news with everything going on. A light in the darkness if you will." We're both smiling ear to ear and now it makes sense as to why she wanted the water.

"How far along are you?" I can't believe it! She's right, of course, the timing could have been better, but this is honestly the best distraction from everything wrong in my life right now. I am so incredibly happy for her and Isaac.

My frustration and sorrow over my mom's issues is still a bitter taste on my tongue, but it's lessened by the happiness of becoming an auntie.

"I'll be 12 weeks on Wednesday. The morning sickness has been killer, but other than that everything has been really good." We talk about all things baby until she abruptly interrupts that she has to pee. She gets up to go to the bathroom and I use this opportunity to text James:

"I love you and I'm sorry."

It's not enough to erase the terrible things I said to him, but it's a start.

Jayden comes back to the living room and sits down. "I told Isaac he could come back to the house. He should be here soon. We can stay if you'd like, or we can go. Whatever you need, Haz."

"Stay, let's have supper. I could use your company and it's been forever since we've hung out. Even if we have to be sober for it, it'll be a great time." I need this break from thinking about my mom. Jayden and I have both had the thought that she's hiding out at Sandy or Paul's and is too stubborn and hurt to say anything, so that's probably where she is, and I have to accept the fact she's not going to reach out.

I make the conscious decision to just let it go. I'll hear from her when she needs something again. In the meantime, I can't live my life in desperate fear for her. She's a grown woman who can take care of herself.

Even as I tell myself that, the anxiety in the back of my mind is like a tornado threatening to tear an entire town apart. I push it down and focus on the people who *want* to be here.

Miranda is going to be so proud of me for this breakthrough. I was going to call her this morning, and I probably should have, but I didn't even think about it with everything going on. I send her a text:

"Monday at 10?"

She responds almost immediately:

"Got you down."

Jayden and I discuss what to do for supper while we wait for Isaac and James to get back, he had texted her saying James was with him. We can't come up with anything, so we wait for the guys to get here before deciding.

I check my phone to see if I missed a text from James. I see I have a notification and get so excited, but that excitement dissipates when I realize it's just from Jack. He looked over our plan and says it looks good. Thank God because I can't delve into it again.

James didn't respond because he's probably still upset with me for how I acted this morning. I hope he's not too upset; I need my best friend in the worst way right now. And I don't mean Jayden. Sure, she's my girl best friend, but James is more than that and always will be. Jayden understands because she has the same relationship with Isaac.

We go to the kitchen to scour for snacks to hold us over until the guys get here. We find some Oreos and Nacho Cheese Doritos and are getting ready to sit at the island and stuff our faces when we hear the front door open, and the guys' voices carry through the house. I turn on my heel and run into the living room to James. Isaac nods to me, smiling and walks past to go to the kitchen with Jayden. I give James a questioning smile and he holds out what I assume are flowers with a plastic sack over them. "I got you some flowers. I'm really fucking sorry, Hazel."

I take the flowers from him and set them on the coffee table. I turn back to him and hug him so hard I don't know if he can breathe.

"I know you are. I'm sorry, too. I'm still upset, but I'll get over it. I missed you and it wasn't until you left that I realized how badly I needed you this whole time. And I, of course, was too stubborn to call you."

He kisses the top of my head and squeezes me harder to his body. "It's okay. I'm here forever. No matter what. I forgive you and I love all of you. Even your stubborn side that makes my life hell." I can hear the smile in his voice. *God, I missed him.*

"I love you, too. Jayden and Isaac are going to stay for supper. She's pregnant!" I release him from my death grip and step back but grab his hand. I'm not ready to break contact with him yet.

"Yea, Isaac told me while we had coffee. I'm happy for them. You hear anything about your mom?" He squeezes my hand that's tightly clutching his.

"No, but I'm assuming she's at Sandy or Paul's and just refusing to speak to me. You know how Sandy is when mom is in her moods. That woman can act like no one's business." He laughs, having been on the receiving end of her deceiving ways more than once.

"Yea it wouldn't surprise me. Did you ladies figure out what sounds good for supper yet? I'll run to the store if we need anything." We join Jayden and Isaac in the kitchen as we talk. They turn to look at us, their bodies visibly relaxing when they see us holding hands.

"No, not yet. We wanted to discuss it with you guys." I shoot Jayden a questioning look, needing her input on what to eat. She's in recovery from binging and purging so some foods trigger her really bad.

"I could make some burgers?" James' burgers are my absolute favorite and I know he's still trying to sweeten me up to him with this suggestion. I would be lying if I said it wasn't working.

"That sounds amazing. Jay, what would you like? We have some pasta and whatnot I can cook up for you." I look at her closely so I can read her facial expression. She tends to agree to food she doesn't like so she's not a burden to us. With her being pregnant and having morning sickness, I'm not sure what sounds good to her anymore.

"No, burgers sound great!" She's smiling and seems really excited for them. Weird, as she's usually not a beef person.

Beef is one of her trigger foods, so I'm shocked she said that.

"Pregnancy making you enjoy beef again?" Pregnancy is such an interesting thing; it can make you love things you hate and hate things you love. I can't wait to be pregnant and experience it all for myself. Maybe we should start trying, I'll have to talk to James about it tonight when Jay and Isaac leave.

"Ugh, yes. It's all I want to eat lately. No gagging, no nausea, nothing. It's like the only thing I can eat and not feel sick immediately after consuming." Isaac is standing behind her, shaking his head in disbelief. He was there for the worst part of her eating disorder and stood beside her through all of it, rooting for her to get better. The doctors said she may not ever have babies, but here she is almost to her second trimester with her first baby. What an absolute blessing.

"It's true. I don't think we've had any of her weird vegetarian dishes in months." While Jay isn't a vegetarian, she really loves some of the recipes she found while she was dabbling in it. She also says it's better for her weight loss. She may have recovered from binging and purging, but she is still really insecure about her body image. She's getting better, but it's a process. I'm worried that pregnancy will cause her to go back to her old ways, but she seems so happy and excited so I think she'll be all right.

"What? That's absolute craziness." My eyes bulge out my head at this revelation from Isaac. James is just as shocked and can't find words to express how he's feeling about the whole situation, or maybe he's just walking on eggshells to not trigger me into yelling at him again. It's probably both.

"Yea, it's weird. And I don't know how to feel about it, but I'll give this baby whatever it wants." She's rubbing her belly and smiling. I can tell how at peace she is with where her life is. I couldn't be happier for her.

"Burgers it is! I'll get some meat out." James finally breaks out of his shocked stupor and lets go of my hand to head to the deep freeze on the back porch to get out some hamburger.

"Can you let Kiba out while you're over there? I'm pretty sure he's going to start destroying things if he doesn't get rid of some energy soon." He stops midway through opening the deep freeze and whistles for Kiba, who's already coming into the kitchen, having heard me talking about him. He runs full speed to James, almost knocking him over.

"Calm down, Boy. Let's go potty." He opens the back door to our fenced in backyard and Kiba doesn't hesitate to run full speed out into the snow. It doesn't bother him at all, he prefers the snow, but with it being so cold, I don't want his paws to freeze and crack. I need to order those shoes for him that I showed James the other day. He thinks they're ridiculous, but I want to make sure Kiba is okay.

Chapter Sixteen

James

I'm relieved that Hazel seems to be in better spirits. I wish I was the one who got her there, but I'll take what I can get. Sometimes you just need an outside perspective, and Jayden has always been able to get through to her when I couldn't.

It must be a girl thing.

I do really hope Lynn is okay, despite how much I dislike her. I know it would tear Hazel apart if she were in danger or hurt—or worse.

I go over to the island and grab some Doritos from the bag after putting the meat in the sink to thaw. I pop a Dorito in my mouth as Hazel comes over to me and wraps one of her arms around my back, I put mine around her shoulders, glad she's being so loving. I need this physical affection to show me she's okay. I can't talk to her very much while Jayden and Isaac are here. I'm sure Jayden will hear all about it, but it's just awkward for me. "Do you guys want to play some *Cards Against Humanity?* We have about 45 minutes before I can start on burgers."

"You know I'm always game to kick your ass, James." Jayden hops off her chair and goes to the hall closet to get the game out. We have been in a battle of who's the best game master for years now. It's too close to tell who is better, but I think it's me.

"You wish, Jayden!" I yell at her back, and she flips me off. That gets a good laugh out of Hazel and Isaac. She comes back with the box and sets it on the island.

"Are we playing in here or at the dining room table?" Jayden asks as she comes back into the kitchen, game box in hand. If we play in here, I'll have to go get a couple more chairs so everyone can be comfortable.

"Definitely the dining room table. There needs to be more room between you and James or else fists will go flying and I don't want to clean up that disaster." Hazel makes a good point. Jayden gets violent when I beat her sometimes. I once had a bruise the size of Texas after I beat her at *Monopoly.* It's all in good fun, but that girl knows how to hit. They head to the dining room as I'm attempting to get Kiba to come inside. He refuses and I have to go out and pick him up. He'd freeze out there if I'd let him.

--

I'm in the lead with five cards when I call a pause so I can go start burgers.

"I'm not cheating, Jayden. I'm just funnier than you are." She rolls her eyes at me.

"If you weren't about to feed me, I'd tackle you. But since you're the chef this evening, I'll let you escape. Damn pregnancy, anyway." I laugh as I head into the kitchen, Hazel follows me to get a round of drinks for everyone.

"Hey, have you heard from Jack? How's all that coming along?"

"Yea, actually. He texted me while you were gone. He says it all looks good and gave the go ahead. I need to text Alex so he can start on it tomorrow. Jefferson won't be pleased I'm not taking the lead on this, but I have faith in Alex. I'm just not in the right headspace to deal with it right now. I'm probably going to take this week off just to give myself some time to process everything."

"That sounds like a great idea. I'd take time off with you, but Jack would have my balls if I took time off right now with all his shit going on."

I throw the burgers in the air fryer, I'd grill, but I'm not trying to be out in the cold for twenty minutes. Already did that once today, that's enough for me. "Hey, can you go ask them if they want some cheese?" She's in the fridge getting some tea and bottled water for Jayden and Isaac.

"Sure thing." She heads back to the dining room while I wash my hands in the sink. I'm really happy she seems to be okay. I'm still uneasy about the whole thing, but if she's happy then so am I.

Hazel comes back a few seconds later and wraps her arms around me, I can't help but feel like she's trying to compensate for not wanting to be touched earlier.

"Isaac would like cheese, but Jayden says that dairy has been making her shit her brains out so to hold off on hers." Laughter erupts out of me. I wasn't prepared for that insight into Jayden's food issues as of late. Not surprising, though. She's never been one to hold things back.

Hazel lets me go to check her phone. Her brow is furrowed. "What's up, Haz?"

"Sandy says she saw my mom down by Teller's Liquor Mart." I freeze on my way over to her. Teller's isn't a good place to go, druggies and the homeless like to hang out in the alley and try to get people to buy them booze.

"Maybe they're having a sale on Paul's liquor."

"I don't think so. If Sandy saw her, that means she didn't take her and she walked. She'd just go to the Corner Store in this weather, wouldn't she?" I walk over to her and rub her back. When she's calmed down a little, I start the oven to cook some French fries.

"I'm sure she has her reasons. Maybe she stole something from the Corner Store or degraded a new person and they won't let her shop there for a while. You're probably just still upset that she left to begin with." Lynn was really rude to new people; she said it was her way of making sure they had the gruff to work there. It was embarrassing.

"That wouldn't surprise me." She shakes her head, trying to rid herself of the negative thoughts floating around. "I don't want to bring the mood back down. We're having fun. If she wanted to be here, she would be." She smiles at me as I lean down to kiss her. I throw the fries in the oven and set the timer. They should be done about the time the burgers are.

"Exactly. Let's go play another couple of hands while the burgers cook. I need to keep Jayden in her place: beneath me, The Master of Games." She smacks my chest as she scoffs at me.

"Be nice, James. She's hormonal." She grabs my hand, and we head out to the dining room.

"All is fair in love and war, Baby." I chuckle as we get to the dining room. Jayden hears this and smiles a wicked smile. She's up to something and I'm not sure what it is.

Kiba stayed in the kitchen, laying down on the rug in front of the sink, waiting for the burgers to be done. He knows I always make him one with no seasoning. He's spoiled rotten.

By the time the air fryer is beeping, Jayden has made a comeback and is one card ahead of me. I'm not sure how she did it, because some of my cards were pure gold. I think she kicks Isaac or Hazel under the table when they read her card and they pick her out of pity or cowardice, but I have no proof. "Let's eat!"

"It's about time. I'm starving." Jayden complains as she stands from her chair to go get her burgers and fries.

"How? You've eaten an entire row of Oreos and half that bag of chips." I'm blown away at how much food she's put away in such a short amount of time.

"I have a growing baby in my stomach, James. It needs sustenance. Don't food shame me!" She seems actually offended and I feel slightly bad about it. I just can't help myself sometimes, she's so skinny.

"My bad. I wasn't trying to. I was just shocked, that's all." She rolls her eyes at me as she passes me to go to the kitchen. I follow her to grab the fries out of the oven, but Isaac stops me.

"Hey, man. Don't talk about her food consumption. It's been bothering her and with her being pregnant, it's a slippery slope. I don't need her going back to her old ways." I feel like the world's biggest asshole.

"Fuck, man. I didn't mean it like that. I'm sorry. I tend to forget about what happened. I won't say anything else." He nods his head and claps me on the back, heading into the kitchen. Hazel is still in the dining room with me, watching me. "I really didn't even think about it. That was so insensitive."

"Yea, it was. Thankfully Jay is pretty thick skinned and knows you don't mean it like that. Just do what Isaac said and don't comment on her food choices and it'll be okay." She squeezes my hand and heads to the kitchen.

I am royally fucking up today and I don't know how things got so out of sorts.

Hazel beats me to the kitchen. She sets paper plates and condiments out while I grab the fries out of the oven. Isaac is cutting up an onion for his burger, making the kitchen reek.

"Oh, breaking out the fancy stuff today, Haz!" Jayden hates paper plates. She says they're bad for the environment. She's the reason Hazel insists on reusable grocery bags.

"I know, Jay. You're going to hate it, but it's fine. It's not doing *that* much damage. Plus, it's not like you're going to do all of our dishes after supper." Jayden rolls her eyes at Hazel but takes the plate from her anyway. Jayden doesn't do dishes, she hates them. It's quite ironic that someone who refuses to use disposable plates or utensils demands using regular dishes, but then refuses to wash said dishes.

Jayden grabs a bun and then a patty from the air fryer. She loads her burger up with pickles, ketchup, mustard, and mayonnaise. It's the most disgusting thing I've ever seen. "Sorry we don't have lettuce or tomatoes. I need to run to the store."

"It's fine. This will work just great." She's practically drooling. She loads her plate up with fries and slathers them with some ranch. I'm appalled at her choices, but I keep my thoughts to myself and avert my eyes from her plate. I don't want to hurt her feelings or piss off Isaac and Haz.

I throw Kiba his burger before making my own burger. I don't even think he chews it; it just disappears.

When we're all loaded up with burgers and fries, we go back to the dining room to eat. While we eat, Hazel fills Jayden and Isaac in on the text she got from Sandy.

"She probably got kicked out of the Corner Store, knowing your mom. Don't think too much about it, girl." I nod in agreement with Jayden; It's the exact same thing I told Haz in the kitchen.

"That may be true, but last week Phil Darrins got picked up from there for dealing fentanyl. Has your mom relapsed, Hazel?" Isaac wipes his mouth as he talks. I wish he wouldn't have brought that up. The last thing I need is for that thought to go through Hazel's mind right now. *Too late now, I guess.*

"Not that I know of. But I have this nagging feeling that something isn't right. I can't help myself. I'm going to go down there tomorrow and see if she's there. Worst case, she is and I have to take her to rehab. Best case, she was just getting Paul some booze and that's it. I just need some answers."

"Are you taking some time off?" Isaac is a workaholic, which works great for Jayden's lavish lifestyle, but makes him somewhat insensitive to family situations. His dad was the same way, so it makes sense. He doesn't believe in taking time off unless absolutely necessary and even then, he's usually on his phone sending emails and quotes to potential partners. He's a big wig contractor for Weiss & Wishman. He makes enough money that Jayden will be able to be a stay-at-home mom if she wants, and still afford her impulse buying and luxe vacations.

"Yes, I'm going to take this week off. Alex is capable of taking point for anything. I'll still be available if they absolutely need me, but I just can't go sit in that office in my current state of mind." Isaac shakes his head. He'd rather be at work than sit around and stew in his thoughts and feelings. When his grandpa died last year, he wasn't home except to sleep. Jayden was here a lot because she got lonely. We all grieve differently, I guess.

"I think that's a good idea, Hazel. Don't listen to Isaac. The man will begrudgingly take time off for ultrasound appointments and the birth or else I'll castrate him." Jayden throws a pointed look at Isaac.

"The only thing I'll take time off work for is that baby and you, Jayden. You know that. I'm just as excited as you are. But I'm not going to be at every appointment like you want me to be. I can't. We have things to buy for the baby and doctor bills to pay."

"I know. I'll get over it. I just wish you weren't so work oriented. I get bored without you." Jayden whines as she pouts at him, and he grabs her hand and kisses her knuckles. This is a serious topic of contention between them, and always has been. As much as she hates him working so much, she knows she wouldn't be able to afford her lifestyle without him. It would be close, but she'd have to budget right. If there's one thing Jayden is bad at, it's budgeting.

"That's enough, you two love birds. I have one more card to get before I win, let's finish this up." Jayden rolls her eyes at me and gets up to help Hazel clear the table of paper plates and napkins. When they get back, we resume playing.

Jayden ends up winning, much to my dismay.

"Take that, loser." She sticks her tongue out at me.

"I let you win. I felt bad for you, being pregnant and all."

"Be nice, James." Hazel slaps my arm as she admonishes me. I laugh incredulously at Hazel's scolding. When it comes to being competitive with Jayden there is no being nice or she'll eat me alive.

"Fine, you won fair and square. But I'm onto you, Jayden. I know what you're doing. I just need proof." I stare at her menacingly.

"I don't know what you're talking about." She feigns innocence and pretends to toss her hair over her shoulder, her messy bun flopping around on her head.

"Psh. Yea, right. You know exactly what I'm talking about. You're just too stubborn and bull-headed to admit it. It's fine, I'll catch you slipping one of these days." I laugh while I talk. I talk a lot of shit to her, but she's really the only one in our group who can keep up with my competitiveness. It's nice not having to take it easy on her when we play games. Hazel and Isaac let us brawl it out and are there to play referee when it gets too intense.

"Good luck with that." She looks at Hazel, "I'll help you clean up and then we have to go. Herschel needs to be let out before he shits all over my floor again." Herschel is their pug. He's an ugly little thing and just as stubborn as Jayden. They've had him since he was a puppy and despite discipline and training, that dog is still not fully housetrained.

They get everything picked up and put away. Jayden hugs Hazel tight as they say goodbye. Before Jayden can zip her coat, Hazel bends down to rub her belly, cooing at it, then kisses it. "Bye, Baby. I can't wait to meet you." I slap Isaac on the back in farewell.

"Congratulations again, you guys. You'll be great parents. And thanks for coming over today. We really needed the company."

"Yea, man. No problem. Thanks for supper. The invitation still stands for the dinner next weekend. Just don't tell anyone about the pregnancy. Don't want to ruin it."

"Of course, we won't say anything. This is your news to share." Hazel gives Isaac a hug as she reassures them their secret is safe with us. "I'll let you know by Thursday if we'll be there or not."

"Sounds good, Haz. Text me tomorrow with what you find out at Teller's." Jayden says as she puts on her boots.

"Will do. Drive safe, guys. I love you, Jay." She hugs Jayden before she turns to leave.

"I love you too, Hazel. See ya, James." I wave them out the door.

As soon as the door closes, Hazel jumps into my arms, wrapping herself around me like a koala. She smothers my face with kisses and whispered sorry's. It's the sweetest thing ever. I wrap my arms around her, holding her to me. I walk to the couch and sit with her still wrapped around me. My face is wet, and at first, I'm grossed out because I think she's drooling on me. But then I realize she's crying, and I pull her away from me so I can look at her.

"I'm so sorry, James. I really thought I'd pushed you away when you didn't respond to my text. I thought that was the end. It wasn't until you came into the house that I knew we were still okay. I was just so overwhelmed and upset at the whole situation and I couldn't communicate the way I should have."

"Babe, it's okay. Shit happens. I've told you a million times, and I'll tell you a million more: I'm not going anywhere. I'm here to stay. We may not be married yet, but it's 'til death do us part for me. Always has been, always will be. No matter the crazy shit your mom does. Because I'm not in a relationship with her, I'm in a relationship with you. You're working on yourself more and more every day and I'm so incredibly proud of you, and you should be too." I kiss her passionately. Silencing anything else she has to say. "You still haven't looked at your flowers. I'm sure they're droopy by now. Poor things."

"Shit! I forgot about them between apologizing to you and having Jayden and Isaac here." She gets off my lap and takes the bag off the flowers. Sure enough, they're starting to droop. Honestly, though, it's not as bad as I thought it would be. Sturdy little suckers. "They're beautiful! Thank you. I really love them. I'll put some fresh water in them and stick them on the island so they get some sun tomorrow. They should be okay." She starts to walk toward the kitchen, but I stop her by calling her name while I walk towards her.

"Don't forget to call Jefferson about this week. I know he's a cool dude, but you are cutting it pretty close with how late it's getting. I'm going to go take a shower while you do all that." I kiss her head.

"Shit, I also forgot about that. I'll do that quick, but wait for me to shower? I would like to join you." She smiles coyly at me.

"Oh, I'll definitely wait for you. Hurry it up." I smack her ass as she turns away, making her squeal and then giggle. I head to our bathroom, getting a couple towels out for us and take off my clothes while I wait for Hazel to join me. It only takes her a few minutes. "All good?"

"Yea, Jefferson was cool. He just said he wished I would have called him earlier, but I explained the whole thing and he was understanding. Thank God. I really cannot go into that office tomorrow. I might be fine by Wednesday, though."

"Don't, Haz. Just take this week to chill and relax. You haven't had any real time off in a while. You could use it." She starts taking off her clothes.

"You're right, per usual." Goosebumps cover her skin, and her nipples harden, the sight causing my dick to harden. I start the shower, not making it too hot, but a little hotter than she likes it to help warm her up. She puts her leg in to test the water's temperature and I must have done well because she hops on in. I follow her, staring at her ass the whole time. I don't think there's a better sex than make up sex and I'm not about to miss out on this opportunity.

I grab her shampoo while she wets her hair and squirt some into my hand. When she steps from beneath the spray I massage it into her scalp, taking my time. We don't do this often, and that's something I regret. I make a mental note to do this more with her.

After a few minutes, I rinse my hands in the spray of water and grab her body wash and start washing her body. As with her hair, I take my time, massaging deep into her muscles while I wash. . I start with her forearms and work my way up her right arm. When I get to her shoulder, I make sure to get her neck too. Her moans don't help my growing erection. I add just enough pressure that she knows what's about to happen.

Just as she's getting into it and writhing under my hand, I release her and move down to her chest. I lather her chest in soap and massage her nipple with my finger, she elicits another moan. I grab more soap and start on her left arm, repeating the process, but this time when I get to her neck, I skip it. She sulks in disappointment. *Just wait, Princess. You'll get what you want.*

I get down on my knees to get her stomach. Her bald pussy in my face, just waiting for my tongue and fingers to work their magic on her. I can't resist myself. I grab her left leg and put it on my shoulder, kissing her inner thigh before lightly nibbling her. Her right leg is shaking, not from exertion, but because she knows what's coming. I move towards her center, taking my time kissing and nibbling. I want to look at her face, but the water spraying around her body makes that impossible, so I close my eyes and begin my feast.

My tongue finds her clit within seconds, rolling in circles. I rinse my right hand off and slide my index finger into her. Her left hand grips my hair, pulling me further into her, needing me to be closer. My middle finger joins my index as I work her clit with my tongue, her hips undulating against me. I circle her clit a few more times with my tongue, my fingers moving in and out of her wet pussy and she clenches around me while calling out my name. I remove my fingers and stand to grab her soap to finish cleaning her.

Still taking my time, making her wait for what she really wants as she pouts. "I don't want to finish showering; I want you to fuck me."

"All in good time, Babe. Be patient." I kiss her forehead and gently push her under the water to rinse her off. When she's rinsed off, I hurry to wash myself. I want to be inside of her as badly as she wants me to be. My cock is rock hard and there's a steady stream of precum leaking from the tip. As I'm rinsing my hair, I feel her hand grab my cock followed by her tongue licking the head.

"Fuuuck." Then her lips are around my cock, and she starts sucking, her hand matching her movements. I reach down and grab a fistful of her wet hair, pulling her back. She looks up at me, despite the water splashing in her eyes. "Mouth open, tongue out." She does as she's told without hesitation. I push my cock into her mouth until I hit the back of her throat. I pause there, letting her get used to the intrusion, then I push further. She gags but doesn't push me away. I pull back out so just the head of my cock is in her mouth. "Again, Haz. But this time I'm not going to be easy on you." She moans around my cock. I shove all the way in and face fuck her until I start to feel the signs of my release. I pull my cock all the way out and release her hair.

"Turn around. Hands on the wall. Feet spread." She follows orders so well. I line my cock up to her pussy entrance and shove all the way in. She cries out and almost face plants the wall from the abrupt movement, the only thing stopping her is my hands on her shoulders holding her in place. When she rights herself, I pull back a bit before shoving in hard again. She keeps her balance this time, ready for what's to come.

Taking my cue, I fuck her mercilessly and she's squirts around my cock after three pumps, yelling out my name. She's not done yet though. I want two more orgasms before my release. I wrap my right arm around her throat and rub her clit while I continue my assault on her soaking pussy. She cums again, this time harder, and I have to hold her up because her legs give out. I pause while she catches her bearings. My balls are so tight, my release just around the corner.

She gains her composure, breathing rapidly. I let go of her neck and smack her ass with my left hand. She whimpers at the contact, and I slam back into her while I circle her clit again.

"Hold on, baby. Almost there." I push my left thumb into her ass as I shove my cock all the way into her pussy, increasing the speed of my right hand. She arches her back, moaning. I pound into her two more times and we cum at the same time, our moans echoing through the house. She sags against the wall as I pull out of her. I rinse off my body and move out of her way so she can re-rinse hers. When she's done, she shuts off the water and I reach out to grab her towels. I hand her the one for her hair. When she has it secure, I start drying her off with the other one.

"I can do that, James." She hates being doted on sometimes, but like hell I'm going to let her do this right now.

"Shh. It's okay. Let me." She shakes her head at me. When I'm done drying her off, she steps out of the shower and puts her robe on. I dry myself off and do the same. She's already lying in bed, naked. I stand there for a moment in awe of her perfect beauty.

"What are you looking at, Weirdo?" She cocks an eyebrow at me, but I can see the blush in her cheeks.

"The most beautiful woman in all the land." I walk over to the bed and drop my robe onto the floor. I climb in as she laughs at me.

"You need glasses."

"I have 20/20 vision, Baby." She rolls her eyes at me as she scoots over to lay her head on my chest. "I love you, Hazel. With everything I am."

"I love you too, James. I'm sorry again for today."

"Stop apologizing, babe. It's over and done with. Let's move on." She tilts her head up to kiss me and then we settle into bed and throw on a movie. She falls asleep within 15 minutes.

Chapter Seventeen

Lynn

The last 24 hours have been a whirlwind. Never did I think Steven would still be around here. Let alone there in that alley, sellin' dope. He used to sell it out of his house, my how the mighty do fall.

How ironic that as my life was falling apart, he would find a way to sneak in. My heart got hopeful that he recognized me. It's been decades.

"Souls recognize souls."

He said that to me once, I thought it was so romantic at the time. And then he fucked my whole world up and left me pregnant and alone. Granted he didn't know I was pregnant; I didn't find out until two weeks after I walked in his house and find him with that whore.

"Steven. It's been a while." I wanted to turn around and leave, but he'd know it was because of him and I couldn't give him that power over me. Not again.

"Yea, it has. I heard you got out of the pen a few years ago. Thought about lookin' you up, but y'know, life." He shrugged his shoulders, hands spread wide. I nodded my head, knowing exactly what life does to people. "What brings you here during this monster storm?" His voice sounded like sandpaper, his voice box rubbed raw from years of drug use and drinkin'.

"I—I was just gonna go in and grab a bottle quick." I couldn't help stuttering. My nerves were eatin' me up. I didn't want him to know how big of a shitshow my life is, even though he clearly ain't much better, given where he's hanging out these days. But his clothes looked clean, nice. And his face was clean-shaven, as opposed to those guys that were hangin' around the fire pit a few feet away.

"You should come over by the fire and hang for a while. We can catch up and just chill." He gestured to the bin where the other guys were standin'. The part of me that was still in love with him begged me to stay, but the part of me that was scorned was yellin' at me to tell him to fuck off and to go back to Hazel's. He smiled at me cruelly, tauntingly, as if he could read my thoughts. "Just come over here for like five minutes. Then you can go back to wherever you're staying.

Five minutes, Lynn. Ain't gonna kill ya." His eyes were pleading and my stupid, young heart won.

I followed him over to the fire and he introduced me to his friends. I wasn't paying any attention to them. I couldn't when he was standing so close to me after all this time. Mere inches away from me; if I was brave enough, I could have caressed his hand with mine.

But I didn't, I couldn't. 'Not again' is a mantra I kept telling myself, wanting to remind myself of the heartbreak that tore my world up, but he was there and I'm broken, so I gave in.

The guy standing across from me pulled out a glass pipe and a lighter. In the glow of the light, I thought he was just gonna smoke some weed and that sounded mighty nice right then. He flicked the lighter and held it under the bulb and I realized what it was-- meth. I hadn't done that shit in a long ass time. It tastes bad and makes me feel even worse. He passed it to the left.

When it got to me, I hesitated. I didn't want to do it, but I also didn't want to not do it.

"You need some help with that, Doll?" One of the nameless men asked me. Steven was watching me, judging me. My life was so fucked, it didn't even matter anymore. *Fuck it.* I glared at him, then put the pipe to my lips and before I could flick the lighter to melt the rocks inside, Steven smacked it from my hand.

"What the fuck, Steven?" I spun towards him and the guys around the fire started protesting, pissed that he broke their pipe. He glared at me like I did somethin' wrong, failed some test of his.

"A lot has changed, Lynn. I know if you go back down this road, you're gonna regret it. I won't let that happen. Not today, not when I'm here to stop you." I couldn't help the way my heart leapt into my throat, poundin', makin' it impossible to breathe. This was the Steven I wanted back when I was alone and pregnant with our daughter. This was the Steven I knew he was back then. This was who I've been in love with for decades.

He reached into his coat pocket and handed a new pipe and a small bag of crystals to the guy on my right. "For your troubles." Then he grabbed my hand and drug me out of the alley.

"Where are we goin?" My voice was shaking as bad as my body. I didn't want to trust him, not now, not ever again. But my stupid heart wouldn't let me tear my hand from his and run away, run back to that fire bin, and smoke my life into oblivion.

"We're going to my house. You can crash there for the night. If you're out here in the middle of the night, I can't imagine you have a good place to crash." I started to protest, but he interrupted me. "I have a guest room you can crash in. No worries, Lynn. We can talk more in the morning."

We arrived at what I assumed was his house. It wasn't as nice as Hazel's, but it wasn't a shithole like Paul's.

He walked up the steps to the front door, passin' by a couple of wicker chairs with decorative pillows and a glass table between them. He opened the screen door and put his key in the door when he realized I wasn't beside him anymore. He turned back to me,

"You coming?" He just stood there, waitin' on me to make up my mind. If this goes badly, I don't know if I'll survive it again.

I bounced from foot to foot, fighting off the cold and my nerves, trying to make up my mind. He saw my hesitation and came back down the steps, abandoning his keys in the door.

"Look, I know we have a bad history. I know this is a lot for you, and if it's too much that's okay. You can leave and go back to that alley. But if you come into my home, there are no strings attached. Just a place to crash for the night, warm and dry. The choice is yours, though. I won't force you." He stared in my eyes and patience is all I saw in his face. His words were genuine, so genuine I could feel it in my bones.

This is a safe space. Some instinctual part of me knew that, but my brain was blaring warning alarms in my head.

I nodded my head and gestured for him to go back up the porch, this time I followed him. This is why I've gotten myself into so many terrible situations. I never listen to the logical side of my brain, and just impulsively jump into things.

I pushed those thoughts away as we walked into his living room and he flipped the overhead light on, revealing a cozy place. The couch looked so soft it would swallow you whole. A gray throw blanket thrown over the back of it. Two chairs on either side of it, separated by side tables with lamps on them. One of the side tables has a stack of books on it and the other a bowl of potpourri.

Nothin' like the house he used to live in: a couch from the curb, worn and filled with holes, the stuffing coming out. Beer cans and liquor bottles covering the floor, drug paraphernalia everywhere.

I guess I judged him too harshly for bein' in that alley, because he didn't fall. He flew.

He made somethin' of himself, and I had never felt as small as I did then..

"I'll give you a tour tomorrow. It's late and we both should get some sleep. I'll show you where the guest room is." He went down a hallway off the right of the living room. The walls are lined with pictures that I couldn't focus on. At the end of the hall, he opened a door on the right, "Here you are. I'm right across the hall. There's a bathroom in here. And some clothes in the dresser. Nothing fancy, but there should be something that fits you in there. Do you need anything?"

I struggled with telling him about my accidents, but it was far too embarrassing.So I shook my head and pushed past him into the bedroom.

"Get some sleep." I nodded my head at him and shut the bedroom door, pressed my back to it in case he tried to open it. I needed space, the whole day had been too much and I couldn't deal with him lookin' at me the way he was.

I took in the quaint little room with a twin bed. Everything in its own place, no dust; clean. I started taking off my layers, putting them in a neat pile in the corner of the room. When I was down to one, I went into the bathroom. I turned the light on and stood there in shock and wonder. A clawfoot tub was on the far wall, a toilet with some sort of contraption on it with dials and a hose. The walls were lavender, the towels and rugs were teal.

The artwork was of fields of flowers, chrysanthemums, lilies, roses, and so many flowers. It's the exact bathroom I had told him I dreamed of when we were together all those years ago, talkin' about our future.

I didn't realize I was cryin' until I walked over to the counter and looked at myself in the mirror. My eyes were red from the tears, and my wrinkles looked deep. I looked as tired as I felt.

I sighed as I turned on the sink, splashin' my face with water. I used the toilet and then had the realization I was probably goin' to piss in this bed. I doubted he had a mattress cover like Hazel. The last thing I needed was to admit my problem to him.

I looked under the sink to see if there was anything I could use, but found nothin'. My head dropped to my chest, I felt so defeated. When I brought my head up again, I saw a cupboard behind the bathroom door. I crawled over to it, desperate for somethin' in there to help me.

I opened the door, the hinges squeaked loudly in the quiet, makin' me cringe. I paused, waitin' to see if Steven came in to wonder what I was doin'. After a few minutes of silence, I went back to lookin' for somethin' to help me. At the very back was an open package of women's Depends. I sighed in relief and pulled them out. They were a little big, but it was better than nothin'. I slipped one on, then went to find some pajamas.

I left the light on as I went back to the bedroom. I found some pajamas in the dresser— a pair of purple plaid ones, I put them on. They were the softest thing I'd ever felt. I turned the light off and got into bed, falling asleep as soon as my head hit the softest pillow in the world.

When I woke up this mornin', I was groggy as all hell. It took me a few minutes to remember where I was, and whose house I was in.

Then last night's events unfolded in my mind, and I didn't know what to do. I was thinking about just hiding in here all day, but that might be weirder than getting up and leaving.

I stretched out on the bed, contemplating my next move. I didn't want to talk to Steven. I didn't want to hash out our past and mend what's broken. I just wanted to leave things as they were and go about my life. Even if I didn't know what to do with my life right now.

Sighin', I got up out of bed and found some clothes to wear in the dresser. I went in the bathroom and take off my clothes to take a shower. I am grateful I found the depends, even though I hadn't pissed as much as I had at Hazel's there's still enough that it would have made a huge mess.

As I was washing myself up, I started planning out my day. I was hoping he was still sleeping when I got done, that way I could slip out the door without any awkward goodbyes.

I got out of the shower and as I was drying off when the anxiety crept up on me. I didn't know what to expect if he's awake. Will he regret havin' me stay here last night? Will he hate me for needing him? Well, not *need*, but he won't see it that way. Will he expect my gratitude? Don't get me wrong, I am grateful he gave me a place to stay, but I didn't need it. I could have gone to Sandy's, *should* have gone to Sandy's.

I just need to get dressed and leave. That's that.

I grabbed all the clothes I wore last night and went out to the kitchen to find a bag to haul them in. As I turned the corner to enter the kitchen, I halted my steps. Steven was standing with his back to me, makin' eggs. If he knew I stood there frozen in place, he didn't acknowledge it. I tried to quietly turn back and go back to the room I was sleeping in, but he turned at the same time.

"You're up! Good. Are you hungry?" He sounded genuinely pleased that I was still here, and it made my insides turn to mush. My brain was screaming at me to leave. But my heart wouldn't let me.

"I could eat, I guess." He nodded to me and gestured for me to sit at the table in the dining room. I set my clothes on one of the chairs in the living room and went to the dining room.

There was a hutch in the corner with some nice blue dishes in it. The table looked like it's made from oak, the chairs made from the same are upholstered with some beautiful black and white fabric. There was a rug under the table that looked like smoke with black and white and gray intertwining.

It's peaceful in this house and seems like it has a woman's touch. He's probably married by now with more kids; they're probably out of town or somethin'. I wanted to ask, but I didn't want to seem like I was interested in his life. That would give him an in and that's the last thing I need.

He set a plate of eggs and toast down in front of me, along with a glass of orange juice, then handed me a fork. It smelled delicious. He sat to my right and leaned back in his chair, watchin' me. His own plate was in front of him. I took a bite of the eggs and I had to hide a moan. They were the best eggs I've ever had. He smirked like he knew just how good they were.

"These are really good, Steven. Thank you…you know, for all of it. You didn't have to help me, but thank you."

"It's not a problem, Lynn. Anything for an old friend." He smirked at me and then dug into his own breakfast. We ate in silence until every bite was gone. I picked up our plates and took them to the kitchen, rinsed them off in the sink. "Just leave them in the sink, I'll clean them up later." He called from the dining room. I did as he said and went back to the dining room.

"Do you have a bag I can use? I layered up yesterday and it would be easier to walk with a bag." He was still sittin' in his chair, lookin' at me.

"You don't need a bag, Lynn. Sit. We have a lot to talk about." My heart sank to my toes; I didn't want to talk to him.

"There's really no need for all that, Steven. I'd just like to go." He leaned forward and braced himself on his crossed arms on the table.

"All I ask is to talk for a while. That's all I want from helping you last night. Just to talk. Then if you still want to leave, I'll drive you wherever you want to go." I sighed, knowing he wasn't goin' to let me leave unless I talked to him. At least not peacefully.

"Fine, but when we're done, I'm leavin'." He nodded and pointed to the chair I was sittin' in. "We both know this is goin' to take a while. How about the living room instead?" He smirked and nodded at me. I went to the living room and sat on one end of the couch, making myself as small as possible, hopin' I'd just disappear. He sat on the opposite end of the couch and kicked his feet up on the coffee table.

"What the fuck happened last night?" Just like him to cut to the chase like that. No beating around the bush, just get it over with. As much as I didn't want to tell him anything, he just has a way with me, always has. I told him everything from Paul hittin' me and kicking me out of his house and goin' to Hazel's and gettin' into the fight with James to leavin' and trying to find a way to just forget everything. It didn't take all that long to tell him everything. He just sat there, starin' at the TV like he couldn't believe what had all happened.

We sat in silence for a while, him thinking about what to say and me not knowing anything.

He finally looks at me and asks, "Are you going back to Hazel's today?"

"No, I can't go back there after leaving the way I did. It would be too embarrassing. Not to mention too much of a burden on her. I'll just go back to Paul's and hope he's not still mad at me." He laughs a humorless laugh. "The fuck are you laughin' at?"

"You're not going back there, Lynn. Ever again. I'll take you to Hazel's if you want, but I will not take you to Paul's. Not unless you want me to go to prison." I'm staring him in his eyes, confused as all hell as to why he's sayin' this. The confusion must be written plainly on my face because he continues.

"You remember the last time I saw you? The day you walked in, and that blonde bitch was on her knees in front of me?" My heart is beating so fast I feel like I'm havin' a heart attack. I don't want to relive that day, even all these years later. I just nod because I can't trust my voice to sound strong, resilient. "You thought she was sucking me off, but she was begging me to help her dad with some money. He found out he had cancer a week before and they couldn't afford the treatments. Instead of asking what was going on, you left. I followed you, but by the time I got outside you were already gone. I told everyone to get the fuck out, but they took their sweet ass time. I went to your house after, and your mom told me to never come back and then she spit on my shoes. She said I was not worthy of you and if I ever showed my face at her house again, she'd call the cops and have me arrested on whatever charge she could. I didn't have a choice. I couldn't go to jail. But I watched you, had people watch you for me."

I'm speechless. Steven wasn't a rich man by any means, but he was a successful drug dealer and had plenty to go around with the possibility of making more. It makes sense someone would be asking him for money, he was a generous man.

"I loved you." My heart is breakin' all over again. My life would have been so different had I not been such a dramatic little girl. I wasn't ready for his love then; I know that now. "I never would have done what you thought I did. It killed me when I realized I'd never talk to you again. Then I found out you were pregnant, and I lost my fucking mind. That was *my* baby. I went to a really dark place. I did more drugs than I sold and got into really bad debt with some really bad people. I got caught by the cops one day while I was higher than a kite on some heroin. I had two options, rot in prison or sell them out and work with the pigs. I'd still go to jail for a while if I helped them, but nothing compared to the sentence I was facing. I took the easy way out and snitched. I'm not proud of it, but I wouldn't change a thing about it.

"I got clean in jail, went to rehab when I got out just to make sure I wouldn't go down that same path. I went to school for psychology and became a drug and alcohol counselor." My eyebrows scrunch together, thinkin' about what he did last night.

"But last night you gave meth to those guys. Why?" He runs his hand down his face and then he pushes his hair back, turnin' to me.

"It wasn't meth. They have plenty of that. It was Narcan. There's been a lot of overdoses lately and a lot of Fentanyl going around. I help when I can, and those guys are doing their best to get clean. I've been there, I've watched people I care about deeply go through the same shit. But I know I can't save everyone, so while I wait for them to *want* the help, I hand out Narcan, I give out clean needles, pipes, whatever I can." I don't know what to think anymore.

Everything I thought I knew is out the window. So I say the only thing I can think of.

"Your wife must be very proud of you." He chuckles at my assumption and leans back on the couch.

"I'm not married. Never have been." For some stupid reason, those words make my heart soar, but just to be sure I have to know if he has a girlfriend. The last thing I need is for her to come here and see me and cause all types of drama.

"Your *girlfriend* must be proud of you then." He just shakes his head at me.

"No girlfriend either, Lynn. It's just me in this house since my mom died two years ago." I'm both happy and sad at this revelation. I don't have anything to say so I just nod in his direction and lean my head against the back of the couch. "So, what's been going on in your life before all of this shit this weekend?" He seems genuinely interested. Better for him to know my past and hate me for it than to not know and think I'm innocent. But we both have dirty laundry to air to each other and I don't have anywhere else to be, so I fill him in, all while hoping he doesn't find me absolutely repulsive when I'm done.

Chapter Eighteen

Hazel

I had the same dream from the other day: we're trapped in a shack and those men come to visit us. Only this time they didn't make me hurt James. They just keep asking where my mom is and when I say I don't know, they punch James in the face. I quit speaking after a while, not wanting them to hurt him anymore. The only thing that stopped them was the distant sound of police sirens. The two big guys got scared when they heard it and urged their boss to leave. As soon as the doors were closed and locked, I jerked awake.

The police siren had been James' alarm. He was still dead to the world despite it blaring a few inches from his head.

I nudge him, "James, your alarm is going off. You have to get up." He moans something indecipherable to me and doesn't move. "James, come on. You have to go to work."

"Nuh uh." He rolls over and throws his arm around me, pulling me down and into his body, the alarm still wailing behind him.

"Babe, I would love for you to stay home with me today, but you said Jack would have your balls if you took time off this week. You need to get up." I tap his arm and try to wiggle free, but he tightens his grip on me. "At least shut that shrieking alarm of yours off. I don't know how you deal with that; it drives me nuts!" He releases me and shuts his alarm off.

"It's the only way I wake up." His voice sounds so sleepy that I feel bad for him having to go to work. He rubs his eyes and opens them wide, trying to fight off the fuzziness that sleep leaves in the morning. He closes them again and snores within seconds.

"A lot of good it does you." I grumble to myself as I get up and grab my phone. I'll give Jack a call when I'm done peeing and tell him James isn't feeling well. He can go one day without my fiancé.

I unlock my phone while I'm on the toilet to check my notifications. There are various emails that I need to tend to later, and some app notifications that I really don't care about at 6:45 in the morning. It's the text notification that catches my attention. I don't recognize the number, but that doesn't matter because I have a horrible tendency of not saving people's numbers. I open it and gasp as I read it.

"Hazel, it's Steven, your dad.

I just wanted you to know your mom is with me.

She's safe and everything is okay."

Why the hell is she with Steven? When did he start calling himself my dad? What the actual fuck is happening right now? The last time I saw him he was drugged up and begging me for money. I haven't heard a single word from him since then. I knew he lived here, but since he hasn't been a part of my life ever, I never made it a mission to meet up with him. I could pass him in the grocery store and never even know.

I wash my hands and go back to the bedroom and see James sprawled across the bed. I debate whether I should wake him up or not and choose not to. I can handle this on my own…right?

I head to the kitchen to make some coffee and give Jack a call.

"Hazel, good morning. Is everything okay?" He sounds nervous, but wide awake.

"Hey, Jack. Yes, everything is fine. Well, as fine as they can be I suppose. James won't be in today.. He's been up all night sick." He huffs into the phone.

"That's not ideal, but I can't have him in here puking his guts up or running to the bathroom every few minutes to shit." He sighs heavily. "I'll figure it out. Thanks for letting me know, Hazel."

"No problem, Jack. Have a good day." He hangs up and I let out a sigh. One problem taken care of and a million more to fix today. Kiba comes trotting into the kitchen and heads to the back door, so I let him out and then grab my mug of coffee and set it on the island. I add in my creamer and sugar, then stick the cup in the Keurig. After it spits out the last few drops, I take the first life-giving sip. *Ah, so delicious.*

I grab a notebook and pen from the junk drawer and start making a list of things I need to do this week. It may be a week off from work, but it won't be spent relaxing. The top of my list is to text Steven back and find out what the hell is going on, then I have my 10 o'clock appointment with Miranda and man is she going to love me today. Then I add in all the boring house stuff and renovations I can do upstairs with this time to myself.

I resolve to finish my first cup of coffee before I text my father back, giving us both time to process everything and wake up a little bit. I don't even know what time he wakes up normally, but it at least gives *me* more time to wake up.

I wrangle Kiba back in before I grab my coffee and go to the living room, turning on the lamp by my chair. I set my coffee on the side table and wrap myself in my blanket. I sit down and grab my book. A little reading and coffee will help me calm my nerves.

I get lost in my book, my coffee mug long since empty. I yelp when James comes into the living room and says good morning to me.

"Sorry, Babe. I didn't realize you were so engrossed in your book." His hair is wet, so he must have just gotten out of the shower. How I missed the sounds of him moving around and showering I don't know.

"No, you're fine. It's just a really good book. I just didn't realize it was *that* good." I chuckle as I say this, standing up and stretching my body. "I need some more coffee. What time is it, anyway?"

"I'll get you some. It's 9:30." I'm pretty sure my jaw is on the floor.

"Holy shit. I didn't realize how long I'd been sitting here." I follow him into the kitchen and hand him my mug. "I called Jack for you; told him you were sick all night. You wouldn't wake up this morning and I just thought that was the best decision all around." His back is to me, but he turns his head and smiles at me.

"I appreciate that. I woke up at 9 and realized how fucked I was and hoped you had done something brilliant like that. I'm sure he's pissed as hell at me." He turns all the way around to face me, handing me back my now-full mug.

"He didn't sound too thrilled, but also not completely pissed. It probably helped that I'm the one who made the call, at least for now. You'll probably hear about it when you go in tomorrow." He grimaces at the thought of Jack yelling at him for a fake sickness I called him in for. "Don't worry, he can't get too mad at you, my job is saving his ass right now."

"You're right. Thank God for small favors, huh?" He sits next to me at the island, and I wish I had time to tell him about the text I got from Steven, but it's almost time for me to call Miranda.

"I have to go get set up for my call with Miranda, but I do have something I want to talk about with you when I'm done." His eyes are inquisitive, but he doesn't push me to tell him. "I love you and I'll see you in an hour." I wrap my arms around his neck and kiss him. He tries to deepen the kiss, but I pull away. "We don't have time for that right now, Mister. Plus, I haven't even brushed my teeth yet." I grimace as I share that information with him. I absolutely hate morning breath.

"Like I give a shit about your morning breath." He rolls his eyes at me. "I love you, go talk with Miranda and then we can discuss whatever it is you want to talk about." He kisses me again, this time just a quick peck. As I turn away from him, he swats my ass making me yelp. He chuckles to himself, and I know from the sound of that chuckle that I'm going to be in the best sort of trouble later. My thighs clench at the thought, but I shake my head to clear it of dirty thoughts of my fiancé before my call with my therapist. The last thing I need to talk to her about today is my sex life.

I go into my office, turn on the light, and shut the door. I put my coffee on my desk as I sit in my chair. *Mom, work, text from Steven. In that order.* I repeat it as a mantra in my head so I don't forget anything. At 9:58 I call her. I get put on hold for a few minutes and start doodling on a piece of paper to pass the time. When she answers I put the phone on speaker and set it on my desk. I lean back in my chair to get comfortable, there's a lot to unpack and only one thing to celebrate in this phone call. I'm hoping she doesn't tell me what everyone else does, but knowing they're right, she probably will.

An hour later and my hopes faded. She told me the same shit as everyone else. Why pay her for her time if I get the same guidance from James and Jayden? *You know why, quit being a bitch.* I didn't get to tell her about work or the text from Steven because we were so wrapped up in all the shit that happened with my mom and James over the weekend.

Defeated, I trudge out of my office to go find James. He's lying on the couch watching something on Comedy Central, but when he sees me come into the living room, he shuts it off and sits up. "How did it go?" I sigh and sit down next to him, grabbing his hand.

"As well as I thought it would, which equated to a waste of my time. Don't get me wrong, I love Miranda, but she told me the same shit you and Jay did. I didn't even get to tell her about my breakthrough, which is probably on me for not starting with that, but it's still a bummer." I can't help but feel so defeated with everything. I slump against the back of the couch, already wishing it was bedtime so I could avoid the world and my problems for a while.

"Hey, it's okay. Not every session is going to be mind-opening or eventful. This just shows you that those close to you are also a good support for you when you can't meet with her. That's it. Don't beat yourself up over it, Haz. It's all good." He kisses the side of my head and I give him a small smile.

"Not to be pushy, but you did say we needed to talk about something before you went in there and I haven't been able to stop thinking about it. So..." He leaves it open for me to start the conversation and while I do need to tell him, it's just going to be so complicated. I don't know if I'm ready to deal with all of the implications. *Might as well rip off the band-aid and get all the shitty things out of the way so I can enjoy the rest of my week.*

I turn to face him more fully on the couch. "Steven texted me last night." James sits up straight and stares at me wide-eyed.

"How did he get your number?"

"I wish I knew. I've never given it to him. I also don't think anyone who has it would give it to him. But a lot of people have it, so it can't be that hard to track down."

"What did he want?" His look is guarded and inquisitive. The last time we saw him it was not a great time.

"Apparently my mom is at his house." I wince at the words. Those two together can't possibly be good, but he says she's safe, he gave her a warm place to sleep after she left here, so I guess we'll see.

James lets out a low whistle. "Wow. That is not what I was expecting. Have you messaged him back? Should we go over there to check things out? Shit, I don't even know where he lives, do you?"

"I haven't. I don't know what to say to him about the situation. I haven't spoken to the man in forever, I have no idea where he lives. He could live in a different town for all I know, but that doesn't make much sense." I can tell both of our minds are going a million miles a minute, but my parents being in the same house and 'safe' at that, is just weird. "I don't think I want to go to his house. That's like crossing some imaginary boundary and it feels all types of wrong right now. But maybe I could get them to meet us somewhere and see how she looks. If it's bad, then we take her back or call the cops or something. Ugh, what a nightmare." He rubs my leg absentmindedly.

"That sounds like a good plan. But if you plan to meet in public, you'll have to go alone since I'm 'sick'. You may have Jack by the balls, but that only goes so far for my job security." I know he's right, but I need him there. "If you need someone with you, call Jayden and have her go. She's never been scared of confrontation, and I think the hormones might help quelch that fear even more." We both chuckle, knowing that Jayden is like a bloodhound when it comes to my mother.

"Shit, okay. Let me text Jay and see if she's available and then we'll decide what to do from there." He nods and gets up from the couch to go grab us a couple waters. I send Jay a text filling her in and she responds almost immediately as if she was about to text me:

Hell yea, I'll go with you. I'll be at your house in 15.

James comes back and hands me a bottle of water. I open it and chug half of it before turning to where he sits on the couch, watching me patiently.

"She'll be here soon. I guess I should text him and figure out what we're going to do." My hands shake as I pick up my phone; dealing with them both at the same time is making me question my sanity. I've never had to do this.

I'm glad she's okay. I'd like to meet with you guys somewhere.

In half an hour if that works. Let me know.

I set my phone in my lap and let out a breath. James' hand is on my thigh, and I focus all of my mental energy on the feel of that connection: calm, safe, loving.

"If you need me, call me. I don't give a fuck about Jack if it comes down to an emergency and you need to get out of there. I know Jayden won't let things get too out of hand, but just in case." He squeezes my leg, and I can't take the small amount of contact anymore; I lunge at him, knocking him back into the arm of the couch. "Woah, Haz, I think you broke my back." He's laughing so I know I didn't actually hurt him. I squeeze him tight as he wraps his arms around me.

"I love you, James Archibald. Thank you for choosing me even when things get shitty and complicated. Thank you for not running at the first sign of drama from my mother. Thank you for allowing me to be me authentically and without need for apology. You're the best." He squeezes me tight against him but doesn't get a chance to respond because my phone chimes and I leap from his arms and grab my phone.

That works. We'll meet you at Rudy's Café.

Rudy's has been around for forever. My mom used to take me there on the rare days she had the night off or was feeling generous with her money. Maybe she was making up for being a shitty parent, who knows. I can't help but wonder if she picked the meeting spot. Neutral ground, but full of nostalgia. It helps that it's two blocks from my house.

I turn to James who is watching the emotions flitting across my face. "Well?"

"We're meeting at Rudy's." He shakes his head incredulously. He knows the history of that place. In fact, I took him there for one of our first dates because it meant so much to me back then. If I'm being truthful with myself, it still means a lot to me now.

The front door opens, and Jayden comes walking in. Kiba loses his mind, bounding over to her, tail wagging a million miles a minute. She gets him calmed down and looks at me, sees the look on my face. It's almost as if she's preparing for war, the way she steals herself for what we're about to endure.

She nods to me, "Let's get this shitshow over with." Most people would find that offensive, but it brings me a sense of relief to have my best friend coming with me. It makes me feel unstoppable, untouchable.

I give James a kiss and he holds me to him for a few minutes as if he's trying to imbue me with all of his strength. I pull away and he gives me a reassuring smile. I take a deep, steadying breath, "Let's do this."

Jayden is driving us because who knows what's going to happen and I need to have a quick escape plan on top of not wanting him to know what I drive. It's not that I don't trust him, but I don't know him and that does mean there is some mistrust there. He could have been a part of my life a lot sooner than this and he chose not to. Some would say better late than never, but this is cutting it pretty close in my book.

"It'll be okay, Haz. You have me and if we need reinforcements, you can call James and I'll call Isaac. I already filled him in on my way over. We'll be just fine." I try to smile at her, but it comes out as more of a grimace.. I'm a nervous wreck and I just want to make sure my mom really is okay.

It only takes us a few minutes to get to Rudy's Café. There are only five cars here and I know three of them belong to the employees. The two that belong to customers are nondescript enough; not too beat up and not too nice. I don't know if either of them belongs to Steven. "We should come up with a safe word, just in case it's too much for you and you don't feel comfortable saying so or getting up and leaving." I could kiss her for her ingenuity.

"Popsicles." She lifts an eyebrow at me, so I explain further. "They don't have popsicles here and it's a fitting metaphor for their hearts." I can feel tears trying to break free of my eyes.

"Popsicles it is. If you want to go back, we can. No one will judge you for doing so." She grabs my hand and she squeezes it.

"They would judge me. I know that shouldn't bother me, but it does. I don't want to appear weak to them. I want to be strong and fierce." I take another steadying breath, "Let's go." She releases my hand, we get out of the car, and walk into Rudy's. I look around and spot them sitting in a booth in the back. Steven waves to me while my mom keeps her gaze on the menu in front of her, completely unphased by how freaked out I've been.

Chapter Nineteen

Lynn

We spent all of Sunday chatting and watching movies. Steven filled me in about all of the bad shit he went through to get to where he is. I don't know why he's being so kind to me. I've tried to tell him to let me leave, but he refuses to take me to Paul's. I could walk, but that seems a little unreasonable. *You want to be here.* Yea, I do. He's as nice as I remember him. He didn't judge a single thing I told him about what I did to raise Hazel. He doesn't yell at me or look at me any differently for the life I've led. In fact, it's the opposite; it's empathy I saw on his face when I told him about all of it. I told him before I started that I don't want no sympathy and he didn't give me any.

We walked down to Teller's to get some soda and I could have sworn I saw Sandy's car, but she didn't stop. Probably because she didn't see me, or she didn't recognize me. I'm not mad at her for not stopping. I'm glad she didn't because she would have taken me away from Steven and I'm not ready to go back to reality yet.

When we got back, he asked if I wanted to watch a movie and I said sure. He sat in his chair, and I laid down on the couch. He turned on *The Breakfast Club*, one of my favorites. I ended up falling asleep about halfway through and woke up hours later to a blanket over me. I smelled food so I got up and went to the kitchen where he was making lasagna and garlic bread.

"Hope you're hungry. This is my mom's recipe. It's not as good as hers, but is it ever as good as a mom's cooking?"

I couldn't help but smile at this whole situation. Years and years have passed and he's just so smooth with everything. I leaned against the counter and watched him as he cooked. I had offered to help, but he wouldn't let me.

"Just so you know, I text Hazel to let her know you're here and safe. I knew she was probably worried about you." And just like that, the serene feeling in my chest disappeared.

"You shouldn't have done that. She doesn't give a shit and is probably relieved I'm gone." My appetite left me and I just wanted to lay down in bed and go to sleep.

"You know her better than I do, obviously; maybe you're right, but I still felt it was the right thing to do."

"How did you get her number? Have y'all been talkin?" I was suddenly very suspicious of the whole scenario. Something wasn't adding up and if they had been talkin' and planning this would make a whole lot more sense than me randomly runnin' into him in that alley.

"No, we haven't been talking. I've been meaning to get in touch with her and try to form some sort of relationship with her. I was just worried she'd turn me down. I just looked her up online and called her office one day. She wasn't in so they gave me her voicemail where she gives her clients her cell number. I've had it ever since. That was about three months ago." I still didn't believe him, but I decided to leave it for the time being. If he was misleading me, I'd find out soon enough.

The rest of the night was peaceful, and we didn't talk about Hazel anymore. I was glad because it just soured the short time we would have together.

I woke up this mornin' and he had breakfast waiting. I figured he'd have to work today, but he informed me that he had taken a couple days off, until we figured out what was goin' on with me. My traitorous heart soared at that revelation. One part of my mind turned over the idea that he was making time for me, that he wanted me to be here and see me safe and cared for. The other part of my brain was telling me I was being stupid and I needed to think logically and get the hell out of there.

Naturally, my love sick brain won the argument, makin' me stay here, torturing myself further.

While we were cleanin' up the kitchen, his phone dinged with a message. I'm not one to pry so I didn't ask any questions. "Hazel is going to meet us in a bit. Go get ready."

"What? Why is she meetin' us? Is she comin' here?" My nerves were out the window, and it was apparently clear as day on my face because he came over to me and rubbed my arm, the first physical contact we've had since he brought me here.

"She wants to make sure you're okay. We're going to Rudy's Cafe. Go get ready so we can go." The mention of Rudy's and his hand on my arm had my emotions feeling like they were in a tornado. I used to take Hazel there when she was little. It was our favorite little spot, and the service was always delightful. I'm not sure if he knows that, but it brings me a little peace knowing we're goin' there.

Now we're sittin' here waiting on Hazel to show up and he's calm as can be. I'm trying to steal some of that calm for myself, but I don't know what to expect from Hazel. I know she's pissed at me. I know I made her worry for no reason. I know I fucked up again. But I just don't know how to fix any of it. Steven nudges my leg with his knee, and I assume it's because Hazel just walked in. Sure enough I take a quick peek and there she is with her bitch of a friend Jayden. I never liked that girl. She's opinionated and rude. My guard is instantly up. I return my eyes to the menu I'm lookin' at even though I'm not hungry.

"Hey, mom." Her voice sounds relieved. "Steven." I can hear how reserved she is when it comes to him. If only she knew everything I now knew, she wouldn't be speaking to him like that. But she doesn't and I don't know how to tell her to not be a bitch to him, so I just look up at her. She's beautiful, always has been. Probably because she looks so much like Steven. Her brown hair is down and wavy around her shoulders, the emerald sweater she has on really brings out her green eyes. "Are you okay? Like really, okay?"

Before I can answer the waitress comes over and asks what we'd like to drink. Steven asks for a pot of coffee for the table and Jayden asks for water. Of course, she's too good for coffee. I refrain from scoffin' at her like I want to. I want this meeting to go well. The waitress comes back with our drinks and asks if we want anything to eat. We all decline. She leaves again, getting the hint that we wanna be left the hell alone.

"Yea, I'm okay. More than okay, actually. Thanks to Steven." The hurt that crosses her face makes my stomach knot up even more. "I didn't mean it like that, Hazel. I was just in a really bad place when I left your house. Steven stopped me from making some bad decisions and has been real nice." She looks relieved to hear that, but there's still somethin' in her eyes that tells me she's not completely okay.

"Why did you leave?" I feel awkward havin' this conversation with Steven and Jayden sittin' here, but I guess I only have myself to blame for that. If she wants the truth, I'll give it to her, no matter how ugly it is.

"You didn't want me there. I was causin' you a lot of stress from what James told me and he pissed me off with his mouthiness." She opens her mouth to interrupt. "Let me finish. I have a lot to say and I want to get it all out before I lose the nerve." My voice is stern, leaving no room for arguments; she sits back in her chair and nods to me. "My feelin's were hurt that you wouldn't tell me how much stress I was causin' you. My life felt like it was nothin' more than an inconvenience and I put myself in that situation. I wanted to escape all the bad shit that was happenin'.

"I went to that alley over by Teller's to find some drugs. Steven was there, helpin' some guys out. When they passed me the pipe and I put it to my lips, he smacked it out of my hands and took me to his house. I've been there ever since. He's got clothes for me, he's been feedin' me, I've been showerin' every day." It feels like a weight is lifted from my shoulders and I can breathe easier than I have the last however many hours it's been.

Chapter Twenty

Hazel

Her voice portrays her happiness and the hope I know she's harboring. I try to find a supporting bone in my body, but all I feel is resentment.

I try to force a smile, but it gets stuck somewhere. Jayden picks up on my emotions, and she reaches over and squeezes my knee. I can't give them my blessing for this, not with all the heartache and frustration these two have caused.

"Well, at least someone can get you to act right. It just sucks that it isn't your daughter who's been going to bat for you for the last umpteen years." I give a dry laugh. "Imagine, everything I've done for you; everything I've endured for you; for you to turn around and change your ways for a man who broke your heart when you were a fucking teenager." I glare into Steven's wide eyes. I can tell he wasn't expecting me to go off like this, but the whole situation makes me sick to my stomach.

"Now, Hazel. Don't—"

"Don't you dare lecture me about what I'm saying right now, Mother. I have spent thousands and thousands of dollars on you, put myself through emotional hell to help you. He comes traipsing in like not a day has gone by and miraculously you're okay? You're all better now? Because he 'saved' you from making a stupid decision when you couldn't face the consequences of your actions at *my house* where you were already safe and fed and had anything you needed? Fuck that and fuck you." Jayden's gasp tells me enough about my outburst, but I don't stick around long enough for anyone to say anything else. I can feel the eyes of the employees and other patrons on me, but I'm too pissed off to care.

I get out of the booth, ready to leave, but Steven decides that's a good time to put his two cents in. "Hazel, sit back down. Let's talk this out. We can all come to an understanding." Steven's voice is pleading and calm. I spin around to face him, my anger is a palpable thing at this point and it takes everything in me not to pour the hot coffee on his lap.

"You *especially* have no right to speak to me. The only reason I responded to your message was because of her.

Because even though I'm the child, I've had to take the parental role and make sure she's okay. For *years* after what you did to her. You have no idea the shit that she put me through. So don't you say another fucking word to me. Enjoy being her crutch. She'll be crawling back to my house in no time. Just you fucking wait.

"Things will go well for a while. Then one day she'll have a change of heart, and nothing will be okay. She'll walk out like she always does." I turn to my mother, "And I won't be there to bail you out this time. I'm done." I turn and walk outside, waiting for Jayden to catch up. I pace around the parking lot by her car, taking deep breaths trying to calm down. All I want to do is go back in there and punch him in his stupid face and tear my mother down, so she knows what I think of her at this moment, but I know it won't do any good. So, I pace, and I wait.

Jayden comes out about 5 minutes later looking smug. She smiles at me, and I know she let them have it. She wraps me in a hug, "It's all good, Haz. I'm proud of you. Fuck those assholes. Let's go." She releases me and we get in her car to go back to my house. I try to get her to tell me what she said to them, but she told me she wants to see my and James' reaction together. I know she's savage, but this makes me nervous.

Chapter Twenty-One

Lynn

I can't believe Hazel went off like that. She's never been one
to lose her temper or yell. Hell, she rarely cusses and gets
mad at me if I cuss too much around her. Steven keeps
trying to talk to me, but I can't hear him. I'm so shocked at
how she acted. I really pushed her away this time. I thought
my life was falling apart before, but now it's abundantly clear
that it's completely down the drain. *What the hell am I doin'?*

Steven grabs my shoulder and gives me a little shake,
"Lynn, are you okay?" I shake my head to clear my thoughts.

"Yea, sorry. I—I just…I just don't know why she reacted that
way." There are tears in my eyes, but I refuse to cry in
public. "Can we go back to the house? I need to get out of

the public for a while." He squeezes my shoulder and nods at me.

Once we get back to his house I sit on the couch and put my face in my hands. My mind is racing a million miles a minute and I don't know how to fix this shit.

"Don't worry about it. She just needs some time and she'll calm down." He sits next to me and rubs my back. His touch does things to my body and I can't tell if I like it or hate it. In a normal situation I would love it, but things are so fuckin' confusing right now.

"No, I don't think she will. No offense, Steven, but you don't know our daughter like I do. She has never, *ever* talked to me like that. Or anyone like that, for that matter. I really fucked up. I should have left Sunday mornin' and went back to her house and explained everything. Apologized for my behavior. But bein' here with you has been so damn nice. I could just forget things for a while. I could pretend things never ended the way they did. Despite us sleepin' in other rooms and you never sittin' next to me on the couch. I could still pretend that it was just years of bein' together that let us have this space from each other. I got lost in a fantasy while my—our daughter was upset and lookin' for me. God knows what she was thinkin'."

He stops rubbing my back as if my words broke some spell on him. I don't blame him, I just admitted to a whole bunch of

226

fucked thinkin' and he's probably repulsed. But I can't lie to him, he knows me, and I know him. I've always said what I was thinkin' with him. Despite the years that have passed, he still feels like home.

"I'll handle it, Lynn. Don't worry about it. Go take a bath and relax. It's been a day." His voice doesn't leave room for arguin' and somethin' about his posture told me he's not in the mood for my mouthiness. I don't know what I could say anyway. I get up and head to my bedroom to take a bath. It really does sound nice after that altercation with Hazel.

As I'm relaxin' in the bath, I can hear him talking on his phone. I can't make out what he's saying, though. I don't know how he plans on handling this shit with Hazel. But I hope whatever it is fixes it. I can't lose her; she's been the only constant good thing in my life.

After an hour in the tub, I decide it's time to get out and see what he's come up with. I need answers. I s'pose that's where Hazel got it from. My fingers and toes are pruned, but my body has never felt so relaxed. If my mind could follow suit I'd be in business. But it doesn't, it's runnin' a million miles a minute, goin' over every different scenario of how I can patch things up.

I go to the living room where he's sprawled on the couch, a glass with amber liquid in one hand, the other draped across the back of the couch. His eyes travel my body as I walk out in the shorts and tank top pajama set I'd found. I don't know what he's thinking, but he's making my heart race with the way his eyes seem to devour me. I'm nothin' like I used to look like. I have wrinkles in the wrong places, saggy skin in others, scars littering different parts of my body. But the way he's lookin' at me tells me he doesn't see the imperfections. I gulp in a breath, "Did you figure out what to do?"

He sits forward and puts his glass on the coffee table, clearing his throat. "Yea, I'll get it all sorted out tomorrow." His voice is gruff, like he's been screamin'. It's hotter than any voice I've ever heard. "Come sit with me, Lynn." My breath catches in my throat.

"It's okay—I was just goin' to go lay down for a bit." He glares at me. "Uh…I guess I could come sit with you for a bit." I scratch the back of my head, a nervous tic I picked up in my time with Paul. I don't want to piss him off, but I also don't want to push him to do somethin' he'll regret. I take a deep breath and go join him on the couch. He's sittin' in the middle, so I sit as close to the edge as I can, to give him some space. His eyes never leave me.

"I'm not going to bite you…" His voice trails off as if he was goin' to add somethin' to the end, but second guessed it. I look everywhere but at his face, I can't look in his eyes and hold myself back. Not with how unhinged I'm feelin'. I pick mindlessly at the couch, my nerves making themselves abundantly clear.

He moves faster than I can process. One minute he's sitting forward on the couch, the next my hair is wrapped in his fist and his mouth is on mine. I might die from a heart attack; my heart is beating a wild rhythm and I can't calm it. When he finally moves his mouth away from mine, I say, "We don't have to do this. I was just talkin' earlier. I shouldn't have said anything. I'm sorry."

"Shut up. Do you know how hard it's been to keep myself away from you? I've *missed* you. You and I had something special. And your wild imagination stole that from us. I've dreamed of you every single night since. That's why I'm not married with more kids. I've fucked other people, sure. But none of them meant anything to me." My heart melts into my stomach at his words. I've been dying to hear him say this since I walked away from him all those years ago. I wanted him to beg for me to come back to him and apologize for his actions.

Now I know why he didn't, my mother wouldn't let him. I can't fault him for that, my mother is a scary woman. Well, she was, now she's just withering away in that home. "I don't ever want you to apologize to me for speaking your truth, Lynn. I am a safe place for you to voice anything and everything you have to say or feel or think. I'm just tired of wasting time by holding myself back from you. If you have any objections—"

I cut his words off by putting my mouth on his and kissing him deeply. He's always been my everything, even when I hated him so much I could have killed him. We have passion and understanding between us. Something no one else has ever been able to pull out of me. Our hands explore each other's bodies and before I know it, our clothes are coming off and getting thrown who knows where. The only thing we care about is feeling each other again.

He pulls me to him and throws one of my legs over his lap so I'm straddlin' him. *Some things never change.* He taught me a lot when we were together, one of which was how to ride a man properly. It was his favorite position, and apparently still is. But I hold off on that and just grind against him as we continue making out. It's been a long time since I've let myself go like this. Sex has always been either a job or somethin' I felt obligated to do. With Steven it's the opposite. I can take my time, explore, let go completely. He doesn't rush me, doesn't guilt me, he just lets me be.

His hands are all over my body, sending goosebumps in the wake of his fingers. I'm a shiverin' mess in his hands; putty beneath his fingers; he owns me body and soul.

My hands are in his hair, then down the sides of his face, down his neck, resting on his chest. I break our kiss and look in his eyes. "Are you sure about this? I don't want you to do somethin' you don't want to."

"Lynn." He laughs incredulously at my hesitation. "I'm rock hard beneath you. If that's not enough of an indication of how much I want you, then listen to me. I want you, and only you, for the rest of my life. I've gone far too long without you. I loved you then, I loved you during our years apart, and I love you now." Tears fall down my face at his words, but I nod in acceptance.

I sit up on my knees and line him up with me and slowly slide myself down on him. We've always been a perfect fit, and time hasn't changed that. He fills every inch of space inside of me, makin' me feel full, complete. I sit there for a moment, revelin' in the feel of our bodies connected again. I take a steadying breath, readying myself to be destroyed by him yet again. I know what he said, and a part of me believes it, but my life doesn't work that way.

Something will happen, and we'll be torn apart again.

I'm just too much of a masochist to stop myself from barrelin' straight into that heartbreak. *Maybe this time it'll kill me.*

As if he can tell my thoughts have carried me away, he gently kisses me while grabbing my ass and liftin' me up and easin' me back down. He's just as desperate as I am, he just hides it better. "Come back to me, Lynn. Be with me here, in this moment." He kisses me again, quieting the thoughts runnin' through my head.

I kiss him back and rotate my hips as I slide myself up and down his length. I've missed him inside of me; I've missed him being with me; I've missed *him.*

Although me ridin' him is his favorite, he picks me up and lays me on the couch; never breakin' our connection. He worships my body like I'm a Goddess sent from above to give him salvation.

When we're done, we lay there intertwined for a few minutes, breathing heavily. He looks in my eyes and whispers, "I love you." He says it quietly, as if speaking it too loudly will tarnish this moment.

Chapter Twenty-Two

Hazel

We walk in the door and James is pacing in the living room. He looks up at me when I walk in and runs over to me, cupping my face in his hands. "How did it go? Are you okay?" He kisses my forehead.

"Let us take off our coats, Mr. Knight-In-Shining-Armor." Jayden taunts from half-way in the door. She can't come in further given where we're standing. James laughs and apologizes, releasing my face and going back to the living room. Once we're stripped of our winter gear, we go sit on the couch.

"Well? I'm dying here. I thought about saying fuck it and going there with you so many times. I was about to leave when you walked in." He's bouncing his knee so fast the whole couch is vibrating.

"It went as well as can be expected, I guess. She's fine." My face must give away my anger and hurt.

"What happened, Haz?" I can't tell him, I don't know if it's embarrassment or shame, but the words won't come out. I look at Jayden and she nods at me.

"She was an absolute badass. She told them both to fuck off and cut Lynn off in the process. She didn't give them room to argue or say anything. Just laid out her truth and then walked away like some action movie heroine." Her smile is radiant as she retells what happened. I can feel her pride radiating off of her, coating my soul in such warmth.

"Wow. I'm shocked. No offense, Babe. But we've all been telling you to do that for years now. What changed?"

"I—I...I was so pissed off that she accepted his help so graciously, seemed so happy to have him there and be her savior after everything we've done for her, everything I've been through. I just lost it. Then he tried to get me to calm down and talk to them and I flipped my lid. It took everything in me not to pour coffee on him or punch his stupid teeth in." My glare is hurting my face, but I can't get my face to relax. I'm still so mad at her and appalled at Steven's audacity to even open his mouth about anything.

"I really thought she was going to swing on him. I wouldn't have stopped her. But I'm glad she didn't." Her words remind me she still hasn't told me what she said to them.

"Apparently after I walked out, Jay had words with them." I turn to her, "Spill." Her answering smile is cruel and wicked, I know it'll be good.

"They were stunned. They sat there gaping for a few seconds and then they turned to me, as if I had answers. I'm not going to lie; I was stunned too. But I pulled myself together faster than they did. I told them they both deserved everything you said to them and more. I looked Steven dead in his eyes and said, 'You don't get to come in here after having nothing to do with either of them for three and a half decades and pretend it can all be patched up. You're a worthless deadbeat in her eyes and mine. I'll be damned if I let you sit here and try to parent her, try to calm her down when she is valid in how she feels.' His head whipped back as if my words physically slapped him.

"Then I turned to your mom who was trying to kill me with her eyes. I said to her, 'This has been a long time coming. Are you aware that every time you need a place to stay James and I try to convince her not to let you go to their house? We've tried telling her to inform you of how much of a terrible mother you were and are. You failed her time and time again. You're failing her again and you can't even get your head out of your ass long enough to see it. She deserves better; she deserved better. Thank God she had Rose, or else she may have ended up just like you. How disgustingly sad would that have been.' Her eyes were teary when I got up and walked away. I'm pretty sure I heard her call me a bitch behind my back. Of course, she didn't have the balls to say it to my face." She cackles like a maniac.

My mouth is gaping open, but I feel such an overwhelming sense of gratitude and love for my chosen family. Because that's what James, Isaac, and Jayden are, my chosen family. They've never let me down like my mother has. They've never made me question their loyalty or their priorities. They show up and they show out for me, just as I do for them. I've searched for this my whole life, and in this moment, I vow to myself to never let them go.

 I fling myself into her arms and sob, "Thank you, Jay. You're the best and I don't know what I did to deserve you, but I'm so glad that you're my best friend."

She squeezes me to her, one hand smoothing my hair, "I love you, Girl. I'll always be there for you. No matter what, no matter when. I meant it when I said you deserve better. You're so strong, Hazel. You've been through so much. I'll be damned if I let her continue doing it."

I release her and look at James who's sitting on the coffee table with his mouth still hanging open. He shakes his head, "I'm so jealous I wasn't there to witness this happen. I've been waiting for years for this to happen. I'm so fucking proud of you two. We need to celebrate. Jayden, call Isaac, we're going to go out to eat tonight. I don't care if Jack finds out, this is too monumental." He kneels on the floor in front of me and wraps me up in the tightest hug. "I'm so damn proud of you, Haz. You are utterly amazing in every way. I never want you to question that." He lets go enough so he can kiss me. I get lost in the feeling of his mouth on mine, his tongue caressing mine, until Jayden starts making barfing noises. We pull away from each other, laughing.

"Sorry, Jay." I give her an apologetic smile.

"If y'all need some time, I can go for a bit. We can meet up later." Her disgust is written on her face. She hates PDA, even though technically we're not in public. I start to protest, but James cuts in.

"Yea, that'll work. We'll meet at Bunberry's at 6." He smirks at me.

"Bunberry's, huh? Festive, indeed! All right, I'll see y'all later." James releases me so I can get up and give her a hug. "I love you, Hazel. Don't have too much fun." She winks at me. I laugh and walk her to the door.

"I love you, too, Jay. See ya later!" When the door closes, I turn to my fiancé, wondering what deliciously devious activities he has planned for us.

Chapter Twenty-Three

James

I pull Hazel to me as soon as she turns from the door. My hand twisting in her hair and pulling so her head tilts up. Her big green eyes meet mine, the hurt and frustration apparent; but so is the lust she feels in this moment. I grin at her devilishly. "I plan to worship you today, Baby. We have two hours before we need to get ready, but I plan to continue when we get home later." Her body shivers against mine, I can feel her nipples harden against my chest. I bend down, lightly brushing my lips against hers, teasing her.

"James, please." Her body is already trembling with her need. I love it when she begs.

"Please what?" My lips graze hers again; she's putty in my hands.

"Please just kiss me already." I chuckle darkly.

"So needy and impatient. But if you insist." I roughly push her against the wall in the front hall, her breath knocks out of her for a moment. But before she can gulp air, my mouth is violently on hers. My tongue invades her mouth, her tongue scrambling to match the pace. I break the kiss to move to the corner of her mouth, trailing down to her neck, giving her a reprieve from the onslaught she asked for.

"I thought you said you were going to worship me?" She's breathless, but I can tell she doesn't mean it in a negative way. Hazel doesn't do worship other than me telling her she's taking my cock like a good girl. We've tried several times and she just can't get into it.

"You know as well as I do that you love this. You prefer this. Unless of course something has changed?" My words are broken up by kisses and bites on her neck. Goosebumps are peppering her skin and her hands are wrapped in my hair.

She answers me by pushing my head lower. "I need your mouth on me." I growl against her skin, moving away so I can take her clothes off. If she wants my mouth on her, she needs to be completely naked. Otherwise, it feels cheap and she's anything but.

I rip her sweater over her head and yank her bra off her arms after I unclasp it. My mouth finds one of her nipples while my hands pull her leggings down. I refuse to let her nipple out of my mouth, so she has to bend with me while I take her leggings off.

When she's bared to me, I release her nipple and continue my descent down her body. Kissing, biting, licking. She whimpers and begs, and even though I know she doesn't like to be worshiped, I *do* want to take my time pleasing her today. My hands skate up her legs to the precipice at her thighs, lightly skating over her sensitive skin, and then skating back down. She tries to get them back up by bucking her hips. My eyes meet hers and I shake my head, letting her know this goes at my pace today, not hers.

I grab her left leg and throw it over my shoulder, opening her up for me. I can see how turned on she is by the sheen on her pretty pussy. It takes everything in me not to jump right in and have a feast. I turn my head to the side of her knee, kissing gently up her thigh. When I'm at the meatiest part I sink my teeth in, and she cries out. I let go and kiss the reddened area lovingly. I continue up her thigh, lightly kissing, my other hand grasps her ass to give me a good handhold on her while I eat my fill.

I get to her pussy and pause, spreading her lips with my free hand. I lightly blow on her clit, causing her to moan and thrust her hips towards my face. At the top of her thrust, I dive in. I can't hold back anymore, she's too much of a temptation for me.

I start off with nice, slow, small circles to ease her into it. She lets me know when she's ready for me when she yanks my hair towards her. I, being ever the gentleman, give her what she wants. My tongue moves viciously against her clit, rough flicks that have her legs shaking against me, her hips rotating in synchronization with my tongue, chasing the release she's so desperately searching for.

I put two fingers inside of her, finding her g-spot instantly and massaging it in time with my tongue. Within seconds she's spasming around me, her leg holding her up giving out. I catch her and grab her other leg and throw it over my shoulder and push her back further against the wall. Both of my hands now under her ass, holding her up while I slow my tongue ever so slightly.

Once she calms down from her orgasm, she starts grinding my face again. Her nails are digging into my scalp, and it'll be a miracle if she doesn't draw blood. If she does, I don't care; it'll be totally worth it. This time I let her find her rhythm against my tongue, make her work for her own release. It takes a few minutes, and my shoulders are starting to get sore from holding her here, but then she's coming again. When she comes down from her high, I set her on her feet. I keep a hold of her in case her legs are unsteady, but she's all right.

I stand up and remove my own clothes, adding them to her pile. I reach out to her, running my hands up her body. I pinch her nipples as I pass them making her chest heave and her fists clench at her sides. I release them just as fast as I pinched them and grab her throat with one hand and the other turns her towards the wall. "Be a good girl and spread your legs for me." She hesitates and tries to look at me over her shoulder, but I tighten my grip on her throat. "Are you defying me right now?" I growl in her ear. I press my hard cock against her ass. She whimpers and spreads her legs, putting her hands on the wall above her head, bracing herself. "That's what I thought." I slap her ass hard, then rub it to soothe the sting.

I push her forward slightly, making her ass push out. I grab my cock and line it up to her. She braces herself against the wall and I slide into the sweetest wetness I've ever experienced. I swear her pussy is like a drug that I can't get enough of.

Once I'm all the way in, I have to pause so I don't come already. She's so tight. Once I have control over myself, I start to pump in and out. Her hands slide on the wall causing her to have to reposition herself several times. "Fuck, you feel so amazing." As soon as the words leave my mouth, she tightens around me, moaning my name.

I release her throat and pull out. She sags against the wall and looks at me over her shoulder, "You didn't come." She's pouting about it.

"Did you think I was done with you already?" I cock an eyebrow at her, and she shudders against the wall. "Up. Go to the living room. I'm going to fuck you in every room of this house before I finish." Her eyes close as she moans. Once she composes herself, she does as she's told.

An hour later and I have succeeded in my mission. While I wanted to continue this tonight, I don't think either of us has it in us. We barely have the energy to get ready for dinner. But we do need to celebrate what Hazel accomplished today, so we make ourselves presentable and head to Bunberry's.

"Two of you tonight?" The hostess is a high school aged girl, wearing a white button down and black slacks.

"There will actually be four. We're just waiting for our friends to get here." Hazel usually takes point in restaurants, but I want her to have a relaxing evening.

"Of course. Right this way." She grabs the menus and turns to walk us to our table. On our way I spot Ryan. *Fuck.*

I beat Ryan for the position I have at Jack's gig. It was a grueling process, and I still don't know how I lucked out, but I'm glad I did. He'll only be too happy to inform Jack that I was out and about after my fiancée called me out of work this morning. Not to mention his history with Hazel. I despise that man, but I try to keep my personal feelings out of our working relationship. Although some days I'd pay big money to punch his face in.

Hoping he doesn't see me, I quicken my pace behind the hostess. She takes us to a back corner booth, out of Ryan's line of sight. I let out a sigh of relief as the hostess goes back to the stand.

"What's that about?" Hazel puts her phone down as she questions my sigh. She was probably letting Jayden know we're here and have a table.

"Ryan is here." The look on her face tells me she's just as worried.

"Maybe we should go somewhere else?" She reaches to grab her phone, but I put my hand on her to stop her.

"No, it's done now. If he didn't see me coming in, he'd definitely see me when we left. We'll just play it cool and hope he doesn't see me."

Our waiter comes over and Hazel orders a glass of chardonnay and I get a scotch on the rocks. I need to take the edge off and it's a celebration, after all.

Jayden and Isaac arrive at our table as the waiter brings our drinks. He tells us the specials and gets their drink orders then leaves again. "Soo…How was the sex?" Jayden shoots a wink at Hazel whose face is beet red.

"Jayden. Lower your voice! The whole restaurant doesn't need to know about our sex life."

"Oh, please. These fuckers are probably 10 times dirtier than the two of you." She's laughing loudly and drawing attention which makes me nervous. She sees it written on my face, "Calm down, James. Jack isn't here. It's fine."

"No, he isn't, but Ryan is." It was worth it to see her shocked expression. It takes a lot to make her speechless, but I seem to have found a way.

"I—I'm sorry. I didn't know. Why didn't you tell me, Haz?" The waiter arrives with their drinks, an Irish ale for Isaac and a water for Jayden.

"I didn't have time. We almost left, but James said it would cause more suspicion if we did. So, we stayed." She turns to the waiter who is getting ready to turn around and leave, but she stops him. "Sorry, I'll have the Shrimp Alfredo and Italian dressing for the salad. Can we also have an order of bread and oil for the table?"

"Sure thing, Ma'am." The rest of us give our orders and he leaves to put our order in. As soon as he's gone, Jayden raises her glass.

"A toast to my best friend, the most badass of all bad asses, Hazel." Her toast works in lifting everyone's spirits from the terrible vibe the dinner started out with.

"To Hazel!" Isaac and I echo her. We all clink glasses and take a drink. I throw an arm around Hazel's shoulders, leaning back in the booth. We fall into normal conversation, the girls talking about their girly things and Isaac and I talking about the newest iPhone coming out. He's a fan, I'm not. I prefer Android, something he drags me about whenever he gets the chance.

Dinner is going smoothly until we're almost done, then I hear Ryan's voice call my name. "James! What a surprise. I thought you were sick today. We really missed you in the office."

I look up and he has the smuggest look on his face having caught me at dinner with Hazel and company. I smile back at him, "Yea, I wasn't feeling very well this morning. But I feel loads better now. How was your meal?" I don't know what to say to him. He probably wants me to beg him to not tell, but I'm not going to stoop to that level.

"Good, good. Bunberry's never disappoints. We're actually out celebrating. Jack made the decision to step away for a while. With his shit storm of a life right now he hasn't been making very good decisions." He looks at Hazel disapprovingly as he says this, and my insides turn to molten lava.

"Oh, wow. I didn't know he was thinking about that. I guess we'll all have to step up a bit to make sure things get done properly." He meets my eyes and smiles. The smile tells me everything I need to know. He's going to be in charge. Why? I have no idea. Don't get me wrong, the guy is a genius, but he's not one to run a company. Not to mention I'm higher up than he is, so it should go to me. But I'll back Jack's decisions, no matter how maddening they are.

"That we will, James. I'm going to need you to work some extra hours to ensure things are done in a timely manner." I'm about to say I can't when he interrupts the words coming out of my mouth. "But that's something we can discuss tomorrow. When I'll see you at the office. Make sure you're there. You missed a lot today and it's going to take a little bit to get you caught up. Enjoy your evening." He turns and leaves.

I can't finish my food. I feel like I'm going to throw up from the war being waged on my insides. This cannot be good. Hazel puts her hand on my thigh and squeezes, bringing me back to the present. They've been having a conversation that I couldn't pay attention to.

"That guy is such a fucking prick. Don't worry about it, man. If you need to quit, you can come work with me. I could use some extra help." Isaac nods his head to me.

I force a smile, "I appreciate that. Well, I guess I didn't have to worry about Jack finding out after all." My chuckle is strained as I look at Hazel. Her eyes show her concern plainly, but she tries to cover it with a smile.

The waiter chooses that time to come deliver the check and before I can reach it, Jayden snags it off the table. "My treat. For Hazel being so brave today and finally telling her mom to fuck off!" Her smile is infectious and even though it feels strained at first, by the time we're leaving the restaurant I feel better.

We part ways once we're out the door, all exchanging hugs, or pats on the back. They remind us of the dinner on Saturday and since things are resolved with Lynn.

I grab Hazel's hand and walk to my car. There are people milling about out here, probably going in to eat or some other shop or restaurant on the block. Once we reach my car, I open the passenger door for her and shut it once she's tucked inside. I go around the back of the car to get in, and see a man standing at the back of the vehicle next to mine. I don't know what causes me to falter in my steps, but the menacing presence of the guy is overwhelming. I know at this moment, we're in danger.

Before I can yell for help or turn to get Hazel to safety, he rushes me.

Chapter Twenty-Four

Hazel

What the hell is taking him so long? I've been sitting in the car for a couple minutes now and James still isn't in the driver's seat to take us home. I unbuckle my seat belt and get out of the car to see if maybe Isaac stopped him as they were leaving and they were just chatting in the parking lot, forgetting about me in the car. *Wouldn't be the first time.*

As I round the car, I see James laying on the ground before a man leaps from the ground and tackles me. I try screaming for help, but he clamps his hand around my throat, cutting off my voice. It wouldn't have done much good anyway, it seems all the people that were walking when we left the restaurant a few minutes ago had gotten to their destinations. "Shut your fuckin' mouth or this goes a lot worse than it should. It's all up to you, Princess." His voice is low, the way he says 'Princess' is degrading and full of contempt. I nod as best I can.

He releases me and tells me to help him carry James to his truck that's a couple stalls down. I do as I'm told, but I'm not much help as I'm trembling, my legs barely able to carry me—let alone my fiancé. He cusses me out the whole way, calling me useless and a waste of space. As if my helping him abduct us would somehow strengthen who I am as a person.

We get to his truck, and he lurches James into the backseat. It's not until now that I see James' face is a bloody mess. *Ryan is going to have a hay day with that tomorrow…if there is going to be a tomorrow.* I try to get in the back with James, to cradle his head in my lap—but our abductor whistles at me to get my attention. "You're in front with me. I don't need you gettin' any ideas about tryin' to strangle me from behind while I'm drivin'." He tosses me a black cloth bag. "Get in and put this over your head. Once we're done with you two, someone will bring you back."

"B—but our car will get towed." He laughs as if I told him the funniest joke he's heard in his life.

"Listen, Princess. No one gives a fuck."

My shock is settling in deep, so I just nod my head and climb in his lifted pick up, putting the bag over my head and sitting back. I'll try to remember turns and such so if we get out of this somehow, I can find our way back. That's what they do in movies, so there must be some truth to it.

The sound of his door shutting makes me jump, all of my senses are on high alert. My hands are twisting in my lap, my leg bouncing. I have to find a way out of this, I have to get James help. What if he has a concussion? What if he has an aneurysm and dies? I can't live without him. I can't do this life without my best friend beside me.

The truck jolts into motion and he turns right. I take a few deep breaths to calm the panic ravaging my body. I try to keep track of all the turns, but after a few minutes my mind keeps playing tricks on me, and I've lost all sense of where I am.

20 minutes later the truck comes to a stop. I don't know if this is our destination or if we're waiting in traffic somewhere, but when I hear his door open and close, I assume this is it. We'll get our answers finally.

He opens my door and grabs my arm, leading me into a place that smells like rotting wood and leaves. The scent is cloying in my nose despite the bag over my head. It makes me gag in the bag. He shoves me to the ground, and I land on my side, my hands not catching me fast enough because I can't see. I hear him talking to other men, and then I hear a body get dropped to the ground next to me—James. "Please, I don't know what we did to offend you or whoever, but we're sorry. We have some money, please just let us go. He needs to go to a hospital."

I'm met with a kick to the stomach. "I told you to shut the fuck up. Jesus fuck, you don't listen, do you? Just like your fuckin'—"

"Trey…" One of the other men cuts him off. I have no idea what he was about to say.

Trey rips the bag off my head, and I try to take in my surroundings, to see if I recognize where we are, but he grabs my cheeks, making me look at him. I've never seen this man before in my life. Granted, it was dark in the parking lot, and he wears a baseball cap low on his head to help obscure his features. I try to pull free, but his grip is like iron. "The Boss will be here in the morning to talk to you. Sit tight for tonight, don't cause any trouble, and all will be well tomorrow…" His words don't make me feel reassured. If anything, I'm more terrified than I was before. Who's this 'boss' he speaks of? What the fuck do these guys want with us?

"P—please, we need to go home. We have lives…please." Tears are running rivers down my face, my voice shaking. I can't help but beg for these men to release us. Kiba will need to be let out and fed. James needs to go to work in the morning before he gets fired. I just—I have to find a way for them to let us go. "Call your boss, tell him to come now. We can figure this all out now and go our separate ways, please!" But I say it to their retreating backs; they're already heading out the door. One of the men turning slightly to shut the door, and I know I know him from somewhere, but my mind is racing too fast for me to place him. The thought is that of one far, far away, passing like a dandelion seed on the wind.

Then the doors are shut and what sounds like a chain pulled through the door handles on the outside. We're trapped here.

I crawl over to James and sit down, putting his head in my lap, absentmindedly playing with his hair. Tears are still falling down my face, splashing his forehead. I can't help it; our lives are so fucked right now. I don't know what we're going to do. I know we'll be okay even if he gets fired from his job, but this whole situation right after everything with my mom is just too much. This was supposed to be a week of relaxation after I found my mom. Now I've been abducted with my fiancé who probably has a concussion and no way out.

I need to call someone, but my phone is in his car. But his phone should still be in his pocket. I gently lay his head back on the ground and scurry down to sit next to his body. I dig in his pockets, but I can't find his phone. I deflate, that fucker probably took it. I start crying harder, sobbing, and cursing the guy who abducted us. I almost don't notice James stirring through my breakdown.

He groans, and I hurriedly crawl to his head, gently lifting it and putting it back in my lap. "James? Are you okay?" He groans some more.

"Haz? What happened?" His voice is weak, and he sounds like he's half awake. The only light source here is the moon peeking from the small window by the door.

"Oh, Baby. It was terrible. I don't have answers. All I know is we were taken from the parking lot at Bunberry's. I don't know where we are or why we're here. But it sounded like they chained the door shut. How's your head?"

"Jesus Christ. What the hell is happening, Haz? This is insane. This is the type of shit you watch on TV, not live through. Do you know who they are or what they want?" He avoids my question about his head, and I don't blame him. He knows I worry a lot and if he tells me it hurts, I'll freak out more than I already am. The one good thing about the poor lighting is I can't see the damage to his face or try to clean his wounds with my shirt. I'm sure I'd do more damage than good if I tried.

"I—I don't know. One is called Trey…he's the one who attacked you and took us. I don't know the other's names, but I recognized one of them, I think. I don't really know. I was panicking, but I'm fairly sure I've seen him before. They wouldn't say what they wanted, only that their boss would be here in the morning."

He tries to sit up, despite my protests, but immediately lays back down. "My head is killing me. I'll be fine, but he really did a number on me. Do you know where we are? Do you have your phone?"

"No, he made me put a bag over my head. I tried to count the turns, but I was too freaked out and my mind was racing and I just don't know." I say this in such a rush, I'm sure he had a hard time comprehending it. My emotions are still raging too hard for me to think rationally.

"It's okay, Haz. I don't blame you. But what about a phone? Do we have one of those?" He redirects my thoughts, thankfully; making me think about one thing at a time.

"No, my phone is in my purse and I think he took your phone or it fell out of your pocket at some point. I looked while you were passed out."

"Shit. Well, I guess that's that for now then, huh?" My heart deflates at the sound of disappointment in his voice.

We spend a while in silence, both of us thinking of different options out of this, what life will be like when we get out—*if* we get out. After about an hour of silence, he finally sits up. "Careful, James. We don't know the extent of your injuries." He grunts a response, then makes his way slowly to his feet. He sways a little but manages to stay upright. He walks over to the door and tries opening it. It doesn't budge other than moving back and forth a little bit. Then he goes to the window. He stands there staring for a while, not moving. I start to get worried, but then he turns and starts looking for things in the dark. "What are you doing?"

"Well, there's a lake out there. Which means this is probably some sort of maintenance building. There's either flashlights or something we could use as weapons, and I mean to find them. It'll improve our chances." His words send my mind spiraling. I shoot up off the ground and run to the window. My heart stops dead in my chest, I can't catch a breath. I think I might pass out.

James seems to sense the change in my body and comes up behind me, putting a hand on my shoulder. "Haz? What's wrong?"

"I—I..." I can't formulate my thoughts into words. I think I might pass out from shock; this is too unreal for me to even comprehend. This place…this building…

"Haz? Talk to me, please. You're starting to scare me. Remember, I'm here to help you. We can figure it all out together, but you have to talk to me, Babe." I turn to him and look up at his face cast in moonlight.

"You die here. I've seen it."

Chapter Twenty-Five

Lynn

Steven and I ordered take out from a Chinese restaurant downtown and had a *Rambo* marathon last night. Although, most of the movies went unwatched as we were too obsessed with each other. We were like hormone-crazed teenagers all over again. When I couldn't keep my eyes open any longer, he picked me up and carried me to his bed. Clearly all I needed to say was that I still cared for him and wanted him, and it brought all his walls down. I tucked that information into the back of my brain, to keep it for later.

He was gone when I woke up this mornin'. He left a note that said he was goin' to fix the situation with Hazel, and he'd be back by lunch.

I look at the clock: 10:20. Sighin', I fix myself a bowl of cereal and take it to the livin' room to watch some TV to pass the time.

At 11:30, he comes rushin' into the house, worry creasin' his face. "What's wrong?" I stand from the couch and go to him, but he stops me with a shake of his head.

"Sit down. I'll explain everything. But you need to be sitting." I'm confused as to what could be so terrible that I need to sit. My brain goes to my mom, thinkin' she died or is in the hospital. I wouldn't need to sit for that. Sure, she's my mom, but there's no love lost there. At least not for me. But I do as he says.

He takes a few breaths as if what he's about to tell me is the hardest thing he's ever said in his life. He clenches his fist and raises his arm like he's about to hit somethin', I shrink away from him. He notices and drops his arm, keeping his fist clenched at his side.

"What's goin' on? Did I do somethin'? Is my mom okay? Just tell me what the hell is happenin'!" He comes and sits next to me on the couch, grabbing my hand and holdin' it as if his life depends on it. He looks me dead in my eyes as he tells me the most terrifying thing I've ever heard.

"Hazel is missing. And James." A choked sob rushes out of me, but he continues on as if the words are burning him from the inside out. "I got ahold of James last night and asked him to meet me. I think he only agreed so he could tell me off, too. But he agreed. Only he didn't show up. So I went to their house, unless their cars were in the garage, no one was home. I rang the doorbell; I banged on the door. The only answer was their dog barking. I tried calling them both and it went straight to voicemail. Odd for people who use their phones for their jobs, right?" I manage to close my gaping mouth and nod at him. I don't dare interrupt him when the words are rushin' out of him like a waterfall. "I was on my way home and I saw his car at Bunberry's, so I went in to see if he was there. The host informed me they had been in last night, but he wasn't there. I asked to see their video cameras, just because, you know. And wouldn't you know, their cameras haven't been working for a month. Their boss keeps saying he's going to fix them, but just hasn't gotten around to it." He laughs dryly. "So, I go back out to the parking lot and go have a look in the car, When I got to the car there, I noticed blood on the ground. I rushed to the side of the car and looked inside; Hazel's purse was in there with her phone sticking out. I don't know where they are, but I have some people looking into it."

I break down cryin'. My baby girl, gone. I know we don't have the best relationship, and I know that's on me. But if anything happens to her, I can't ever repair the damage I've done. I won't ever see her beautiful face again or hear her laugh. Steven puts his arm around my shoulders and pulls me to him. We stay there for a few minutes before his phone rings in his pocket. He lets me go and stands as he answers it, pacin', listenin'. Then he stills, his body tense and I know in my bones this isn't good. I try to keep my thoughts from runnin' wild with what it could mean. I take deep breaths. I have to have hope that she'll be fine. James will do everything he can to protect her, that much I know.

He shakes his head, but says "Thanks, John. Yea, send them here." He hangs up the phone and turns to me. "They know who took her." I don't know who 'they' are, and I don't care. All I care about is knowing who it is and where she is. My face must give away my feelin's, because without me prompting him, he says, "The Enigmas." The name doesn't ring a bell for me, so he explains. "They're a newer gang, they're mostly hired hitmen. Although their list of killings is small in comparison to other gangs we've had around here. Most of the time they just beat the piss out of whoever they're hired to terrorize. Whether that's part of their gig or not, I don't know. But given that they're still in business and no one knows who the leader is, they seem to do a fine enough job.

"Some guys are coming over to help us find them. Some of them you'll remember: Joey, Nathan, and Ron. The others I became friends with after I got clean. They're all good people and I trust them with my life. Their mission is the same as mine, and their pasts just as fucked up. I don't have to tell you that whatever we say or do cannot be repeated. You remember well enough how this side of life works. We'll get dirty if we have to. I'm hoping we don't, but we *will* get her back, Lynn. I swear to you."

I just nod my head because I don't have the right words to give him. I just want my baby home.

Chapter Twenty-Six

James

"What do you mean I die here, Haz? What are you talking about?" I pause my search of finding anything to help us, her words have rooted me to the spot.

"I've been having this dream for a couple of weeks now, I just thought it was the stress and my subconscious telling me how much you mean to me…but James, I've seen what happens here. I've been raped, you've been beaten…and I've been forced to kill you." Her words are broken off by a sob, causing the spell on my body to be broken. I walk to her, fold her into my arms. I hold her as she loses her composure, my shirt getting soaked with her tears and snot. I smooth her hair with one hand and rub her back with the other.

I have to get us out of here. I'm sure it was just a nightmare, but on the off chance that it's not… She won't survive dealing with all of that, not that she isn't strong. Hazel is one of the strongest women I know, but that's a lot of trauma...and even the strongest mountains crumble sometimes. Not to mention how fucking cold it is in here. We're both shivering from the brisk air and adrenaline flowing through our bodies.

She calms down after a few moments and turns back to the window, staring at nothing, or maybe everything. I go back to looking for things to help us, which is really difficult in the dark. Maybe that's what they were banking on, us being disoriented by the dark and cloying panic, unable to defend ourselves.

What they didn't prepare for is my will to live and fight back. This is not how Hazel and I's time together ends, not if I have anything to do with it. We have too much going for us, too many plans, too many dreams.

I finally find a flashlight. It's old and the light doesn't do a whole lot to help, but it's better than looking by moonlight and feeling around with my hands. I use the dim beam to look around, I find some pieces of wood lying about, one of which has nails sticking out of the end. Perfect. I settle down against the wall and call Hazel over to me. She's hesitant to leave her vigilant position, but she gives in and sits next to me. "How's your head?"

"It hurts. But I'll be fine. I'll even go to a doctor when we get out of here." Hazel stiffened at those words. I don't like doctors; I know exactly what she's thinking, I'm in more pain than I'm letting on. "It's not that bad, Haz. I just know you'll want me to. So, this is my promise to you, when we get out of here in the morning, or whenever they come back, I'll go to the doctor and get checked out." I hope that reassures her.

"Okay, but I'm coming with you to make sure they run all the tests they need to and take you seriously." There's hope in her voice, she's trusting me to get us out of here. I just hope I don't let her down.

We spend a few hours chatting, planning on what to do when we're free. We plan a trip to Cabo; we discuss plans on how to renovate the rooms upstairs. One will be a nursery; another will be a room for plants. We plan to finish the basement and move my treadmill down there and make it a proper man cave with a couch, TV, fridge stocked with drinks, a bar stocked with snacks and my favorite liquor. I don't drink much, but the option to have it at home is nice. We talk about putting a lock on the basement door when we have kids so they can't get down there and mess with stuff or get into the alcohol. We talk about names for our kids, which ends up being much more heated than I had thought—our views on names differ a bit. We'll get it sorted, though.

Hazel drifts to sleep while I'm in the middle of explaining a family name to her, her head is on my shoulder and she's snoring lightly. I'm not sure who's more exhausted between the two of us. I settle against the wall as comfortably as I can and drift off to sleep with her.

I wake up to the sounds of birds chirping. Ironic that they would sound so peaceful while we're locked in this shed, covered in blood, and beaten…well I'm beaten. Hazel is thankfully okay physically. She's not sitting next to me anymore, she's standing at the window, staring out. If breathing wasn't necessary to human life, I'd question if she was doing it because she's so still. I move to get up, the rustle of my body on the ground snaps her out of her reverie. She comes over and tries to help me up. "It's okay. I got it."

"Are you sure? You don't have any dizziness or soreness?" Her concern for me is adorable, but bittersweet. The reason she knows to ask about all of this is from helping Lynn all those years with Paul. This last time wasn't the only time Paul had gotten violent. Of course, Lynn never admitted it to us, but it was pretty clear what had happened.

"I do have soreness, but I can't tell if it's from being beat or from sleeping sitting up on this floor or from the cold." She rolls her eyes at me as she shakes her head.

"That's not the soreness I was talking about, and you know it." I pull her into me and kiss the top of her head.

"I know, but I'm okay. Well, as okay as I can be, I suppose. Plus, I get to see you, so that makes it better." She swats my arm, but I finally get a smile out of her. Now that it's getting lighter out, I can see around the shed more clearly. The wood I found last night to use as weapons might work but looking at them in proper lighting I see they'll be good for maybe one swing. If there's more than one person that shows up, we're fucked. *Here's to hoping.*

Hazel paces around the shed, worrying about what's going to happen. I'm not one to follow premonitions, so I'm not too concerned. These people brought us here for a reason and I don't think my death will solve any of their issues. I don't even know what their issues are. I haven't done anything to piss anyone off. We pay our taxes, our bills are never late, we don't have many enemies. The only thing that comes to mind is Hazel helping all those assholes out at her job. But she's been doing this for a long time and nothing like this has ever happened; to start blaming her for this would be stupid.

My stomach rumbles loudly in the quiet of the shed. If I were to guess, I'd say it's about 9 A.M. I wonder when these people are going to show up. I'm tired of sitting around waiting. Every noise outside has me bracing myself, my heart ricocheting around my chest. But it's just nature doing its business. On top of being hungry, I'm freezing cold. This is not the weather to be leaving people in sheds without heat. We'll probably have frostbite by the time we're out of here, if not hypothermia.

Hazel sits down and I join her. We cuddle up together, our breath making white clouds in front of us. She nuzzles her head into my shoulder, "I love you, James. I want you to know how much, but I don't have the words to describe it to you. I wanted to have a long life with you; grow old and sit on our porch while our grandkids played in the yard. I wanted to go on vacations and see the world with you. I wanted to experience so much with you…" Her words are cut off by a sob, but she takes a deep breath and carries on. "You're the most important person in my life. I don't know how we got here, but I would give anything to get us out of it. I'm so scared. I don't know how to do life without you."

"Hazel, Baby. I love you, too. But you have no reason to be scared. They'll be here soon, and we'll figure it out. We'll be able to experience all of those things and more. It's okay. I know this isn't ideal but imagine the stories we'll be able to tell our kids. How badass we'll sound." I'm trying my best to calm her down, but she's not having it. She's far too distraught. "Hey, deep breaths for me, okay? We need to be calm when they show up. We don't know who they are, but

we've seen enough movies, we know how to handle this."
She takes five deep breaths, the tears are still falling down
her face, but she's not gasping for air anymore. Progress,
not perfection. I stroke her red cheek with my hand. She
flinches with how cold my hand is. "Sorry."

"It's fine. It's freezing in here." Her tears are slowing, and I
see her resolve coming back to her, like a brick wall being
built. "I won't kill you, James. They can't make me. I can't do
it. I'll never survive that."

"You won't have to, Babe. It'll all work out. Just wait and
see."

We drift off to sleep after a while of sitting in silence, both of
us plotting how to get out of here. We're woken up by the
chain on the door rattling.

"Someone's here." Hazel's voice is so quiet I almost don't
hear her words over the chain getting removed. I get up as
fast as I can and grab my piece of nailed wood. Hazel stands
behind me, shaking from the cold and fear.

The chain slides out of the door handle and the door opens,
spilling blinding light inside. I lift my free arm up to cover my
eyes. When they've adjusted, I lower my arm and get a good
look at who's standing just inside the door with that stupid
smug look on his face. My heart skips a beat and I'm so

thankful he found us, even though I have no idea how. But his words stop me in my tracks.

"I've been waiting for the perfect moment for this, for years now, actually." Ryan leans against the door frame, glaring at me.

"Hey, Man. I'm glad you found us. I don't know what the hell is going on." I give a nervous laugh. My brain is trying to process how he found us and how he got us out of here, while also being so grateful we've just been saved. "Haz, I told you. We'd be out of here in no time. Your dream was just that—a dream." I turn to her, and freeze. Her face is ashen, her eyes wider than I've ever seen them.

"Why?" Hazel's flat voice and question confuses me. He's here to save us, why is she being so spiteful to him?

"Oh, Hazel." He gives her a condescending laugh. "He's stolen everything from me. That promotion was supposed to be mine. I may have gotten the company, but with him around, I know I won't be able to properly do the things I need to do. He's too proper for the way things need to be. It has to be this way. I know what you're thinking, 'Just fire him and be done with it.' But I can't. He'd sue me. Somehow, some way, he'd take even *more* from me, and I can't let that happen." His voice is low and level, but I can feel the anger radiating from him now, permeating the thin air in the shed.

"But you know, as well as I do, that's not all he's taken from me, Hazel." He pins her with his stare, and she shrinks from it.

Then it all clicks into place. He's not here to save us, he's here to get revenge. Revenge he has no right enacting.

I'm not going to let him know I know about their past yet; that's a card I'm keeping close to my chest. But I can't let him know I've caught onto his intentions, I'll play dumb and let him dig his own grave.

"What the hell are you talking about, Ryan? What is going on? If you want me gone, just say that I'll leave that company to you. I won't sue you; I won't throw your name in the mud. Just a clean break. To be honest with you, I was thinking about quitting now that you're in charge anyway. We've never seen eye to eye, and it would just be more hassle than it's worth. Just let us go home, man."

He slinks away from the door frame, stepping into the small shed. "Ask Hazel what I mean. Ask her what else you've taken from me. What you *both* have taken from me."

Chapter Twenty-Seven

Lynn

The guys show up and it's been so long I almost don't recognize Joey, Nathan, or Ron. But when Joey comes over and hugs me, I know it's him. He's always been a little love bug. It used to piss Steven off, but he doesn't seem to mind now. Whether that's because he knows I need the extra support or he's just more secure with himself now, it's hard to say. I don't ask because we have bigger issues to work through right now. Nathan and Ron just nod to me as we all head into the dining room to start figuring out how to get Hazel back.

"So far what I've gathered is they have five main places they utilize. Kind of sloppy if you ask me. But they hide them well. It was almost impossible to get this info, it cost me a lot of fuckin' money." Ron seems to be the ringleader here, which doesn't surprise me. He was always the informant for Steven back in the day. He knew things others didn't and almost no one questioned him. The one time someone did, they got proven wrong and then beat so badly they were in the hospital for a month and had to have some reconstructive surgery on their face. No one knew how he knew, but his information was always spot on. The best thing about this was he never gave Steven's information to anyone else, but Ron knew everything that happened in this town.

"I'll pay you back, Ron. I'm really grateful you did this for me." His eyes lock with mine as I speak, but there's no reaction on his face.

"I didn't do this for you, Lynn. I did this for Steven. No offense, but you've been gone for a long ass time, and I don't owe you shit." Steven shoots him a reproachful look and I'm sure they'll get into it later. Ron was always the one who pushed Steven's limits the most, but he was too useful to do much else than get a stern talking to. I just sit back in my chair and listen to all the info. I'm not goin' to be much help in this conversation, and I've already made an ass out of myself, no need to make it worse.

"Who all do we have available to help us look?" Steven's voice is all business, and I know it's taking everything in him to not go to all these places himself. But that would take too much time and by then they could be moved somewhere else...or worse. I shudder at that thought. *Hang in there, Hazel. We're comin' for you.*

"We have us, Jeremy, Caleb, and Remy. No one else wants to touch it, even with everything you've done for them. It's too dangerous for them. Pussies."

"They're not pussies. Everyone has their limits. Plus, if this all goes to shit, we still need people at the shelter and on the streets running Narcan and shit around. We'll make do." Steven and Ron start to strategize on who will go with who and what to do if we catch them. When that's all figured out, Joey puts a big duffel bag on the table and opens it. My jaw is on the floor as I stare at all the guns and communication devices that are in there.

"What are you guys, some super-secret government agency or somethin'?" Joey laughs at my question; the rest just raise their eyebrows at me.

"No, we're just prepared." Joey says plainly. "We don't run drugs anymore, but we do try to help out the community however it needs. Sometimes you need weapons in order to do so. Since I'm the only one with a perfectly clean record, I keep the guns stashed at my place."

I look at Steven and I didn't know my heart could belong to him anymore than it already does, but I'm proven wrong as I just watch him make sure his guns are loaded and ready to go. I'm also a little shocked, because if what Joey says is true, that means Steven no longer carries a gun on him. He always had one, no matter where we went. The change is one I wasn't expecting even though I know he has a record now. I just didn't expect him to follow that rule.

When everyone is strapped up, everyone leaves but Ron and Steven. Steven jerks his head for me to follow him to the living room. He turns to me and wraps me in his arms and kisses the top of my head. "You're going to stay here." I start to interrupt, but he just talks over me. "I know you want to go, Lynn. I do, but it's going to be dangerous if we find them. I can't afford the distraction. I have to get our daughter and James back. If you're there it's too many things to keep track of. We'll be back as soon as we can."

"I'll stay in the car. Please, let me go. I need to be there." He looks at me with so much sadness in his eyes and I know it's useless to beg.

"I can take you to her house if you'd like, or you can stay here. Oh, and before I forget again…" He goes over to the entertainment stand and opens a drawer. He pulls out a box and hands it to me. "I got you a phone. You need to have one. I was going to give it to you last night, but I forgot." He's embarrassed he forgot, but we were a little preoccupied with each other. "It'll keep you a little entertained while we're gone. I don't know if you know a lot about these damn things, but they're pretty neat." He's trying his best to distract me, and I love him for it, but I also hate that he thinks a phone will calm me down while he's out there trying to find Hazel.

"Thank you, but I still want to come with." Instead of entertaining me with an answer, he just pulls me into a hug and kisses me. I know I can't stay here and stew in my feelings. "I guess take me to Hazel's. Kiba probably needs to go outside." He releases me and smiles.

"I knew you'd come around." He lets me go and we head out the door.

A few minutes later we're pullin' up to Hazel's house. Anxiety is clawing at my chest. I don't know if he's comin' back. I don't know if Hazel's comin' back. I may be alone for the rest of my life. I choke back a sob and blink the tears away. I have to be strong for them right now and if I break down cryin', I'd be taking valuable time away from him finding Hazel and James.

He walks me to the door and lifts a plant on the porch, pulling out a spare key. We walk in and are assaulted by Kiba who barks at us, tail waggin'; happy to see people after being alone for so long. I ignore him and wrap myself around Steven. I need one more hug and kiss from him before he leaves. I want more, but this will have to be enough.

"I gotta go. I don't know how long I'll be gone, but the minute I can, I'll call you. So make sure the phone is on. I love you always."

"I love you, too." He smiles at me, and I know he's tryin' to reassure me, but it just makes my stomach churn. I love that smile, those arms, that man. He waves and walks out the door.

I turn from the front door, so I don't run out and demand to go with them. Kiba is standing there staring at me. "What do you want, mutt?" He whines at me and pads to the kitchen. I follow him and let him out the back door.

I'm shocked to see there's no messes in the house. While he's outside, I fill his food and water dish. As soon as I set them back down, he's scratching at the back door to be let back in. As soon as he's in, he's at his dishes as if he was dying without food and water. I go into the living room with my new phone and sit on the couch while he finishes his business.

I'm interrupted from figurin' this damn thing out when Kiba sits beside me, whinin'. "I know, Kiba. They'll be home soon. I promise." I don't know what's happenin' to me, but I feel bad for promising somethin' to a dog that I can't guarantee will come true.

It takes me five minutes to figure out how to turn the damn thing on, but once it loads, I see I already have a message. I open it and it's from Steven:

I love you always. If I never see you again, just know that
you
always meant the world to me. I regret not demanding
to see you that day I went to your mom's. I regret not fighting
for us.
We could have had something great and
been a wonderful family if I had just tried harder.
I'm sorry I failed you and Hazel. But I won't fail this.
And if I do, just know I died trying.

I start sobbing. I can't help it, my emotions are too much right now and I just can't handle all of this. It's all my fault that this shit is even happenin'. I should be the one finding her. But as I think that, I realize that if I hadn't left and gone to that damn alley, I may not even know she was gone. If Steven hadn't been in that alley, I would be drugged out and had no idea she was missing. Things work in mysterious ways and it makes my head spin.

Kiba nudges my hand, trying to comfort me. I set my phone on the coffee table and curl up on the couch, holdin' my stomach so my insides don't come spillin' out on the carpet.

Chapter Twenty-Eight

Hazel

This cannot be happening. James knows that Ryan and I had history back in the day, but I've never thought it would lead to us being abducted and held hostage. I don't even know why he's still holding onto it...that's not entirely true. I do know—and with him here, I'm transported back to a conversation we had a few months ago at the party where James was given the promotion they had both been vying for.

"You know I still love you, right?" His words spear my heart and make me shrivel away, a husk of my own being.

"This is highly inappropriate, Ryan. We haven't been together in years, it's time to let it go." I try to give off an aura of confidence and stability, but my voice is shaking, and I know he hears the scared woman he left all alone in that barren apartment.

"You mean how you let our child go? Just forget everything that happened with us, Hazel? How could I?" His mention of our child has me shuddering under his unrelenting stare.

"I didn't let our child go, Ryan. You punched me in the stomach when you thought I was out with another man when I was with Jayden shopping for you. Or did you forget? Did you forget that I had to lie to the nurses and doctors at the hospital and tell them I fell down a flight of stairs? Even though the evidence was there in the shape of a fist on my abdomen. Even when their pitiful gazes pierced my eyes, imploring me to tell them the truth, to tell them you did this, but I didn't. I didn't because I believed you felt bad, I believed that you were better than this. And then you left me." I try my hardest not to raise my voice and keep my fake smile plastered on my face so no one can tell we're having a heated discussion. All I really want to do is go to James who is standing with Jack being congratulated over and over by other colleagues and business partners.

Ryan releases a humorless laugh before he says, "That's all you were good for anyway, Hazel. Being my bitch: cooking my food, cleaning my house, doing my laundry, and popping out my babies. You looked great on my arm. It was my mistake to let you in any further than that. Now I have to see you with him all the time, rubbing it in my face that you've moved on. I could have changed. But you're not worthy of

that. Don't be surprised when he treats you the same way."
He turned and went to James, shaking his hand and
congratulating him with a devilish smile on his face.

I had stood there, rooted to the spot, the only function I could manage was short shallow breaths as I had watched him interact with James. And then I ran to the bathroom and threw up everything in my stomach. I rinsed my mouth as best I could, but my unease must have been clear on my face, because when I joined the party again, James asked if I was okay. I didn't lie to him, necessarily. I told him no, but I didn't tell him why—just that I wanted to go home. He assumed I had eaten something that didn't settle well with my stomach. We said our goodbyes and went home. I changed into some sweats and curled into a ball in our bed and silently cried myself to sleep. Whether it was from the adrenaline dying or the loss of my first child, I didn't know.

Now he's standing here, threatening everything that means the world to me all because of his vindictive ego and inability to let shit go. I'm seething with rage, but also terrified that my whole life is going to come crashing down because of this piece of shit. I refuse to let it happen. I refuse to lose everything all over again because of him. I snap out of my stupor, straighten my spine, and rejoin the conversation.

"Come on, Man. We can work through this. I don't have any ill feelings towards you."

"Ah. There it is." His gaze lands on mine. "I told you it was a matter of time before he was the same way."

"Woah, what way?" James turns to look at me, I meet his gaze and I try to convey that he needs to trust me, that he needs to forgive me for everything before and everything I've kept from him. I don't know if he gets the message because Ryan's words have him spinning back to face him.

"That you'd come to see how worthless she is. That she's not good enough for anything other than basic womanly duties and being a hole to stick your dick—" James swings the piece of wood at his head. The impact is a loud *thunk* in the small room. Ryan stumbles sideways into the wall while his hand goes up to his head where the board hit. It comes away wet with blood. "You mother fucker!" He tries to charge at James, but I come from behind James and swing at his knee with a sturdier board I found this morning while James was sleeping. He goes sprawling along the ground.

His two henchmen were stunned by the act of aggression from us at first, but now they dive into action. The one I recognized last night grabs me by the arms and pulls me away from Ryan. I swing my head back, trying to reach his nose, but he's too tall. My head collides with his chin instead and I'm momentarily stunned from the impact. The result is him holding my arms in one of his hands and wrapping his other arm around my throat, tightening enough that I can't move, but can still breathe.

Then it hits me, who this man is. His name is Johnathan Reinfeld. We went to high school together. I never pegged him to be someone's crony, but here he is.

James is on top of Ryan, somehow, he turned him over and is pummeling his face with his fists. The other henchman is having a hard time grabbing onto James' arms because he's flailing like a madman, but he eventually pulls James off of Ryan, who's lying on the ground groaning; his face covered in blood. James is fighting off the other guy like a bear trying to get out of a cage, but it's useless. James is strong, but he's not built like these guys.

By the time Ryan composes himself, James has gone limp in the other man's arms—whether it's exhaustion or him just biding his time, I have no idea. He hasn't looked at me a single time, instead his gaze is locked on Ryan. If looks could kill, Ryan would be dead a million times over.

Ryan stands up, dusting off his pants, "I didn't expect such vigor from you, Hazel. You've never been one to stand up for yourself like that. But I suppose, self-preservation will do that to you." I try to spit at him, but it just dribbles down my chin with how Johnathan is holding onto me. Ryan looks at the spit with disgust.

"What do you want, Ryan?" James sounds utterly defeated.

"I want to ensure nothing else gets taken from me. I also want revenge. You see, Hazel here seems to be harboring her secrets from those close to her." His eyes never falter from mine, menacingly staring down at me.

"I don't know what you're talking about." James' words are venom aimed at his veins, trying to lance deep enough to kill.

"Of course you don't." He looks at James and laughs at him, as if he knows the secrets of the universe and James is only guessing at a pebble of sand. "Because it's Hazel's lowest point of her life—when she let our unborn baby die in her womb." I freeze at his words. I know what's about to happen and I can do nothing to stop it. I try wiggling free, despite knowing I can't. I have to get free of this suffocating embrace, this shed with its walls closing in on us, this man who has been nothing but poison to everything I've ever loved.

James laughs at him, his head hanging low. The sound sends a shiver down my spine; I've never heard that sound coming from him. It terrifies me, but it also sends white hot desire down to my core. Ryan's eyebrows scrunch together, "What's so fucking funny about that? It was my fucking child!" He yells as spit and blood fly from his mouth. His voice grates my ear drums to the point I think they're going to bleed. I wince, my throat digging into Johnathan's arm, choking me momentarily.

"You're really that fucking stupid, aren't you, Ry?" James lifts his head slowly, the look in his eye deadly. Much to my surprise, Ryan looks taken aback, he takes a step back from James, almost running into a barrel of wooden planks behind him. "You really think that Hazel kept *anything* from me? That I haven't stood by her side through all of the nightmares, all of the crying, the counseling? You think that I didn't fucking know you beat her to the point of her losing that baby? That she was so scared of you, she almost didn't stay in this shithole of a town? The only reason she did stay was because of her grandma, who refused to leave.

"I know what you did. And I've been moving against you this entire fucking time. That's why I worked so hard for that position. Because I knew what it meant to you. Because you didn't fucking deserve it, just like you don't deserve to breathe another fucking breath." On his last word, the fist he'd kept curled at his side swings up and then down into the guy's leg. He's immediately released. But before he can make a step in Ryan's direction, the door swings open and two men walk in.

Johnathan tightens his hold on me, cutting off my air, as if I can protect him from whoever just walked in the shed. It was cramped already, but now there's barely any room to move.

My vision goes cloudy due to lack of oxygen and blood flow. One of the men looks familiar, though. I just can't see him clearly enough to tell.

Chapter Twenty-Nine

James

I spin around when two men walk through the door, putting my back to Ryan. My eyes bulge out of my head as I take in Steven and some other man I don't know.

"What are you doing here?" My suspicion is too high to trust him, I barely know him. All I know is Hazel went off on him yesterday, and now we're in this shed fighting for our lives, seems suspicious enough for me.

Before he can answer there's a sharp pain in my back and I fall to my knees. My breathing turns frantic and I'm not sure what happened. I try to catch myself as I fall face first to the floor, but my arms aren't working properly. Then there's a lot of shuffling and grunting, but I can't tell what's happening. My back is warm, but my limbs are ice cold. I can't catch a breath, and the world goes black. My last thought, *please let Hazel be okay.*

Chapter Thirty

Lynn

I'm curled in a ball on Hazel's couch, Kiba laying in front of it, starin' at the door. He's a nervous mess, every moan and creak of the house has his ears perking up and his eyes lookin' everywhere for Hazel and James.

The TV is on, but the sound is low so I don't miss any sounds coming from around the house. I don't know if they're comin' here to ransack the house and steal somethin' or if Steven will need help carrying Hazel or James into the house. I just know I need to be on guard.

But I can't sit here in silence anymore, it's eating away at my insides. Kiba whines where he lays on the floor, he's lookin' up at me with the saddest look in his eyes. I hate animals; never had 'em growin' up and never had 'em in my adult life either. But the look he's giving me has me softening to him.

"Get on up here, Boy." He doesn't hesitate and jumps up to join me on the couch.

I jump out of my skin as my phone rings from the coffee table in front of me. I hop up to grab it, and Kiba decides it's a good time to go potty. I let him out before checking the thing. I sag to the floor in relief as I read the words on the screen:

We're all alive. James is on the way to the hospital.

I'll bring Hazel home later to shower and get some clothes.

Love you.

A huge part of me wants to call him and demand answers, but the logical part of me knows there's a lot goin' on right now and he probably wouldn't answer.

I let Kiba back inside. He sits and stares at me, cockin' his head from one side to the other. "They're all right, Kiba. They'll be home soon. I didn't lie to you." A smile spreads across my face and I sag to the floor and hug Kiba. It amazes me what a little shared trauma can do for relationships. Never did I think I'd be huggin' this damn dog like this, but he's the only thing here and I have to share my elation with someone. He licks my face and that ends that love fest. *Nasty ass pooch.*

I shoot a text back to Steven telling him I love him too. Then I sit down on the edge of the couch and wait, as if they're gonna come through that door any minute. After about 20 minutes my back starts to hurt, and I realize it will probably be a few more hours before they get back. I'm not sure what's wrong with James, but hospitals always take their sweet ass time, so I shouldn't expect them to be fast with him just because I'm sittin' here waitin'.

I lay back down on the couch and Kiba doesn't even wait for the okay before he jumps up and cuddles with me again. I don't mind as long as he keeps his damn tongue in his mouth.

I jolt awake from my sleep when the front door opens and Kiba jumps from his perch on the couch. I didn't even realize I had nodded off, but it helped pass the time. I check my phone to make sure I didn't miss any important updates. All that's there is Steven sayin' he's on his way to the house with Hazel. My heart stutters as I see the time: 11 P.M. I've been asleep for 5 hours. *Shit.*

I get up and hurry to the front hall, I stop dead in my tracks as my eyes take in Hazel's tangled hair and dirty clothes.

She's sittin' on the floor, her face buried in Kiba's neck, her shoulders shaking from the silent sobs comin' from her. Steven walks through the door behind her and hunches down to rub her back. She doesn't release Kiba or acknowledge his presence. He looks up at me and his eyes are dark with regret and guilt. Steven pats her back a couple of times and whispers somethin' to her that I can't hear and leaves her to cling to her dog. He grabs my arm and pulls me to the living room. "What happened?"

He just wraps me in his arm, inhaling deeply, before he lets go and plops onto the couch. He rubs his eyes and then starts telling me everything I've been dying to know this whole time.

"They were at the park. You know that shed that's there? They were locked in there. I don't even know why they use that place, but I mean it makes sense right now. No one will be in the park to hear them yelling for help.

"Anyway, we found out who the ringleader was, Ryan Branson." The name rings a bell in my head, but I can't place it right away. "He worked with James and apparently Hazel has some history with him." The memories invade my mind when he says that.

"That son of a bitch! I'll kill him myself!" I go to get up from the couch to hunt him to the ends of the earth, but Steven stops me and pulls me back to the couch.

"Just listen, Lynn. There's a lot left to say." Despite my entire body beggin' me not to listen and to go find the sorry son of a bitch, I sit there and let him finish telling me the story.

"When we pulled up, we could hear yelling, and that's probably what covered the sound of us pulling up. We got inside and Ryan was yelling at James, they both looked like Death warmed over. Hazel was passed out in some dude's arms. I think James was about to attack Ryan again, but our entrance distracted him, and he turned to see who had joined the fray. Ryan took that as his opportunity to stab him in the back, literally." My jaw is on the floor, and I have no words. "Ron went after Ryan, and I went after Hazel. As soon as I stepped up to the guy, he threw Hazel to the ground and tried to pull a gun on me. Thankfully, it got stuck in his haste to get it from his holster and I knocked him in his nose and knocked him out." My eyes track to his hand, the knuckles bruised already and covered in blood; whose I'm not sure, but before I can ask, he keeps going.

"Hazel woke up coughing when I leaned down to check her pulse. She opened her eyes and immediately started looking for James. I knew his prognosis wasn't great, but she's my daughter so she was my first priority. She scrambled over to him, screaming his name.

"I used that time to call 911 and a few minutes later an ambulance and a couple of police cruisers pulled up. We're going to have to go to the station to give official statements later, but I'm not pushing her to do so. She'll go when she's ready." He releases a breath like that's the end of it, but it can't be.

"Okay...what about Ryan? Is James alive?" His eyes widen in shock.

"Shit, sorry. There was a lot that happened. Uh—James is alive, he's at the hospital right now. Hazel is going to shower and then I'm going to take her back over there. She wanted to stay, but I made her come back here to get cleaned up.

"Ryan is dead. I don't know exactly what happened. Ron barely touched him, but there was already so much blood all over him. James had fucked him up pretty good. So, we'll have to see what the autopsy reveals about that." He releases a big breath, like his soul is finally clean after all the sins of his life have been wiped away.

"How were none of you arrested?" I'm assuming no one was arrested, given that Hazel and Steven are sittin' here with me, but maybe I'm wrong.

"We didn't do anything wrong. They arrested the guy who I knocked out, his name was Johnathan Reinfeld. His rap sheet is long. The other guy, Trey Reynolds, had a stab wound to the leg and was about to bleed out, but they took him to the hospital too. He's under arrest as well.

"And with the whole Ryan thing...well, I'm not sure. If it wasn't Ron who killed him, then it was James and he was acting in self-defense. He'll probably have to go to court. But maybe they'll let it slide since he's not in great shape.." He shrugs as Hazel meanders into the living room finally.

Her body is curled in on itself, like the air around her is hurting her. She lifts her head, and her eyes meet mine. I stand up from the couch just as she starts to break again. I rush over to her and catch her as her legs give out. The way she's clutchin' me makes me think I'm the only thing keeping her intact right now. I look over at Steven and tell him to go start a bath. He nods his head, concern etched deeply on his face.

I hold Hazel as she sobs and sobs in my arms until Steven comes back in and nods to me. He comes over and helps me carry Hazel into her bedroom. He sets her on the edge of the tub and then goes back to the living room. I help Hazel shed her torn, dirty clothes. She's not cryin' as hard now, but she's so withdrawn it scares me. I help her get into the tub, she sits with her knees to her chest and her head laying on one of her knees.

I wash her back and stroke her hair, singing Mary Had a Little Lamb because it's the only song I can think of right now. When I'm finished with my third time through the song, she finally picks her head up and looks at me. I cup her cheek with my hand, "I love you, Hazel. I'm so grateful that you're here and you're alive. James will be just fine."

Her eyes well up with tears again. "I was so scared, Ma. I had dreamed of it, you know? I knew it wasn't going to be good; I knew I was going to lose him. He could still die. They're going to have to do surgery and probably a blood transfusion. Anything could go wrong. I just want him back. If I had a time machine, I'd go back and change everything. We never would have gone out to eat last night. We shouldn't have gone, anyway. James called out that morning, well I called him out because he was sleeping through everything. Ryan was there and he made some stupid ass remarks to James, but James shrugged it off." She laughs at that, but it sounds like a choked sob. Then her body shudders at what happened after.

"You know, we went out to eat to celebrate me going off on you and Steven. Jayden was so damn proud of me. *I* was proud of myself. Yet here you guys are, saving us." She smiles at me, and I don't know how to respond. Normally I'd have some snarky remark to give her, but her being kidnapped took the wind out of my sails and I just want to fix everything that was wrong with our relationship. I want to take accountability for my actions and really try to be a better mom for her. She deserves it after all this time. And I'm done being some awful, hateful being.

"The only thing I would have changed about it all is not being there when they found you. Although, I can't say the outcome would have been any good. I wouldn't have let the cops have any of 'em. They would've been dead by the time they arrived. So maybe it's for the best. Plus, Kiba needed some company. I think he's starting to like me." I wink at her, and she genuinely smiles at me. It's still a bit strained, but with her fiancé in the hospital, I don't expect her to be a ball of sunshine. "Finish getting cleaned up so we can get you back to the hospital. James needs you by his side. We'll take Kiba to our house so he's not alone while y'all are gone." I stand up and turn to leave.

"Thank you, Ma. I'm sorry I was so awful to you yesterday. I love you mostest." Tears spring to my eyes and I just nod my head as I leave the bathroom, shutting the door behind me. I lean against it for a moment as my heart swells in my chest. We can fix this. We can mend every broken piece of our relationship and become better than we ever were; I've never been surer of anything in my life.

Chapter Thirty-One

Hazel

I'm in shock. That's the only way I can justify the things that are happening around me right now. Or maybe while I was strangled and passed out some vital part of my brain lost too much oxygen for too long. *My mother is being nice to me and caring for me.* Since when has Lynn ever been this way? Maybe when I was a baby and wasn't causing her grief all the time, but the moment I turned two I'm sure her switch got flipped and she retreated into the hateful woman I know her to be.

I'm grateful beyond words that she's not being her normal self, but I can't wrap my head around it. Just yesterday I was telling her I was done, and now she's here acting like nothing bad ever happened between us. A part of me wants to forget the past transgressions and just clutch to this new person she's transformed into, but the bigger part of me is warning myself to not be so foolish. She's been nice before and it hasn't lasted longer than a few weeks. We have a lot of shit to work through before I can let my guard down completely, especially when I just got it built in the first place.

I shake my head to myself and finish washing up. I need to hurry so I can get back to James.

Oh, James. My eyes fill with tears just thinking about him lying in that hospital bed, pale and still. I need him to survive. He has to. God, I'm so thankful he didn't die in that shed. But I can't imagine that his recovery is going to be easy. No matter what happens, I'll stick by his side.

I go out to my room and get dressed. It takes everything in me not to curl up in a ball on his side of the bed and succumb to my sadness, my exhaustion. I may have slept in that shed, but it wasn't restful and then everything that happened after took it all from me. My throat hurts and I have a headache. Once I'm done getting my leggings and sweater on, I go back to the bathroom to take some ibuprofen and pray to God it helps with all the pain. If only they had something to help with heartache.

I trudge my way to the living room where Steven and my mom are sitting on the couch, cuddling together, talking quietly. I envy their closeness right now. I won't get that with James for—I don't even know how long. I sigh and gather myself.

I clear my throat to get their attention. "I'm ready to go."

"Do you want to eat somethin'? I can make you a sandwich." My mom offering to make me food is weird, but she seems eager, and I don't have the stomach to tell her no. I nod my head.

I follow her into the kitchen, and she gets everything she needs to make me a butter and honey sandwich. It takes me back to my childhood. Back to the same park James and I were in last night and some of today. My mom used to take me there sometimes and push me in the swings. When I got too old for that we'd throw a frisbee around. But it became less frequent the older I got, which coincided with when I needed her most. I still visit that park sometimes when I'm struggling with how to help her. I think it might be ruined now, though.

She doesn't talk as she makes my sandwich. I'm not sure if it's because she doesn't have the words to comfort me or if she just doesn't want to upset me. I don't mind the silence, though. It's not awkward; it's more comforting, as if we can pretend nothing bad ever happened and we were transported to the past and get to have a redo.

She hands the sandwich over on a plate, then she just stands there, chewing on her cheek as she watches me nibble away at it. She takes a deep breath and looks me in the eye. "I'm sorry, Hazel. I—I know this probably isn't the time, but honestly after everything happened today, I just can't imagine not sayin' this before you walk back out that door. I'm sorry I wasn't a good mom to you when you needed me. I was checked out. Life had gotten heavy and nothin' I did was workin'. I was tryin' so hard to give you everything I always wanted, but it was never enough. The guilt ate me alive. Every time I saw you upset with me; it killed me more inside.

"I know that I was mean and vile to you and James. I—fuck, I was jealous, Haz. I hated that you had found your happily ever after. It doesn't justify it, no matter which way I cut it, it will never be enough. But I just want you to know that I am so damn proud of everything you've accomplished and everything you will accomplish in this life." Her words are stop and go, there's tears running down her cheeks and I really do think she means it. *What is happening to my life right now?*

"You're right. This isn't the time. Because I have so much to say to you; specific things I need you to apologize for, but I don't have the time to get into it right now. I need to get to the hospital." She just stands there, nodding her head, crying. "Thank you for the sandwich and your words, though. I did hear you, and I have a lot to think about in regard to you and Steven. I'm not a hundred percent ready to forgive you guys just because he saved us, and you suddenly have a change of heart." My words come out harsher than I intended, but it's the truth and I'm not sugar-coating things anymore to spare her feelings. She's never done it for me, so I refuse to do it for her.

I leave my plate on the counter and walk back to the living room. Steven looks up from his phone as I enter. "I'm ready to go. Don't forget to grab Kiba's food, bed, and some toys for him when you come back to get him and Mom. He'll chew all your shoes up if he doesn't have his toys."

"No problem. We'll take good care of him while you're with James. If you need anything, just call me. I called you a few times before I found out you were missing, so my number is in your call logs."

"How did you get my number? We've never spoken, you've never called. God, why can't you guys just be fucking normal?" I'm yelling, but I'm so tired of all these curveballs. My life is in fucking shambles and I'm starting to lose touch with what's real and what's just in my head.

He has the mind to look sheepishly at me. "I had been meaning to call, but I didn't think you'd want to hear from me. I got your office number from your website. I called once and it went to voicemail. You have your cell number on there and I wrote it down and kept it. I dialed your cell so many times, but before I could hit send, I'd shut my phone off. I'm a coward, I know, but I just couldn't face rejection." He looks at the floor, regret hanging off him like a cloak.

I scoff at him and go put my coat and boots on, signaling to him that the conversation is over. I can't mentally handle all of this right now, if ever.

The drive to the hospital is filled with regret and resentment. The only sound is the classic rock music playing softly from the speakers. His tight grip on the steering wheel turns his knuckles white.

I've wanted nothing in my life more than to have my dad be a part of my life, to care about what happens to me, to be interested in what I was doing. But he was okay with hiding in the shadows. I wasn't enough for him to step up and be a man. I thought I had come to terms with that, but him being here now, saving me, has dug up some deeply buried issues. *Miranda is going to love this.*

We pull up to the hospital and he parks his car, I step out of the car as he says, "Remember to take care of yourself. Kiba and James need you. Your mom does, too." The only response I give him is shutting the car door.

I force myself to walk calmly into the hospital. The nurse working at the front desk looks up as I enter, giving me a kind smile. "How can I help you?"

"James Warden, please. I think he's in room 203 unless they moved him."

"Visiting hours are over, unfortunately. You can come back at 9 A.M."

"No, I'm his fiancée and I will go find him if you don't take me right now." Her smile falters, and she pulls up a screen on her computer. Her demeanor completely changes when she reads whatever is on the screen.

"I'm so sorry. Right this way." She nods to another nurse sitting at the desk with her. Then she comes around the desk and takes me to James' room. There's a police officer sitting in a chair outside of his room, two more officers sit a few doors down. I'm assuming the two further down are for the man named Trey, but I'm not going to ask. I can't know or I'll do something stupid and wind up in jail.

The police officer in front of James' door stands as we approach. "Hazel Greene?" The nurse takes that as her cue to go back to the front desk.

"Yes. Can I help you? I'm just trying to see my fiancé."

"I understand, Ma'am. This will be quick." I stare blankly at him, waiting for him to continue. He clears his throat, "A detective will be by in the morning to talk to you and get an official statement. I'm here to protect you both. We don't know if other people will try to get in here and finish what was started. Their gang has an extensive reach in this town, and we don't want to take any chances."

"Thanks." He nods his head and resumes his place in the hard plastic chair. I almost feel bad for him, but I don't have the emotional capacity right now. I go into James' room and the lights are low, as if they would bother him in his medically induced coma.

My bottom lip wobbles as I take in James' state again. A half an inch and he would have lost everything. I can't imagine how lucky we are. We have a long road to recovery, but we made it. We'll be okay. I drag the recliner to the side of his bed and sit down, holding his hand as I drift off to sleep.

Chapter Thirty-Two

Lynn

I clean up the mess from making Hazel a sandwich and then grab Kiba's food from the back hall. I take it to the front door so it's ready when Steven gets back. The hospital is about 15 minutes away, so he should be back any minute.

I think about what Hazel said to me before she left. I do have a lot to apologize for and I know a generic apology won't work. I failed her a lot in her life. I've failed myself a lot in my life. I've never wanted to be better, I always had somethin' else to blame it on. But I'm ready to take accountability. Maybe it's reconnecting with Steven, maybe it's almost losin' Hazel; shit, maybe it's just that I'm so fuckin' tired of living the way I have been.

I have an epiphany when Steven walks in. "I need to see a shrink. Do you know any good ones?" He pauses halfway through the door, blindsided by my statement.

"I do. We'll set you up an appointment in the morning. Let's go home." *Home.* I've never really had a home before. I've had places I've stayed and slept, but nothin' that ever made me feel safe and loved.

He gathers Kiba's things, handin' me a giant ass bed to carry out to the car, while he gathers everything else. Kiba is runnin' around like he's on crack, barking and wagging his tail. We get his stuff in the car, I get in the passenger seat while he goes back in to get Kiba on his leash and back out to the car. He gets in and buckles his seat belt, puts the car in reverse, and does that thing that's always gotten me flustered: puts his hand on the back of my headrest and reverses with one hand. I don't understand why it gets me all hot and bothered, but I don't get a lot about our attraction and relationship. I just know I want forever with him, this life and all the other lives we live, I want him to be the one.

We pull up to his house five minutes later and Kiba is drooling all over himself in the backseat. I cringe at the sight of it. That's gonna suck to clean up. I get out and grab his leash, taking him into the house. "Here's your home for a while, Boy." I take his leash off and he hauls ass around the house, sniffin' and investigating everywhere. "You better not piss anywhere, Mutt. I'll kick your ass!" He ignores me, tail waggin', lovin' his temporary home.

Steven comes in and gets Kiba's things situated. It would be nice for us to get a dog when all of this is over. Kiba hasn't even been here five minutes, but already his presence makes the house feel better. Maybe it's just my sense of doin' somethin' good and helpful for once, but it just feels right. Steven turns to me, "We're going to have to take him for walks; there's a hole in the back fence I haven't fixed yet. I'll get it fixed within the next few days."

"I'd offer to fix it, but I don't know the first thing about how to do it." We both laugh, and he winds his arms around me and holds me for a few minutes, releasing all the bad from the day and letting in all the good that happened.

"I can show you. I can show you whatever you want me to." He kisses my temple and heat floods my body.

"I know what you can show me right now." I smile devilishly at him.

"You're insatiable." His lips catch mine and we're swept up into our passion, our thankfulness for life. A small part of me wants to hold off because of everything that transpired today, and the fact Hazel is at the hospital with James, but I've waited long enough to have my happiness, I don't want to waste a single second.

We're like animals, tearing each other's clothes off, hands grabbing and exploring each other's bodies. Nails and teeth digging into skin. I've never known the passion I have with Steven. No one has ever made me feel this good in my own skin, this comfortable in who I am.

He wraps his hands around my thighs and lifts me from the ground. I wrap my legs around his waist as he pins me against a wall. His lips drag from my lips down to my jaw, nibblin', then to my neck where he bites a little harder and I swear I might get off just by his closeness and touch alone. He hasn't even gotten to the good part yet. "Please; I need you."

He grunts in response and slides in effortlessly. The wall digs into my back, the pictures on the wall rattle on their nails as he pounds into me. We're so desperate to be with each other and alive that it doesn't take long for us to both find our release. We're breathless and have a hint of sweat along our bodies. He releases me from around him, then takes my hand and leads me to his bathroom. I've never showered with anyone before. This has always been my personal time. I don't hate it, it adds a level of intimacy I've never known, even with him.

He takes his time washing my hair and exploring every inch of me as he rubs me down with soap. His hands are gentle, yet firm. I'm slightly embarrassed havin' him on his knees, washing my intimate regions, but this man is everything to me, so I let him see it all.

He rinses me off and starts to wash himself, but I stop him. I take the soap in my hands and return the favor. He's already hard again, or maybe he never went soft. I was too distracted to really notice. The sight of him is enough to have heat pooling inside of me. But I'm tired and I'm sure he's exhausted. Today was long and full of tumultuous feelings and hardships. There will be time tomorrow; and the day after that; and the day after that. I rinse him off and he grabs us both towels.

We dry ourselves off, and then go to bed with nothin' between us. No unsaid words, no clothes, just us as we are. It's the best night of sleep I've ever had.

I wake up the next mornin' to light shining through the cracks in the blinds. I stretch in the bed, reachin' for Steven, but his side of the bed is empty. Not surprising as he likes to get up early and have a good breakfast before starting the day. Plus, I'm sure he needs to get some work done. Although, I think he should take today to rest. But he's never been one to take time for himself.

I meander to the kitchen and he's not there. I don't see any sign of him or Kiba. He must have taken him for a morning walk. I spot my phone on the counter, plugged into a charger. He must have done that before he left. I go over to it and there's a text on it:

I took the dog for a walk, be home soon.

Here's a good therapist, give her a call.

Theresa VanDam

555-9393

I love you.

My nerves start eating me up. I know I need to see a shrink, but openin' up to the people I love is hard enough, how the fuck am I gonna do it with someone I've never met before?

To put off the inevitable, I make myself a cup of coffee and drink it before making the call I know I need to. Her receptionist seems nice enough and they have an opening tomorrow. I thought I'd have more time, but when I said my name the receptionist's attitude completely changed and she seemed eager to get me in sooner. Steven must have called ahead or somethin'. I suppose it's good it's so soon, otherwise I might find a way to get out of it.

Steven walks in with Kiba as I hang up with Theresa's office. As soon as Kiba is free of his leash, he comes runnin' over to me and licks my arm. "Damn dog. That's disgusting!" Steven laughs while I wipe off the slobber coating my arm. "I don't know why you're laughin', that shit is gross! He licks his asshole with that tongue!" This just makes him laugh even more.

"He's just showing you he loves you and comforting you."

"I don't need no comfortin' from him." I shoot the dog a glare, but his tongue is hanging out of his mouth and his tail is wagging as he looks at me has my anger disappearing. Then he barks at me and starts running laps around the house. "What the hell is he doin'?"

"He has the zoomies. He's excited. Have you never been around a dog before?"

"I've been around him, but he's never acted like this when I've been around. He usually growls at me and stays far away from me."

"Hm. Maybe he can sense something new with you and he approves." My chest inflates with hope, and I pray he's right. "I need to head into the office for a while. You gonna be okay here?"

"Yea. Can you take me to Sandy's later? I need to fill her in on everything and get a few things from Paul's. I should also tell him it's over officially. He's probably wonderin' where the hell I am."

"Of course. I'll stay in the car while you're at Sandy's. But I don't want you going into Paul's on your own." When I had filled him in on everything with Paul the rage that was on his face was terrifying.

"Okay. Have a good day. I love you."

He wraps me in a hug, the smell of his cologne and the crisp air outside mix to make the most delicious scent I've ever smelled. "I love you, too. I'll text you." He kisses me and then walks out the door.

I decide to do some cleaning around the house, not that there's much. Steven is a neat freak, apparently. It only takes me an hour to get everything done. "Well, now what, Kiba?" He raises his head from where he's laying on his bed and wags his tail at me. "Wanna cuddle and watch talk shows?" He barks happily at me. I hate this dog—but he's growing on me.

We curl up on the couch and watch mindless TV for the rest of the day, only breakin' for potty breaks and a couple walks for Kiba.

My stomach growls as soon as Steven walks into the house. When I hear the front door open, I look at the time on my phone and my heart crumbles. I get butterflies in my stomach, but not the good kind. The bad kind that makes you want to throw up from being such a fuck up. "I'm so sorry, the day got away from me." He's taking his shoes off in the front hall; he turns to me, eyes wide.

"What are you talking about?"

"I didn't make dinner. I was just hangin' out with Kiba all day and I lost track of time. I—I did do some cleanin'." I wring my hands together, trying not to get too carried away so he doesn't get madder at me. He just stands there, shocked.

"Lynn, what is going on with you? Why are you freaking out about not having dinner ready?"

I release a sigh, "I—I…" He walks over to where I'm standing in front of the couch, shoulders scrunched up, hands shaking. I'm waiting for him to yell at me and tell me how worthless I am, maybe even hit me a few times. I can't even have supper ready for him. I'm a fuckin' mooch.

"Lynn, I never said I wanted you to cook dinner for me. I mean, sure it would be nice, but it's not necessary. You've been through a lot the last few days…hell, the last few years. Just relax. We can talk about what you can do around here if you want. But I won't ever get mad at you if it's not done when I get home from work." He envelops me in a hug, and I immediately relax.

"O—okay. I'm still sorry. It's the least I could do for you. Especially after everything you've done for me so far. But I would like to discuss some things I can do around here. I tried to do some cleaning, but there wasn't much to do."

He gives a soft chuckle. "Sorry about that, I get bored and just clean. My mom would roll over in her grave if I let this house go to shambles. She worked really hard to keep this place nice. It also helps me keep my head clear." He has a soft smile on his face as he thinks about his mom, it only strengthens as he talks about his sobriety.

I release a large breath and step out of his arms, "Okay, so what are we gonna do about supper? I'm starvin'." He chuckles as he runs a hand through his hair.

"I was thinking about getting some Dairy Queen on the way to Sandy's. We can eat in the car." I pause at that because I had forgot we were goin' to Sandy's tonight. "You still want to go, right?"

"Y—yea, absolutely. I just kind of forgot." I rub the back of my neck with my hand. "Let me just freshen up real quick and then we can go."

"Okay, I'd like to do the same. Can't look like a bum meeting your best friend." He shoots me a wink and heads to his room—our room. I go into the guest room where the clothes I've been borrowing are and find somethin' nice, but not too nice. I don't want Sandy to be suspicious or nothin'. I'd really like some of my own clothes, but I don't want to seem ungrateful. Not that I think Steven would consider me ungrateful, but I just feel bad asking.

I go out to the living room where Steven is sitting in his chair waitin' for me. His eyes track me up and down, takin' in the black jeans and cream cashmere sweater I found in the dresser. "You look great." His smile is infectious, and I find myself smiling in return. My heart stutters in my chest.

"Thank you." I tuck a strand of my hair behind my ear. "It isn't too much, right? I don't want her to think I'm tryin' to be better than her or anything."

"No, it's perfect. If she has an issue with it, is she really your friend?" He raises an eyebrow as he asks me that. It makes me wonder if she really is my friend. I have sometimes doubted it, but I really don't think Sandy is someone that would do me dirty.

"I don't suppose she would be if that's the case. Wouldn't that be a hoot?" He stands and takes my hand, leading me to the door to put on our coats and boots.

When we have our Dairy Queen, he parks the car at a park down the street so he can eat without driving. "Why are you nervous?" He wipes his mouth with a napkin as he turns to me.

"I—I just don't know how she's goin' to take me just showing up at her house in some strange car, lookin' better than I have in years. She's not judgmental, but at the same time she is. I don't want her lookin' down on me is all."

He nods his head as he takes that tidbit of information in. "Well, if she doesn't think you looking better is a good thing, she's not someone you need in your life. I won't make that decision for you. I'll let you do what you want. But I do want you to consider your own happiness for once. You've never had it and it's long overdue."

I put the rest of my food in the bag on the floorboard, not able to stomach it anymore, and stare out the window. When Steven finishes his food, he asks for her address. When I tell him, he shakes his head and whispers, "Jesus."

"What?"

He shakes his head as he glances over at me. "I used to sell a lot of dope in that trailer park. Now that you mention it, I think Paul was one of my buyers. I just hadn't thought to consider that it would be the same person." His jaw clenches.

"Wouldn't surprise me. He's had issues for a long time now, I just didn't know about them when I was in prison. Shit, it took a while for me to figure it out when I got out and moved in with him. By then it was too late to do anything else."

He reaches his hand over to grab mine and doesn't let go until we get to Sandy's.

Twenty minutes later, we pull up to Sandy's. I see her front blind open slightly and quickly close again. I take a deep breath, preparin' myself for whatever may come. Steven squeezes my thigh in reassurance. "I'll be quick. I just need her to know I'm okay."

"Take your time; I'll be right here when you're done." He smiles at me as I get out of the car and make my way up her rickety steps and knock on her door.

Chapter Thirty-Three

Hazel

This chair is the most uncomfortable thing I've ever slept in; aside from the night spent in the shed, but it's the least I can do for James. I can't leave his side just in case something bad happens. I'd never forgive myself.

After sleeping for a while, I called Jayden and told her everything that happened. She offered every type of assistance she could think of, but I declined most of it. The only things I accepted from her were her visiting and bringing me good coffee and our pillows and blankets from the house. She was shocked when I told her my mom took Shiba. I don't blame her. My mom is a selfish woman, usually, but something has changed, and I don't know what.

James has had two blood transfusions so far and they say his prognosis is good, so I'm just left here to make sure he's absolutely okay…as okay as he can be, anyway.

A knock at the door pulls me from my reverie of the last few hours. "Come in." A tall, African American man in a suit enters. I stand up and walk over to greet him.

"I'm Detective Andrews." He shakes my hand with a firm grip, his eyes are kind, but his body language gives off an aura of 'no bullshit'. "I just have some questions. I know this isn't the best time, but you know how these things go, I'm sure."

My first instinct is to be offended by his presumptions, but I take a steadying breath, and tell myself that he's just doing his job. "Of course. Please have a seat." I gesture to the hard plastic chair by the door.

"We don't have to do this here;. there's an office area we can go to that will give us privacy."

"I'm not leaving him." He nods his head as walks over to it and sits as if it's the softest throne in the world. I turn the recliner I slept in to face him, but I leave it at an angle so I can keep an eye on James as well.

"Understandable." He says as he pulls out a little notebook and pen, flipping open the notebook. "Tell me what happened the night of the 13th." I take a deep breath, not really ready to rehash all of it, but he's not leaving me much of a choice. *I'm going to have to pay Miranda triple pay to help me deal with this shit.* I start off with the morning, giving him all the details of an ordinary-ish day, turned into a nightmare.

"So, James and Ryan worked together?"

"Yes." I can't help the exasperation that douses that single word. I just went over all of this and I have better things to do than answer stupid questions...well, not really, but that's besides the point.

He makes a humming sound, apparently the information I just confirmed is super interesting. "And they both worked for Jack O'Connell?"

"Correct, at O'Connell's Commercial Enterprise."

"Did you have any involvement with Mr. O'Connell?"

"I did. He asked me to be his Personal Relations Assistant with the issues he was having with his personal life. We managed to come to an agreement and then I handed the case over to my assistant Alex Manera. I was dealing with some personal issues, as you know from the story I just told you. I took some time off and knew Alex was capable of handling what needed to be handled."

"And where do you and Alex Manera work?"

"Civil Relations."

"Do you have any suspicion that Mr. O'Connell was working with Ryan in his gang activity?"

"I mean…not really. Jack is a piece of work, but gangs? It just doesn't seem to be his thing. I could be wrong, though. I don't know Jack very well, to be honest."

He nods his head. "So James was the one who attacked Trey Monaghan?"

"If that's the man's name who abducted us and then was holding James while Ryan prattled about, then yes, he was. James did it so he could get free and go after Ryan. It was to protect us."

"I don't have any doubt about that, Miss Greene. And James hit Ryan with a board and punctured his head?"

"As I already told you, yes. And then beat the piss out of him, which he deserved." Detective Andrews looks like he's about to agree with me but decides otherwise. Probably the best to keep the professional persona going.

"Steven Matthews and Ronald McDaniels were also there?" He looks up from his notepad, his gaze could pierce my soul if I'm not careful.

"Yes. Steven is my father. I don't know who Ronald McDaniels is, but I'm assuming they're good friends." I wring my hands in my lap. I'm still reeling from everything that happened, but after everything…I think I forgive my dad. I think I want him to be a part of my life finally and give him an actual opportunity to be there for me.

"All right. Well, I don't have any further questions. When James wakes up and is clear-headed, please give me a call. I need to verify this information with him. I'm also going to need you two to submit official statements on what happened. The sooner the better." He rises from his chair and hands me a card. I take it from him with a shaking hand. "For what it's worth, I'm impressed with both yours and James' resiliency and determination to get out of there. You're a force to be reckoned with. Have a good day, Miss Greene." I murmur a thank you as he leaves the room.

I don't feel resilient or determined. I feel weak and stupid. Given my line of work, most people would think I could read people well. I've said I can read people well myself, but I never once thought Ryan would be capable of this, despite our previous relationship issues.

I have an ungodly headache after speaking with Detective Andrews. I don't want to go over it all again, but I know it'll happen at least one more time. I text Jayden:

Detective was just here asking questions.

Have a major headache. Send help!

I hope it's okay for her to bring me some Tylenol, but if not, I don't really care. What I really want is some wine and my bed. But it can wait for when James is better. My phone dings with a text from Jayden:

What room are you in? Bringing coffee, bagels, and Tylenol! Anything else you need?

What would I do without this girl? I text her back:

Room 243.

That sounds perfect! Maybe a couple books.

Thank you. Love you!

A nurse comes into the room as I set down my phone. "Just checking everything is okay and changing his bag of fluid. Are you holding up okay?" Her name tag reads 'Rebecca'.

"Yea, I'm okay. As okay as I can be, anyway." I give her a small smile.

"I'll be James' nurse for the rest of this afternoon. If you need anything let me know. I can sneak you some stuff." She shoots me a wink and then turns to change his bag of fluid.

"Actually, I have a question. My friend is bringing me some Tylenol because I have a headache; is that okay?"

"Absolutely. We can't give you anything like that because it's not prescribed, but your friend can definitely bring you some."

"Okay, cool. I just wasn't sure what the policies were." I relax back into the recliner.

"No worries, Hon." She gives me a bright smile and a part of me feels shitty that I can't be as cheery as she is right now. "He's looking pretty good. As soon as another nurse is available, we'll come back in to check his bandaging and turn him a bit."

"Sounds great. Thank you." She nods her head and leaves the room to continue her rounds. "She's really nice, James. I think you would like her a lot. Please wake up soon, Babe. I miss you so much." I lean forward and grab his hand, bringing it to my lips and pressing a kiss to it. "We have a long road ahead of us, but we'll get through it. I'm not going anywhere. I vowed to myself once I realized how great you and Jayden were that I would never let you go and I meant it. I love you to the ends of the earth."

In the books and movies, they say people in a coma can hear when you speak to them. I don't have much else to say, so I sing "Dandelions" by Ruth B. My voice isn't good, but it's not the worst either. James loves it when I sing, so I hope this helps him somehow.

Thirty minutes later, Jayden comes in, weighed down with coffee, bagels, and a tote bag full of books. "Oh my gosh, Jay. You should have said you needed some help!"

She scoffs at me. "I'm pregnant, not disabled. I'm more than capable of carrying this to an elevator and down a hall. You have enough to worry about than to worry about me." She sets the bag next to the recliner and the café goods on the tray at the foot of James' bed.

"How many books did you bring me?!" I go over and look into the tightly packed tote bag of books. There's probably thirty of them in there.

"Girl, you read so much. I didn't want you to get bored. There's probably thirty or so in there, though. Hopefully you haven't read them." I pull her into a hug now that she's free of her burdens.

"Thank you, Jay. I love you so much." She squeezes me hard against her and I can't help the tears that start falling from my eyes.

"I love you too, Haz." She holds me, rubbing circles on my back until I calm down.

"Sorry about that." I laugh off my over emotional state.

"About going through a traumatic experience and having an emotional response to finally having someone safe to lean on? Girl, stop. If you need to cry, you can cry. I'd say you can scream if you need to, but that would probably cause a panic." We laugh at that idea.

She pulls the plastic chair over from the door and grabs her tea and bagel from the tray and sits down, sighing as her feet are relieved of pressure. Before digging into her breakfast, she digs in her purse and tosses me a bottle of extra strength Tylenol. "You're a godsend." She smiles at me. "How's the pregnancy going?"

"As well as it can. I know that sounds awful, but for real. This shit is awful. I miss alcohol and eating whatever I want. I miss not eating meat mostly. My conscience is eating me alive, but the baby gets what the baby wants. I've gained probably 10 pounds already and I just hate it. My feet hurt constantly, and the morning sickness is for the birds."

"You poor thing. It'll be worth it though, right?" There's no way she's already gained ten pounds, she isn't even showing yet.

"It fucking better be, Haz. Or I'm going to go get some milk and not come back." She laughs at her own joke. Jayden isn't one to abandon a baby or her husband. I join her in her laughter, thankful I have something to genuinely laugh at and be happy about.

"You're going to be the best mom, Jay. I'm so happy for you guys. I know it's hard now, but it'll get better. I want to throw a baby shower for you." She squeals and we fall into talk about what she wants the theme to be and game ideas. We have a few months to prepare, but the distraction is nice, and she knows I need it.

Chapter Thirty-Four

Lynn

I knock on Sandy's door and then stand there feeling stupid. I've never knocked on her door, why am I doing it now? I know she's my friend, but things are different now; what if she doesn't want to be my friend anymore? I'm pulled from my thoughts fallin' down the toilet when she opens the door. "Lynn?"

"Hey, Sandy. I—I just wanted to come fill you in on everything that's happened. I realized I didn't have your number so I couldn't call you."

"Well, come on in and get comfortable, Girl. It's colder than a witch's tit out there and I don't need you catching a cold or getting frostbite!" I smile gratefully at her and throw a glance at the car idlin' by the curb, hopin' she doesn't notice my glance.

We sit on the couch as usual, some soap opera is on the TV and Sandy mutes the TV so we don't have to talk over it. She hands me a bottle of water. "Here's this unless you want some tea. I need to get to the store this week."

"This is just fine; thanks, Sandy." She hums her approval and then pins me with her stare.

"Spill the beans. I've never seen that car around here or Hazel's before and if you were with Hazel, you would have had my number. What the hell happened? I saw you outside of Teller's the other day and we both know the kind of people who hang out there. Did you relapse? No judgment if you did. Lord knows you've been through hell and back with Paul."

I lean back onto the couch before answering her. Might as well get comfortable as I fill her in on everything. "No, I didn't relapse. I almost did, but Steven saved me from my own stupidity." Her eyes are as big as dinner plates on her face.

"Steven? Like ex-lover Steven or some new and mysterious Steven?" She raises her eyebrow at me, the corner of her mouth curvin' up in a devious smile.

"Ex-lover Steven. He runs a nonprofit that helps junkies with Narcan and clean pipes and shit. He believes in harm reduction or something like that. Real wild." Her mouth is gaping open like a bass fish, and it would be comical if this whole thing wasn't so wild to begin with. "Anyway, he took me back to his house and we caught up the next day."

"Didn't he leave you alone to raise a baby?" She raises an eyebrow at me. That's her look that tells me I'm the stupidest person in the world.

"That's what I thought. He told me he tried to come talk to me when I found that girl blowin' him. My mom stopped him and told him she never wanted to see him at our house again or she'd call the cops on him."

"Okay, but what about the girl who blew him? You're just gonna excuse that?" She crosses her arms across her chest and I hope she's actually willing to listen to what I have to say. I think she dislikes Steven more than Paul and that's really sayin' somethin'.

We go through all of what has happened the last few days, which takes longer than I thought it would. I don't know why I thought this would go fast, Sandy is nosey and asks millions of questions. As if she can sense my worry of how long this is takin', she asks, "Is that who's in the car out there, Steven?"

"Yes. He's waitin' for me so he can take me home. I need to go to Paul's and get a few things as well. He's here not only to be my ride, but to be my bodyguard if need be." She sucks her teeth at the mention of Paul. "Has he been over here?"

"Yea. He knew you came here to get a ride to Hazel's. It was right after I saw you at Teller's. I didn't tell him I saw you wandering around, but I did tell him I hadn't heard from you other than to give you a ride. He was pissed; talking about how he needed you to clean your shit up in the house and needing to be laid or something. I don't know, I tuned him out for the most part, counting down the minutes until he left. I ended up shutting the door in his face because he wouldn't shut the hell up." I can't help the laugh that escapes my mouth at that.

Once I compose myself, I close my eyes and let out a sigh. "This is gonna be a shitshow, isn't it? Why can't my life just be easy?"

She reaches over and squeezes my hand, somethin' she doesn't do often. "No one's life is easy, Lynn. It may seem that way from the outside, but people hide their shit well. Everyone deals with some type of bullshit. Life's specialty is throwing curveballs. Get through this and maybe it'll smooth out for a while." She gives me a half smile and I'm overwhelmed with gratitude for my friend.

"Thank you for everything, Sandy. You've been the best since I've met you and I know I wasn't always easy to deal with. You never turned me away and never judged me too harshly. I've been very blessed to have you in my life." Her eyes tear up and she blinks a few times to keep them at bay.

"Don't go getting all sentimental on me. I can't handle it in my old age. It was a pleasure helping you even though sometimes your attitude was shit. It kept me on my toes and kept my life interesting. Don't lose touch with me now that you're moving up in the world." At my look of confusion she continues, "Did you honestly think I'd miss you showing up here in a cashmere sweater? Please. I have better taste than that, Lynn. I'm a tad offended you'd think so little of me." She chuckles and swats my arm. "You better get going over to Paul's and back to Lover Boy out there." She writes her number on a piece of paper and hands it to me. "Let's have lunch soon. Be careful over there."

I take the piece of paper from her as we stand from the couch. She walks me to the door a few feet away and I hug her quickly before I leave. "Talk soon, Sandy." She waves me out the door and closes it quickly behind me. I walk to Steven's car, still idlin' at the curb.

I get in, apologetic. "Sorry, that took longer than I thought it would."

"Huh. I thought it would take longer, to be honest." I can hear his smile in his voice, see it in the dim light from the dash. "You ready to go to Paul's? I have a couple guys on call in case we need some help."

"Yea, let's get this over with." He shuts the car off, the motor ticking as it cools off. I walk around the car to his side, and he grabs my hand, squeezin' it to give me comfort and solidarity.

We walk across the street to Paul's trailer, the lights from inside shinin' through the broken blinds on the windows. As we get to his yard, we can hear the music blaring through the thin walls. I can't help hoping he won't hear me knockin' over the ruckus.

Luck has never been on my side, though. As soon as I knock, the music goes quiet as the song changes. My knock rings clearly through his trailer. I can hear his muffled grumblin' through the door; it causes my heartbeat to kick up and my instincts start telling me to get the hell out of here and abandon my insignificant things in his trailer.

As I try to turn, I find Steven blocking my path and the door behind me gets roughly yanked open. I know Steven didn't mean to block my path, it's just the way the porch is laid out. It doesn't stop me from blaming him at this moment, though. My trauma runs too deep.

I try to swallow, but my throat has gone completely dry, and I start choking. "Lynn. What the fuck are you doing here? And who the fuck is this?!" Paul is angry, rightfully so. I abandoned him and then showed up with someone he's never met.

Steven reaches a hand around me, offering it to Paul. "I'm Steven." Thankful for the chance to catch my breath, I turn around and face Paul. His shirt is stained yellow, and his boxers hang loosely off him. He glowers at Steven and his offered hand, offended that Steven is standing on his property.

"And what the fuck are you doing here with Lynn?" If he glowered any harder his face would be stuck in a permanent scowl. Now that I'm thinkin' about it, maybe it already is. The number of times I've seen Paul smile are miniscule at best; maybe twice in the few years we've lived together. Usually that smile meant somethin' bad was comin' my way. I feel stronger with him glowering like that, which doesn't make sense, but I'll take what I can get.

"I just brought her by to get a few things." Paul turns his glower onto me and my heart stalls in my chest. I may die of a heart attack right here, or vomit all over him, either one is highly likely as my insides have a rave inside of me.

"You don't have shit here. I don't know why you're here or what you think you're gonna get here. But it's all gone." I know he's lying. I know I have a few clothes and personal care items here. It's not much, and probably not a good enough reason to have come, but they're my things and I want them.

I finally find my voice, "I actually do. If you just let me in so I can get them, I won't bother you anymore." He closes the door a fraction of an inch, then laughs in my face.

"The fuck you do. I threw all your shit out yesterday. I know people in town, Lynn. I know you've been out gallivanting and using again. Not to mention, running around with this fuckwit. Did you really think I'd keep your shit lying around *my* house while you're out doing God knows what? Fuck that and fuck you." He slams the door in my face. I shrink into myself, embarrassed to have been treated like that in front of Steven. It's different when it happened in the privacy of those walls, but havin' an audience makes it a million times worse, no matter who the audience is.

Steven grabs my hand and pulls me from the porch. I let him guide me back to the car and sink into the seat, my self-hatred rears its ugly head. He gets in and starts the car, but doesn't go put the car into drive. He turns the heater up then turns to me. "I don't know what you had in there. If it was sentimental then I'm sorry he threw it away."

"It was just some clothes and other shit. It doesn't matter. I just wanted some things that were mine." I murmur so quietly I'm not sure he can hear me over the blastin' air from the vents.

"We can go shopping tomorrow when I'm off work if you want. I know it's weird wearing my mom's clothes. We just haven't had any down time to go get you anything of your own. Sorry about that." Tears are falling down my face, and I hate that I'm cryin' over this whole situation. I can't stop them, though.

"You have nothin' to be sorry about. Nothin' that happened the last couple of days or even decades is your fault. You tried back then and you saved our daughter. I'll forever be thankful to you for that.

"But I don't want you to buy me stuff. I don't mean to be ungrateful with what you've already given me. I just thought havin' my own stuff might be nice and put me more at ease."

He puts the car in drive but reaches his arm across to rest his hand on my thigh. It stays there the whole drive home.

Chapter Thirty-Five

Hazel

Jayden left a few hours ago. It was so nice having her here to talk to instead of talking to an unconscious James. It makes me feel terrible thinking that, but I needed the interaction with someone I know, someone I don't have to mask myself around.

I dig through the tote bag she brought full of books. She picked out some good ones and it takes me a while to pick one to read. I decide on *It Ends with Us* by Colleen Hoover. I've heard great things about this book and I'm excited to start it.

I'm four chapters in when Rebecca comes back to check on James and switch his fluid bag again. I set the book aside when she enters, not wanting to be rude. "Your friend brought you some reading material, huh?"

"She did. I love reading and was going a little stir crazy in here with nothing to do."

"I understand that. You can go home if you want. He's in great hands here." I start to protest, but she holds a hand up, "If not, it's okay. I get it. My mom passed away a few years ago from a really bad car wreck. I stayed with her in the hospital the whole time. People told me to leave, but I *knew* if I left, she'd pass while I was gone; or make a grand recovery and I'd miss it.

"I didn't have anyone to bring me anything. We had just moved states and didn't know anyone here. The nurses working weren't very nice to me. When I got hired a year ago, I made it my mission to show kindness to everyone who walked through those doors, no matter their circumstances." She smiles the whole time she's talking.

"I'm sorry about your mom. It must be so hard being nice to everyone. I know some people are mean, especially under emotional distress."

"It is sometimes. I just remind myself that I don't know what their personal life is like, or what they're going through. I remember how alone I felt sitting beside my mom. So, even if they aren't thankful for my presence or cheerfulness, I keep at it. It may help more than they're willing to let on." She fidgets with a machine next to James' bed. "His vitals are really good and the labs we took this morning came back clear. No sign of infection. He's going to wake up soon and it'll all be better. Not right away, but you know that. Just keep holding on for him and talking to him." She smiles at me and then leaves the room.

I sit there for a few minutes contemplating her words. "I don't have much to talk to you about that I haven't already. So how about I read to you instead? I don't know if it will be the same, but it's all I've got." I fill James in on what's happened so far in the book and then pick up where I left off when Rebecca came in. I read to him for hours, until my throat is raw from talking so much. Then I sit the book down and just hold his hand for a while.

I doze off while staring at his face, holding his hand. I wake up to a hand stroking my hair. I shoot up from my hunched position in the chair, eyes looking around for who joined us. A weak chuckle greets me. When I don't see anyone in the room, I slowly turn my gaze to James' face. His eyes are open although hooded with weariness and pain. "Holy shit! You're awake! We need to call the nurse!"

"Just wait a few minutes. It won't hurt anything. Please." His voice is weak, his throat sounds dry; but I agree anyway because he's the one who was stabbed and in a coma for a couple of days.

"I'm so happy you're awake. I was worried sick. I really thought you were dying. I haven't left this room for a second

338

because I thought for sure if I did you would have died or woken up without me here. I didn't want you to be left with strangers." He weakly squeezes my hand, cutting off my rambling. We stare at each other, mesmerized and in awe. He finally nods his head slightly, signaling for me to call for the nurse.

The next hour is a rush of doctors, nurses, medical jargon, and relief that he woke up. No one had any idea when he'd wake up, but they didn't expect it to be so soon. They tell us he'll be taken for MRI's and other testing in the morning now that he's awake, but for him to get rest tonight; our long journey is about to begin, and he'll need his strength.

They bring me supper and James some Jell-o. He's put on an easy diet since he just woke up. They don't want him to asphyxiate or get too full before all the testing he'll be going through. I feel bad for eating in front of him, but I can't leave him as soon as he wakes up. I still can't believe it. I find myself just staring at him, praying to a God I don't fully believe in that this isn't some sick dream.

After the night nurse, Anna, comes in and takes our dishes, James looks at me as he grabs my hand. "I heard you; you know. Everything you said, you singing and reading to me. I couldn't wake up fully, but I heard it all. It was like a tether holding me here. Thank you."

Tears fill my eyes at the implications of his words. "I didn't know what else to do. I missed you so much and I was scared. You see it in the movies all the time and I hoped it wasn't some Hollywood bullshit. Then Rebecca came in and told me to keep doing it, but I didn't know what else to say—I didn't feel like singing, so I read. A lot. We're halfway through the book already." I give him a small laugh; his answering smile is all I need.

He falls asleep shortly after, exhausted from his body healing. I take the time to go into the ensuite bathroom to shower. I brought some clothes with me from home, not knowing when I would leave here again. It was an afterthought, but I'm glad I did now.

As the water flows over my body, tears run down my face; great sobs break free from my chest even though I'm doing everything I can to suppress them. My legs give out and I hug my knees to my chest, holding myself together. I have to keep reminding myself that this is real and I'm not sleeping, not dreaming. We got out of the shed. He's okay, my prayers were answered.

There's a soft knock on the bathroom door, reminding me that there's a constant flow in and out of this room; more so now that he's out of a coma. I pull myself off the bottom of the tub, turn off the water that has gone cold. I wrap a towel around myself and crack open the door. Rebecca is standing on the other side. "Give me a second to get dried and dressed and I'll be right out."

"No worries." I shut the door and hurry through the motions of my after-shower routine. It's already cut short because I don't have everything I use at home, but it still seems like it takes forever anyway.

I exit the bathroom, finding Rebecca sitting in the plastic chair next to the recliner by James' bed. I sit down facing her. "Are you off work?" The question is stupid because she's in street clothes, not her scrubs.

"Yea. I thought you could use some company. I heard he came out of a coma and wanted to come congratulate you." We talk in hushed voices, so we don't bother James while he sleeps. I'm a little taken aback that she's here to visit. A small part of me is warning that this is breaking protocol, but I'm so desperate for interaction from people that I ignore the voice and enjoy the company.

"That's so sweet of you. I really do appreciate you coming here. Sorry I was in such disarray when you showed up." My chuckle is self-deprecating, but I mean the words that come out of my mouth.

"Don't worry about it. I've seen much worse." She smiles at me, but there's something about the look in her eyes that has me on edge. "I had knocked a couple times before. I could hear you crying…I wasn't trying to pry, I swear. It was just bad timing. I thought maybe something bad had happened. But between his stable vitals and Anna stopping by when she saw me standing here, I knew it wasn't James. I just wanted to make sure you were okay."

I groan at the idea of someone being privy to my mental breakdown in the shower. "I'm so sorry for that. I keep thinking this is some sick, twisted dream and I'll wake up any moment and we'll still be in that shed or he'll still be in a coma…or worse. But everything feels real. I was just overwhelmed and unfortunately for me, I'm a crier. I cry at everything." I scratch the back of my neck.

"Don't apologize to me. You have every right to feel the emotions you're going through right now. It's only been a couple days since you went through something traumatic; not to mention James waking up. I just figured you could use some company. Someone who understands sitting here hour after hour. If I'm overstepping, please tell me. I just find you to be very kind and…I—I don't know. I just thought we were kind of kindred spirits." Her cheeks are bright red as she says this and it dawns on me that she's not only friendly to everyone because it's what they need, but she, too, needs someone to be kind to her.

She's lonely.

I grab her hand and just hold it in silence for a few moments. "I don't know why we crossed paths, but I'm so glad we did. You've been a lifeline for me and I'm incredibly grateful. Usually, I like my privacy and if any of the other nurses came in here like this, I'd give them some sort of reason why I wasn't up for company. With you, though, it's different. I enjoy your company and bubbliness." I burst out laughing, covering my mouth quickly to quiet the sound coming from me. Rebecca looks at me like she's suddenly unsure of being here. "Sorry, it just hit me that you're the complete opposite of my best friend, Jayden. She's bitchy and moody, but she has my back like no one's business. You're more like me, friendly and open. I think you two would get along nicely; I'll have to introduce you."

Surprisingly she isn't as put off by that as I thought and we make plans to get lunch in a couple days with Jayden.

I don't know what it is about Rebecca, but something in my bones tells me I've found another life-long friend. It amazes me what you find when your life is in shambles, and you feel like everything is falling down around you.

We visit for a couple of hours before she says she has to go let her dog out. I get her number so we can stay in touch in case I don't see her during our stay here. She hesitates before she leaves, like she wants to say something, but she shakes her head and leaves.

I glance at James who is still sleeping, convincing myself that he'll be fine if I step into the hall to call Jayden. There's been enough talking and laughing to disturb him for now.

She answers on the second ring. "Is everything okay? What's going on?" She sounds like my phone call roused her from sleep. I look at the time and see it's already 11 P.M.

"Shit, Jay. I'm sorry, I didn't realize what time it was. Uhh…James woke up a few hours ago."

"And you're just calling me *now?*"

"It was a little hectic and I just got the chance. I should have at least texted you. I'm sorry, Girl."

"It's fine. I understand. Is he looking okay now that he's awake?"

"I guess? I don't know all the terminology they use. They're going to do some tests tomorrow and we'll have more definitive answers then."

"Thank Baby Jesus." There's a rustling noise over the line as she moves her phone away from her face to tell Isaac the news. "We'll be by tomorrow. Let us know when he's done with tests and up for some visitors. Text me if you need me to bring you anything."

"I will. Love you."

"I love you too, Haz. I'm glad things are looking up." My heart feels full and the smile on my face feels permanent now that I've told her.

I'm about to walk back into the room when I stop dead in my tracks, remembering who saved us and who should have an update as well. My mom has texted me a few times, but I've ignored it, not having the mental stamina to deal with her on top of James' prognosis.

There's a bench across the hall from James' room door, I take a seat, the plastic biting into my flesh as I make the call to let her know what's going on.

Chapter Thirty-Six

Lynn

As we're gettin' ready to climb into bed, my cell phone rings from the bedside table. I'm not about to answer it at this time of night, can't be nothin' good. I go to silence it when I see it's Hazel callin' me, and I can't pick up fast enough.

"Hazel? Is everything okay?"

"Yea, Mom. Everything is great. James woke up a few hours ago. I—I just wanted to let you and Steven know since you guys have been such a big help. How's Kiba?"

"Oh, thank God, Hazel! That is fantastic news! Kiba is doin' good. Damn dog is growin' on me. I never thought I'd live to see the day I liked a damn dog, but here it is." Her laugh is music to my ears. She knows better than anyone how much I hated this furry mutt that found his way into our bed at night.

"I'm glad to hear it, Mom. Hey…I was thinking here soon, within a week or so, maybe you and Steven would like to meet me for lunch?" My heart stutters in my chest, remembering the last lunch we went to. I'm about to decline when she carries on, "I just want to clear the air, apologize to you both in person for…well, a lot. This whole thing has really put things into perspective for me and I just don't want there to be old quarrels not settled."

I don't know what to say. I've wanted so badly for Hazel and me to put our shit aside and just be kind to one another. I know that I'm the one who is mostly to blame, but if she wants to clear the air, I'm okay with doin' so. "I—uh, yea. That sounds really great, Haz.

"Hey, I just want you to know, I start therapy tomorrow. I—I realize I need more help than I'm capable of givin' myself and I have a lot of shit to work through. I just—I just ask that you give me a little more patience as I work through all of this. It's not goin' to be easy, but I'm willin' to do the work." She's quiet for so long on the other end I pull my phone away from my head to make sure she didn't hang up on me.

"That sounds so great, Ma. I'm proud of you. If you need me to take you to appointments or go to appointments with you, just let me know. I'd really love to work through our differences and have a healthy relationship."

"Okay. Yea. Good. Do—do you need us to bring you anything?"

"No, Ma. I'm good. Jayden brought me some things earlier. Thank you, though. I'll let you go so you can go to sleep. I just wanted to update you and ask you and Steven to lunch. Let me know when it works for you guys next week and I'll try to make it work."

"Sounds great, Hazel. I—I love you." I choke on those three words, unsure of how she'll respond. The words shouldn't be that hard to say but it's like they get stuck in my throat.

"I love you, too, Ma. Bye." She hangs up while I'm still reelin' that she said it back to me. I know she loves me, but after the other day I wasn't sure I'd ever hear her say that again.

I put my phone back on the nightstand then collapse onto the bed, a sound of pure elation coming out of my mouth. "Are you okay?" Steven comes runnin' into the room from the bathroom.

"I have never been better. That was Hazel...*Hazel.* She called me to update us on James. He's out of a coma and they'll know more in a few days, but he's pulled out of the worst of it now."

He lays down on the bed next to me, draping his arm over my waist. "That's great news. I'm really happy to hear that."

"That's not all, Steven. She wants to have lunch with both of us to clear the air and apologize to us for whatever the hell she thinks she needs to apologize for. I haven't a clue what it would be other than the disrespectful shit she pulled the other day. But we owe her apologies too. I think this is the start of somethin' truly beautiful."

"Let's not get our hopes up too high. You have a lot of work to do to get to a stable mental standpoint and she's just gone through something extremely traumatic. I just don't want you to have unrealistic expectations." My first reaction is to be pissed at him for that comment, but I know he doesn't mean anything bad by it. I take a deep breath and release the anger and resentment as I let it out.

"Yea, yea, yea. I know all of that. I just—I don't know. Somethin' feels so different with me now and I'm ready to see where it takes me. The first order of business with his new feelin' is allowin' you to take me shoppin' tomorrow. It feels weird sleepin' in bed with you in your mother's old pajamas." He lets out a full belly laugh, causin' Kiba to look at him with his head cocked to the side.

"The clothes would definitely look better on the floor." The smile he gives me is purely devilish and has me curling my toes at the promise that waits there.

He moves his hand to my hair, fisting it in his hand. He uses it as leverage to take me with him as he turns onto his side.

349

His other hand starts sneakin' up my shirt. He kisses me lightly, romantically. There's nothin' rushed about his movements, I'm not complaining; I want to savor this, be in this moment and celebrate all that life has given me after taking it all away.

Our tongues explore each other's mouths, drinkin' each other in. His hand traces patterns over my abdomen as he makes his way to my breasts. My shirt rides up as he makes his way up my body. His fingers pinch one of my nipples, making me moan into his mouth, my back arches off the bed. He rubs circles around the nipple, soothing the small ache there. Goosebumps erupt over my whole body at the feel of his fingers on me, his mouth giving me a reason to live.

"I'm going to take my time and make love to you, Lynn. I want you to remember this moment for the rest of our lives. I want this to be everything you've ever wanted, ever dreamed of."

I can't form words, all that comes out is a small whimper and I nod my head, giving him the go ahead.

He releases me from his hold on me, leanin' back to gaze down at me. My chest heaves with want and love. His smile is lazy as he slowly peels off my pajamas, kissin' his way along my body, his hands taking their time in their exploration. I'm a writhing mess beneath him, whimpers leave my lips without my consent. My hands curl into the mattress, there's an unspoken rule that this is his time, I am not to touch him; my time will come soon enough.

When he's pleased with his exploration of my body he lays back on his side of the bed, hands goin' beneath his pillow. He's the epitome of utter relaxation, yet the bulge in his boxers tells me everything he's feeling. I envy his self-control, but I also rise to the challenge. I want to make him putty in my hands just as I was in his.

I don't have as much to remove from him as he did me, so the undressing part won't take too long. I decide to save that for the very last. I swing a leg over him so I'm straddlin' him.

I run my hands through his hair, down his face. I bend over him, nipping his ear while releasing a breathy moan. His body stiffens almost unnoticeably beneath me. I smile to myself, knowing I'm gettin' him as worked up as I was moments ago.

My hands skate down his neck, nails lightly scratching the skin. His eyes close as he swallows roughly. My hands continue down his neck, stopping at the tuft of hair on his chest. My fingers twine in the hairs there while I graze kisses along his jaw, my tongue lickin' where my fingers scratched his neck.

I make my way down his body, enjoying the feel of him beneath me. My fingers slide beneath the waistband of his boxers, slowly workin' them down. His hard length springs free, bobbin' in the dim light. The sight sets my pulse racing, my throat is suddenly as dry as the Sahara Desert. As much as I want to take his length into my mouth, I force myself to keep removing his boxers.

When they're off, I make my way back up him, scratching his legs, massaging here and there. When my hands get to the apex of his legs, one hand cups his balls and the other wraps around his length. I can't control myself anymore, by the way he stiffens and groans at the contact I don't think he can either.

I take him in my mouth, all the way to the back of my throat. His hips arch up at the contact, the sudden wetness coating his cock. I massage his balls in my hand as I work him up and down, my tongue circling his head.

It doesn't last long before Steven is grabbing me by my hair, yankin' me backwards. He flips me onto my back. "If you keep that up, we won't have much fun." He sits back on his heels and opens his fist. "This probably isn't the best time, but I've never been one to have good timing." He opens a little box. "Lynn, I've gone most of my life without you by my side. Many years were wasted when we should have been side by side. I don't want to waste any more time with you. Will you do me the honor and be my wife?"

Despite the heat of the moment, I burst into tears. This is everything I've always wanted, to be married to the man kneeling naked in front of me.

I sit up and tackle him in a hug that sends us fallin' off the bed. Kiba comes runnin' in barking. When he sees us on the floor, he comes over and starts lickin' us. "Kiba, that's enough, ya damn dog!" Steven is laughing at the whole mess I've made. I'm laughing and crying at the same time; I can't get a grip on my emotions. "Yes, I'll marry you, Steven. It's all I've ever wanted. It's the one dream I've allowed myself to hold onto throughout the years. The fantasy that kept me mostly sane durin' my darkest moments. I've never let go of our love and our passion, even when I thought it was pointless."

I kiss him wildly, all thoughts of tenderness gone. He sets the box aside and makes love to me on the bedroom floor.

One Week Later

"Should I wear my ring to see Hazel? I don't want to upset her." I'm full of anxiety. We're meeting Hazel for lunch in twenty minutes, and I have no idea how it's goin' to go.

"It's completely up to you. I do think, though, that she would appreciate you not hiding it from her. She'll either be happy for us or upset. That's not up to us to decide." Steven is loungin' on the couch in a pair of nice jeans and a blue sweater. He looks really nice. Which makes me feel like a potato left on the counter for a week.

I got my hair done yesterday, somethin' I've never done in my life. Instead of my ashy, stringy hair, it's nice, tame, and auburn. I thought I liked it, but as I stood in the bathroom gettin' ready this mornin', I realized it's a lot. I threw on a navy sweater dress and black tights. I got them last week when Steven took me shoppin'. We spent a lot more money than I was comfortable with, but if I showed any interest in somethin', he put it in the cart. We went through his mom's old clothes, and I kept some stuff, but we donated the rest to the battered women's shelter downtown.

I tried to do my make-up, but I feel like a cheap hooker. The irony of which is not lost on me. I haven't worn make-up since I got out of prison because Paul said it was tacky and I didn't have a reason to wear it unless I was trying to impress someone that wasn't him. It wasn't worth the effort or fight.

But I wanted to look nice for Hazel today—my therapist, Theresa, said it would help me feel stronger. I think she might be full of shit, but she's a nice lady.

My engagement ring is a nice diamond cut with emeralds around the center diamond. It was Steven's grandma's ring from her third, and last, marriage. It's absolutely beautiful. I look at my left hand hanging by my side and take a deep breath. If Hazel has a problem with this, then that's on her. This is my life, and this is somethin' I've wanted since I was a teenager. Granted, I wanted it a hell of a lot sooner, but beggars can't be choosers.

I sit next to Steven on the couch, his hand automatically goin' to my back, rubbing reassuring circles all over. It helps me relax more than he knows. "Do I look okay? I don't want to go too overboard, but I want to look nice. I don't know— somethin' about today just feels different and I'm so fuckin' nervous."

He sits up, grabbing my chin, turning my head to look into my eyes. "You look gorgeous. Everything will work out the way it's supposed to. Breathe and let it go. Remember what Theresa told you, work on those calming techniques if you get overwhelmed." I nod my head, knowing he's right. "Are you ready?"

"Yea, as ready as I can be." He grabs my hand, pullin' me off the couch. We put on our coats and shoes, ready to head out the door to meet with Hazel to have a conversation that I'm not sure I'm ready for.

Chapter Thirty-Seven

Hazel

James improves each day. He's able to get up and up and down the hall a few times before he gets tired and needs to rest. He stays awake most of the day now and only takes the lowest amount of pain meds they'll allow. The doctors said that he should be able to go home by Saturday and as long as he stays up and moving, he won't have to stay at the rehabilitation center, just do outpatient appointments.

I called the detective the afternoon after James woke up and told him to come by on Friday to get our statements. It's not how he would have liked to have done it, but I don't give a shit.

James corroborated the story I told, and we wrote out our stories, starting back at the beginning with my relationship with Ryan. It was awful having to write it all down and let the truth come to light after all this time, but it's long overdue. I just wish Ryan was still alive to reap what he sowed all those years ago.

I've gone home a few times to get clothes and things he needs, which helps me with the anxiety of leaving him today to visit my mom and Steven for lunch.

We're going to Billy's Steakhouse. They have a business room that I reserved for our meeting. I'm not sure they'll appreciate there only being three of us there, but that's their problem not mine.

James is working on his laptop as I lean down to kiss him. "I'll be back later. If you need anything, call me. If anything happens, call me. I will be here as fast as I can." He pauses his work and looks at me.

"Haz, I'll be fine. Take your time visiting with your parents. This is way more important than sitting here in this miserable hospital."

"It's not that miserable." He levels me with a look that tells me I'm full of shit. "Okay, it is. But having you awake helps make it bearable." I give him a hug and remind him to call if he needs anything.

Fifteen minutes later I'm walking into Billy's, Steven and my mom are already standing there waiting for me. I pause on my way to the host stand because my mom looks...amazing. I've never seen her so put together, she dyed her hair, and it complements her skin tone wonderfully. I can tell by the way she bunches her dress in her fist that she's nervous and my heart softens at the sight.

She hasn't seen me yet, her back is to me, but Steven did. He doesn't let my presence be known, but somehow my mom senses I'm here and turns around. She did her make-up, something I haven't seen since before she went to prison. She needs to practice, her eyeliner is too thick on her eyes and her foundation needs to be blended in better, but it looks nice for what she knows. She smiles nervously at me as I walk over to them.

"Hey. Are you ready?"

"Yea, sounds good." Her voice sounds strong, but I don't miss her hands shaking at her sides, or the ring sitting on her left ring finger.

I go to the host stand, letting the young woman there know we're here for our reservation. She smiles and leads us to the back meeting room. "Will there be any others joining you today?" She looks at me expectantly.

"No, this is it." I sit in a chair on one side of the table. The hostess shuts the door behind her, giving us privacy.

Mom and Steven take their seats across the table from me. There is water on the table for us already. My mom drinks hers greedily, the water threatening to slosh over the edges from her shaking. She sets her glass down and meets my eyes for the first time.

"You look beautiful, Ma. I really like your hair." Her hand shoots up to smooth it down, even though there's not a strand out of place.

"Thank you, I started therapy last week and she told me I should try somethin' new. I don't know if I like it very much, but it's sweet of you to say that." Her smile is small, and I know she's feeling nervous. Although that's weird because I've never known my mother to be nervous. She's always trying to be combative when faced with opposition.

"You're welcome. I'm glad you started therapy. It's helped me a ton and I'm sure it'll help you too. Just remember to be honest and do the work. If you don't, it's a waste of your time." I turn my attention to Steven, taking in the slope of his nose and his eyebrows—the same as mine. "You look nice as well."

"Thank you, Hazel." His smile is more genuine than my mom's was. I nod my head in response.

"We didn't come here to exchange pleasantries, as you both know. I just really want to start over with the both of you. There's a lot of history I don't know about your relationship, but given that you're engaged, you must be very important to each other." My mom's eyes bulge out of her head at my acknowledgment of her engagement ring. "No need to look like a deer in headlights, Ma. I'm truly happy for you." She releases a big breath.

"I—I want to say I'm sorry, Hazel. For the way I raised you, for the type of work I did, for my behavior and attitude your whole life. You didn't deserve it, and I didn't deserve to act the way I did. I was sabotagin' everything in my life because I couldn't believe that I was worthy of anything good." Tears stream down her face as she talks, her mascara leaves black streaks down her cheeks.

I suck in a breath, shocked because my mother has never shown her emotions to me. "It took almost losin' you to realize what a shitty person I had been to you. I couldn't live with the guilt. When you walked into your house with your dad that day, I promised God that I would do whatever it took to make things right for us. I prayed that it wasn't too late."

Her admission has my eyes joining the crying party. This is all I've ever wanted from my mom, for her to acknowledge her shortcomings and apologize for the way she's treated me my whole life. I wanted her to be a real, feeling person. "Thank you for that. It's all I've ever wanted, Mom. I used to pray every day that you would wake up from whatever nightmare you were in and just be the mom I knew in my soul you could be. But they were never answered. When I told you I was done the other day it was because I was tired of holding onto hope.

"It took being abducted by Ryan and his crew to realize how fast things can go badly, how fast you can lose someone you care about. When Steven showed up at the shed, I told myself I would try one more time to try to get through to you. I need you, Mom. I need you here, I need you to be present. Let's put the past behind us and just move forward."

She's sobbing so hard across from me that she can't form words, she just nods her head.

"As for you, Steven." He looks at me, worried. "I don't know why you weren't there; I don't know why you never reached out. I expect the entire story. But I am willing to give you a chance. I always wanted a dad, but I never had one. I always wondered what it would be like, but never gave myself the chance to hope too hard. Mom's line of work didn't really fare well for any potential father figures."

"Absolutely." He clasps his hands in front of him and starts telling me about his life. When he's done filling me in, I understand him more. He did exactly what I would have, and I can't hate him for it anymore.

His heroic acts the other day help soften my resolve regarding him.

"I would like to do some family counseling with both of you. This is progress, but there's so much we have to work through and get past, I think it would be more conducive and productive if we did it with a professional present." They both eagerly agree, surprising me yet again.

"I'm glad we had this talk. Do you guys want to eat now? I told them I'd let them know when we were ready for food. I couldn't stomach food beforehand, but I'm starving now."

"That sounds great, Hazel." My mom finally stopped crying and shaking. Sometime during Steven's story, she realized I wasn't going to shut them out anymore, that I was actually receptive to talking to them and ready to bury the hatchet.

I go let the server know we're ready to order and he follows me into the room. We order our food, I get a mimosa to go with my grilled chicken breast—not the best combination, but I need some alcohol in my life.

As we're eating my mom broaches a subject I wasn't expecting. "Have you gone to see your grandmother recently?"

"I saw her a couple weeks ago. She was doing all right. As soon as James is stable at home, I plan on going to visit her. I just haven't decided if I should tell her about the mess of the last few days. I don't know if she can handle it."

Steven sets down his fork and takes a drink before responding. "Your grandmother is a strong woman and can handle more than you know, despite her age. I think it would be a good idea to tell her, but you do what you think is best."

"I appreciate that. She is pretty strong." I smile fondly at him before continuing my meal.

"I think I'm going to go see her on Monday. I haven't been there since the last time I got kicked out. I miss her. I'm not sure she's goin' to be as receptive to our engagement as you are, but she deserves to know."

"She absolutely does. I know she didn't approve of your relationship back in the day, but you're no longer living in her house. It's also been a long ass time and both of you have grown and matured, so maybe she'll be more okay with it. I can go with you if you'd like?" She gasps at my offer.

"I would like that a lot. Hopefully she doesn't die of a heart attack seein' us gettin' along." We both chuckle. Nana has been there through most of our fights, or at least heard about them when I called to bitch to her about my mom.

"James should be home by Saturday, so Monday works great for me." She smiles openly at me, and I feel a little more tension leaving my body and soul at the look she gives me.

We finish our meals and leave the restaurant. As we're walking out, I freeze at the door. Steven almost runs into me because I stopped so abruptly. I can't move, my heart is pounding in my chest and my limbs feel numb.

Steven puts a hand on my shoulder and speaks quietly to me, "Breathe, Hazel. It's a panic attack. No one is out here that's going to hurt you. You're safe." I try to listen to his words, but the thought of going out into this parking lot is terrifying. I don't know why it wasn't hard at the hospital, or when I pulled up and walked in, but now that I'm leaving it's just too much. I feel like I'm going to pass out.

After 15 minutes of freaking out and Steven speaking softly to me, I finally take a few deep breaths. My fists are clenched so hard that my nails are digging into my palm. I release them, my palms stinging where my nails were embedded. "There you go, deep breaths. In through your nose for a count of six and out of your mouth for a count of six." Steven is still talking quietly to me, my mom is rubbing my back softly.

I do as he says because the alternative is turning around and running back to the meeting room, curling into a ball, and never leaving this restaurant. A few more minutes and I'm calm again—at least as calm as I can be. Steven takes my left hand; my mom takes my right, and they walk me to my car. I feel like a little kid again, I allow my inner child to come out and envision her being swung by her mom and dad as they walk to the car after a night out for supper. Something about this act is healing for me.

Steven checks the backseat and under the car to make sure no surprise attackers are there. When he gives the all clear, I give them both hugs and confirm plans with my mom for Monday. My mom kisses my cheek as she releases me from her hug. Steven squeezed me tight enough to bruise some ribs, but I don't mind.

This feels good, this feels right. I feel a hole in my chest disappearing as I drive away from Billy's, getting patched up by every past grievance forgiven.

Epilogue

One year later

James

It's our wedding day. I get to marry my best friend in front of all our friends and family—our full family. Hazel has a great relationship with her parents now, who eloped a month after they got the blessing from Rose. They flew to Vegas and got married in one of those quick marriage chapels. The pictures are priceless.

Lynn's dress is right out of the 80's with its ruffled sleeves and lace. Steven's tux is baby blue and the undershirt matches Lynn's ruffled sleeves.

But today is bigger than that, at least for me. I wonder if this is how they felt on their flight out there. Isaac stands beside me as my best man, looking dapper as fuck in his three-piece suit. I glance at him, and he throws me a reassuring smirk. It feels like we've been standing here for eons, waiting for Hazel's side of the bridal party to make their appearance.

I know it's only been a couple of minutes, but damn; my nerves are eating me alive. He reaches out and squeezes my shoulder, reading the panic in my eyes. "Are you doing okay?"

My back still has some issues from when I was stabbed, but I'm mostly better. I started working with Isaac after I got released to work. Jack took back his business after all the shit with Ryan. He begged me to come back, but I told him he couldn't pay me enough to go back to that shit hole. We're still not sure if Jack was a part of what Ryan was trying to do, but there's enough suspicion that I don't want to risk it.

Trey and Johnathan Reinfeld are in jail awaiting trial. They were denied bond because they're a flight risk, not to mention their safety is at risk from being caught by the police. We go to trial a month from now and I'm so stoked to see what happens, but also hella nervous.

I nod at Isaac, letting him know my issues don't have to do with my back. As I refocus my attention on the doors at the end of the aisle, "as long as i have you" by Foster starts playing, signaling the bridal parties arrival. The doors open and they start making their way down the aisle. I try to find Hazel, but I can't see her. She must be hidden behind the corner. I've never wanted x-ray vision more than I want it now.

As the snippet of the song comes to an end, and the bridesmaids and Jayden, her maid of honor, are on her side of the stage, the doors close. "Dandelions" by Ruth B. starts playing. Hazel refused to use classic wedding songs, it was a huge argument between us, but she won in the end.

At the end of the first verse, the doors open slowly, revealing Hazel in her silver dress, black lace veil, and bouquet. I swear my heart stops dead in my chest. Tears prick my eyes as I take in my fiancée walking down the aisle so she can marry me.

The sunset is bright behind me, so she can't see me crying. This is good because otherwise she'd start crying and then it would be a mess. All she sees is the silhouettes lined up at the front, waiting for her.

Her steps don't falter as she makes her way up to me, never second guessing her decision to do this. She makes it to me at the end of the second verse, the music cutting off as she stands next to me.

I was wrong, she is crying. We're both soaked with our tears and snot. Thankfully, Jayden came prepared and hands

Hazel two tissues. Hazel hands me one and we clean ourselves up as we laugh at how ridiculous we look.

As soon as we're cleaned up, the preacher starts his spiel. I don't hear any of it, I'm lost in Hazel's emerald eyes, my mind reminding me that this is real. I've dreamed of this moment since I first laid eyes on her, and we're finally there.

Halfway through the preacher's speech a baby starts wailing in the crowd, Jayden flinches at the sound and mouths a sorry to us. We just chuckle. Her daughter is teething and going through a sleep regression, so she's been a little fussy lately. Jayden is breastfeeding and doesn't like to be too far from her daughter. Thankfully, her mom takes Emery out to the hall to feed her a bottle, so she doesn't interrupt the service anymore.

It feels like the snap of a finger before the preacher is announcing us husband and wife and I dip Hazel, kissing her deeply. A weight is lifted off my shoulders as everyone hoots, hollers, and catcalls us.

I lift her back up, both of us grinning like idiots. "I love you, James."

"I love you too, Wife."

Lynn

The ceremony was beautiful, but this reception is somethin'
else. The lights are dim, candles light the tables, romantic
music plays from a band up on a stage as we all eat food
catered from Bunberry's. Hazel chose them to cater as a
final closure on what happened a year ago.

Steven sits next to me, relaxed as ever, but he's been the
happiest I've ever seen him the last few weeks. Hazel asked
him to walk her down the aisle, giving him the greatest honor
a father could ever have. My mom sits on my other side,
lookin' so nice in her lilac dress. I took her to get her hair
permed yesterday, then we went out to eat at Billy's. It's
become a new favorite of mine since Hazel had that meeting
with Steven and me there. It was the place where my life
officially changed for the better and as long as they're in
business, I'm going to support them.

Hazel and James are at the table next to ours with their
bridal party surrounding them. James' parents sit at our table
as well. They're nice people, but I just don't have much to
say to them, probably just my nerves. I don't want to say
somethin' offensive or off putting. I'm still workin' on my filter
in therapy.

When everyone is done eating, the band switches from romantic music to upbeat music. Tables are pushed to the sides of the room to open up the dance floor.

The first song that plays after the tables and chairs are moved is some sappy love song, of course. It's the first dance as husband and wife. The way Hazel and James look at each other reminds me so much of how I feel about Steven. I'm so grateful she found someone who loves her the way he does, and vice versa. I still don't much care for James, but we're gettin' better.

After the first dance, the DJ plays a few other songs. Then he announces the father daughter dance and Steven stiffens at my side. I guess he didn't know that was a thing. I nudge him with my elbow while Hazel stands in the middle of the dance floor waitin' for him.

He gets up and makes his way to her. When he gets to her, he takes her hand and twirls her around. It's the cutest thing I've ever seen. I can't help the tears that fall as I watch them. My mom reaches over and holds my hand as we watch them dance to "My Little Girl" by Tim McGraw. I can see them talking from here and I wonder what they're talking about. I hope Steven fills me in when he gets back.

"They're absolutely stunning out there. I know I've already apologized to you for keeping you from him, but I am sorry. He would have made a great dad. He *does* make a great dad. Just look at the way Hazel looks at him. She really loves him, huh?"

"What's not to love, Ma? He's the best." I smile over at her and am surprised to see she's cryin' too. "You're gettin' sentimental in your old age, Ma." She playfully slaps my hand.

"I'm not old enough to kick your ass, Girl." She winks at me.

Things in my life are finally good. I haven't pissed myself in months; apparently I had a major bladder infection and the stress of my life was causing some issues.

Hazel

"You look absolutely beautiful." My dad says as he smiles down at me.

"Thanks, Dad. You don't look too bad yourself." I wink at him as we spin around the dance floor. He clears his throat.

"I wanted to thank you for giving me the opportunity to be here for you today, to walk you down the aisle and to get this dance with you. I don't feel worthy, but I'm thankful nonetheless."

"Of course, Dad. What kind of wedding would it be without you here? It's something I've always wanted, but I didn't think you wanted to be a part of my life. The last year has proven otherwise, and I would be remiss if I didn't extend the offer to you. Thank you for showing up and being who you are. You're great."

He blinks a few times, clearing the tears pooling in his eyes as he clears his throat. "It's my pleasure, Haz. I'll be here for you for the rest of my life. I love you, Kiddo." Even though I'm not a kid, him calling me that heals something deep inside of me. I love it when he says it.

"I love you too, Dad. Mom's staring at us, I bet she's trying to figure out what we're talking about." He chuckles along with me.

"That woman is too nosey. She's always eavesdropping on conversations while we're out shopping or eating. If she doesn't get the full story, she makes one up. It's the most ridiculous thing I've ever seen."

"What's the best one she's come up with?" By the time the song ends, we're both laughing so hard tears are rolling down our faces from the ridiculous stories my mom comes up with. It feels nice having this bond with him, joking, and laughing freely.

Before we can leave the dance floor, he stops me. "I want you to do something for me."

"Anything, Dad. What's up?"

"Take this moment with me. Close your eyes, take in the sounds and feelings of love and joy in this room." I do as he says even though it feels so weird. "Engrave these sounds and feelings in your mind. Never let them go, Haz. In your darkest moments in life, dig this moment out and fight through." I open my eyes and gaze into his eyes. "It's something I learned in the years after my sobriety; having good memories to focus on in the dark times so you have something to be thankful for, something to look forward to, something to fight for."

"That's really insightful, Dad. Thank you."

"Of course." He pulls me into a hug, kissing the top of my head. "Now go enjoy the rest of your night and make more important memories." He joins my mom and nana at their table.

James scoops me into his arms causing me to squeal in delight. "That was quite the dance you had with your dad. Seemed like you guys were having a good time."

"He was telling me about my mom making up stories from snippets of conversations she hears while they're out on the town. It was hilarious."

"You'll have to tell me more about it later. For now, my aunt Christine wants to talk to you about babies, so if you don't want to discuss that, I suggest making a beeline for your friends." I visibly flinch at the idea of talking to Christine about babies. She's the pushiest woman I have ever met. I take his advice and make my way over to Jayden and Rebecca. They get along just as well as I thought they would.

Rebecca is holding Emery and Jayden is drinking a glass of wine, the one she's allowed herself for tonight. Her doctor told her as long as she can hold the baby safely, she's fine breastfeeding the baby, but even the one glass gives her massive anxiety. It was Rebecca who convinced her to have one and she reluctantly agreed.

"Save me from Crazy Christine, please. She's looking for me to ask when we'll be adding a new addition to the family and if I have to hear her tell me to start now, I'll scream at the top of my lungs." Both ladies jump up from their tables, Rebecca more carefully so as not to jostle a sleeping Emery too much.

"Bathroom break!" Jayden leads the charge to the bathroom. When we're safely inside, she locks the door. I slide to the floor, releasing a breath.

"You guys are a serious lifesaver."

"I can't believe we're hiding out in a bathroom on your wedding night." Rebecca laughs as she leans against the wall holding Emery.

"It's not the most ideal of situations, but it isn't the first time we've had to hide out in a shitty bathroom." Jayden looks at me as I peak out behind my hands. We both burst out laughing. "There was this time in college, before Hazel met James, we were at a bar and this creepy ass man was hitting on her and wouldn't take no for an answer. Not even when we pretended to be lesbians. So, we went to the bathroom and hid. Whenever someone else came in, we'd ask if he was still out there. He stood in that hallway for an hour before we finally got tired of it and walked out. When he grabbed her arm to stop her, I flung around and knocked his ass out. I should have done that in the beginning, but I thought maybe he'd get the hint."

I don't think I've ever seen Rebecca's eyes so wide. "That's absolutely terrifying."

"Yea, way more terrifying than Crazy Christine. Plus, Haz…" Jayden looks over at me where I'm sulking on the bathroom floor in my wedding dress. "It's *your* wedding night. So, let's put her in her place and go dance our asses off!" She pulls my hands from my face and pulls me up off the floor.

We make our way out of the bathroom and Christine sets her eyes on me, making her way over to me. Jayden heads her off and tells her to leave me alone for the night. She must have said it aggressively enough that Christine actually listened, because shortly after, she left without saying goodbye.

Rebecca handed Emery over to Jayden's mom so she could come dance with us. As we make our way to the dance floor, the other guests take the cue and join us. As James kisses me surrounded by our family and friends, I know I'll be okay and that this is a night that I'll never let go.

Special Thanks

I would like to thank my husband, Zach, for pushing me to write this book. Without his support, encouragement, and assistance this would have never been possible.

Thank you to all of my friends and family who believed in this and cheered me on when I was doubting I could do this. You're all the bee's knees and I'm so blessed to have all of you in my life.

Thank you to Google and YouTube creators for helping me figure this formatting gig out. Without these two resources, I would have been completely lost.

You can join the Facebook reading group at:

Gina Hejtmanek Reader Group or

https://www.facebook.com/groups/141950632241151

Made in the USA
Monee, IL
13 September 2023

42712757R00219